THE THIRTY DAYS' WAR

The ambassador smiled. 'I don't have to remind you that Britain is fighting for her life and, knowing we're at bay with nothing much with which to defend ourselves except teeth and finger-nails, we feel the Irazhis might well not wait to make their move. There's one other thing.' The ambassador allowed a long silence before he spoke again. 'Fawzi ali Khayyam.'

They'd all heard of Fawzi ali Khayyam... Frontiers meant nothing to him and his arms came from a variety of sources, and if he were around to complicate the issues they could well see why the ambassador had paused before speaking his name.

The ambassador gestured. 'Well, there you have it, gentlemen. All of it. Things are likely to erupt at any time and I've called you here to see what means we have at our disposal.'

He looked at the AVM who indicated Group Captain Vizard.

Vizard rubbed his nose and frowned. 'Means at our disposal,' he said slowly. 'Nothing.'

Also in Arrow by John Harris

Army of Shadows
Cotton's War
Live Free or Die!
North Strike
The Sea Shall Not Have Them
Take or Destroy
Up For Grabs

THE THIRTY DAYS' WAR

John Harris

ARROW BOOKS

Arrow Books Limited
62-65 Chandos Place, London WC2N 4NW

An imprint of Century Hutchinson Limited

London Melbourne Sydney Auckland
Johannesburg and agencies throughout
the world

First published in Great Britain by
Century Hutchinson Limited 1986
Arrow edition 1987

Printed and bound in Great Britain by
Anchor Brendon Limited, Tiptree, Essex

ISBN 0 09 950390 5

Author's Note

Irazh and the aerodrome at Kubaiyah are fictitious, but only transparently so, and this story is based on a series of events which took place in the Middle East in 1941. Nearly every incident described actually took place and they were unusual enough to be described just as they happened – though, for the demands of fiction, they have been concentrated on one or two characters. The affair occurred at a time when, after the fall of France, the British were entirely without allies and were fighting a losing struggle against a strong and confident Germany, which had not up to that time lost a battle and was looking around for new means towards world conquest. With Greece and the Balkans – and eventually Crete – under their domination, their stepping stones to Middle East oil and India were almost in place, the final one, Syria – under Vichy French domination – far from unwilling to help. With all these assets, Hitler and the Nazi generals, who had already filtered their agents and propaganda into the Middle East countries, were ready to strike. Unfortunately, as in the case of the man who intended to blow a pill into the mouth of a sick bear, the bear blew first.

I am indebted for the details to the various RAF officers who wrote so entertainingly on the affair, and to Somerset de Chair's version of the activities of the relieving column in *The Golden Carpet*.

Part One

1

The dazzling plain was bare of trees and hard underfoot, grey shingle like gravel where large stones appeared only occasionally. Almost bare of outcrop, it looked like a pile carpet, the particles of sand clean and polished, the minute facets of the grains catching the rays of the sun in a fierce reflection.

To the right was the steep ridge of Kubish, edged like a set of teeth and narrow as a saw-blade, part of the tableland that surrounded the RAF aerodrome of Kubaiyah. Along its edges, the flocks of long-eared sheep and goats of the Irazhi shepherds dotted the brown sandy slopes that rose ridge on ridge into a series of small hills until they reached the flatter plateau behind. On the northern slopes and in the narrow valleys there was moisture enough for hard wiry grass and shrubs.

Below, however, the desert was barren. Small whorls of dust lifted in the breeze and the yellow-brown parched earth stretched to infinity, glaring in the sun, dazzling in the brilliant light under the brassy sky, endless, scorching, incredibly empty, the few thorn bushes – grey and brittle with white skeletal branches – maintaining only a precarious hold on life. There was no green anywhere, not a leaf nor a blade of grass, and the soft red-gold sand was almost too hot to walk on.

With narrowed eyes, Flight Sergeant Emrys Madoc leaned on the butt of the Lewis gun of the Rolls-Royce armoured car and watched the line of horsemen sweeping towards him. 'You've got to hand it to the buggers, sir,' he observed. 'They know what they're at.'

Flight Lieutenant George Jenno, sitting alongside the driver, said nothing, shifting restlessly in his seat, his eyes squint-ing against the low sun. It was a typical manoeuvre of the Bedou horsemen to come on their enemies out of the sun so that they were hard to hit. It was the very same technique he had learned in the RAF about air fighting: Watch the sun because that was where the enemy lurked. It seemed odd to apply it to the horsemen bearing down on him.

Their faces dark under their pink headdresses, they were swathed in bandoleers of ammunition that were slung across their chests, catching the light, like lines of sharks' teeth. Long silver-handled knives were stuck in their girdles and some had two rifles over their shoulders. Leading them was a lean, paler-complexioned figure with a yellow keffiyeh fastened to his head by the double ropes of a black silk aqal. The men behind him were typical of the country, coarse-grained, harsh, tough but highly intelligent. Irazh was a kingdom, though at that moment in 1941 its king was only five years old – his father having died in a motor accident two years before – and the place was ruled by an uncle, the dead king's brother. And ruled somewhat nervously, too, because there were people, both politicians and soldiers, who itched for power, while both the Germans and the Italians had infiltrated agents to fish in troubled waters.

The breeze was blowing from behind the moving horse-men, carrying the dust they had stirred up ahead of them in pale transparent clouds against which Jenno could see the square shadows of the lorries moving about in the rear. Jenno had stood like this on many occasions since he'd arrived in Irazh. When he'd come to the Middle East early in 1939 he had confidently expected a flying job but instead had found him-self riding in worn-out Rolls-Royce armoured cars, some of which dated back to Lawrence of Arabia's operations against the Turks in 1918. When the League of Nations had handed over the mandate for what had originally been known as Mesopotamia, to avoid stationing a large army there the control of the country had been given to the RAF which ran the place with a few squadrons of aircraft, a few companies of armoured cars and a few local levies.

The horsemen were now almost on top of the cars and, though he had seen it before as often as Jenno, Madoc began to look nervous.

'Always give it the full treatment, don't they, sir?' he said, and Jenno noticed that his hand rested on the cocking handle of the Lewis ready for immediate action.

It wasn't necessary. The figure wearing the yellow keffiyeh lifted its arm and the horsemen wrenched at their reins. Their jaws dragged back into their necks, the horses sat back on their haunches, sliding forward, their stiff forelegs flinging up clouds of dust and stones. As they came to a halt only yards from the line of armoured cars, the riders broke into wild excited yells. Behind them their trucks tore up and down, their crews screaming their delight.

As Jenno drew on his cigarette, Madoc's hand lifted off the cocking handle of the Lewis and he took a deep breath. 'One of these days,' he said, 'the sods are going to come right over us.'

The man in the yellow keffiyeh cantered his mount forward. To call it a horse was really a misnomer and it was certainly never a cavalry charger. It was a wiry pony – to Jenno it looked no bigger than a rat – and the man in the saddle was tall enough to give the impression that, if he wished, he could put his feet down and the horse could trot out from between his legs.

'All right?' he asked Jenno.

'Impressive,' Jenno said. 'Think you'll ever have to use it?'

The man in the yellow keffiyeh grinned. 'Doubt it,' he admitted. 'Especially since I trained 'em to use lorries. Most of 'em are held together more by freaks of fortune than by any recognized principles of engineering, but they go, and the boys are getting quite good with 'em.'

As he trotted up to the armoured car Madoc opened the door of the turret and a dog jumped out. It was small with a dachshund's bandy forelegs. The man in the yellow keffiyeh leaned from the saddle, grasped its collar and hoisted it up so that it squatted chirpily on his saddle with its front paws on the pommel.

'Archie any trouble?' he asked.

'A dog with the flying hours that hound's clocked up is hardly likely to cause trouble on the ground,' Jenno said. 'He went to sleep.'

As the horseman hitched his robe back, it was possible to see that, like Jenno, he wore an RAF drill tunic above khaki riding breeches and boots, and that on his shoulder was the single broad stripe of a flying officer. The RAF in the Middle East, Jenno decided, got up to some bloody queer antics at times.

'Boumphrey's Belles.' He grinned and indicated the Bedou riders, with their flowing robes, long plaited hair and kohl-rimmed eyes. It was a name they'd been given partly in scorn, partly in admiration, and there was considerable rivalry between them and the British regular cavalry in Irazh. It was inevitable that the officers of the staider force never felt quite at ease with Boumphrey, the Englishman who had chosen to 'go native'.

Among his own, however, Flying Officer Anthony Augustus Boumphrey was regarded with the warmth that usually surrounds a happy eccentric. The son of a master of foxhounds who had ridden all his life, he had joined the RAF for some obscure reason which he had long since forgotten. At flying school he had been assessed as a good pilot, steady and capable but lacking dash, and had inevitably gone on to two-engined machines; when the war had started he had been one of the few survivors of the first raids. The RAF had quickly discovered that, contrary to the general belief, bombers in daylight could not properly defend themselves and, though Boumphrey had made it back, it had been touch and go in a limping Wellington with three wounded men on board. He had told the remaining two of his crew to bale out but they had insisted on sharing the hazardous landing and, in the ensuing appalling crash, Boumphrey had been the only survivor. Thrown through the roof,

12

he had been found wandering dazed about the aerodrome with a broken shoulder – and even been ticked off by the station medical officer for getting in the way. The crash had shaken him and he had been sent for a rest to Kubaiyah, where under a treaty abrogated in 1930, the RAF maintained a training school for aircrew.

Since arriving, he had done a variety of jobs. A not-too-clever young man who modestly didn't consider himself especially brave or even especially good at his work, he had done a period of duty with the armoured car squadron, but then the previous commanding officer, who had gone home the year before, had had a brainwave. A keen rider to hounds himself and knowing Boumphrey's skill with horses, he had put him in charge of the Irazh Hunt, a pack of mix-breed hounds which chased anything that would run away fast enough to make it worth following.

When Italy had come into the war the previous summer there had been a change in attitude. Hunting was out and defence was in and, because there was no one else, apart from the regular British cavalry whose duties were elsewhere, Boumphrey had been converted overnight from an airman to a cavalryman and ordered to raise a regiment to guard the long and wandering boundary of the aerodrome. With his intimate knowledge of horses, he had jumped at the chance.

Most of the Bedou he recruited were sons of chiefs and skilled riders and from them as his second in command he had been wise enough to select the son of a major chief, Ghadbhbhan al Husaini. Ghadbhbhan was a very able man. Handsome, educated and intelligent, after a period of acting in Egyptian films he had worked at Kubaiyah for British Overseas Airways Corporation whose flying boats had operated from the lake to the south. Mastering English and French, with his brilliant black eyes and ready smile he was fiercely loyal to Boumphrey.

To begin with, the Bedou Legionnaires' idea of an advance was a wild charge in no sort of order and it had been

Boumphrey's job to show them what was meant by drill. They drew watering bridles, ropes, tethering pins, blankets, belts, rifles, pouches, nosebags and nets, and, though they didn't take easily to uniform, Boumphrey had managed to get them to wear what passed as one. At least their headgear, robes and equipment matched, though, here and there, there were small discrepancies of individual taste which Boumphrey wisely decided to ignore. Some of them had even affected spurs – as large as small windmills which caught in their robes as they walked – and it was days before Boumphrey managed to persuade them to discard them.

Most of the men didn't consider grooming a horse part of their duties – it was normally their habit to ride a horse into the ground and when they needed another to steal it from a neighbour – so he had had to teach them about horsemastership and the reason for currycombs and brushes. It was Boumphrey who had rounded up every horse and pony belonging to the members of the hunt and turned them over to his new soldiers. As a good horsemaster, he had rejected the big hunters favoured by those who had followed hounds in England and had gone in for the wiry little local ponies that were used to the conditions. Some of them were new to the game and when the regiment had first assembled, a mass of excited men with dark grinning faces, the undrilled ponies had turned round and round, bucked, kicked and backed into each other like dodgem cars. A few riders had stacked their equipment on their saddles and as the horses sheered out of line – the well-disposed animals pushed out of place by the ill-disposed – blankets and equipment had bounced off in showers. When they were ordered to move off they went like greased lightning and within half an hour the regiment, known now officially as the Irazhi Mounted Legion, could be spotted on every small rise within a mile. Boumphrey rounded them up by following the trail of lost equipment.

That had been a year ago, however, and they were different now. They had now also been mounted on wheels and excess equipment had been dumped but, though they were by this time disciplined and controllable, they still loved to tear about the desert in their garish robes on their horses or in their light trucks, shouting and waving their weapons.

They thought the world of Boumphrey. Shy, ganglingly tall, schoolboyish in manner and features, despite a nose twisted out of shape by a fall in the hunting field while in his early teens – to his men he was known as the Father of the Funny Nose. He was neither an intellectual nor a theoretician and had no brilliant views on strategy or tactics. He was just good with his Bedou warriors and had made them into a formidable force. But though the job wasn't disgrace, it wasn't a step up either and he knew it.

Boumphrey was an odd character, curiously popular with the rank and file. He played a good game of cricket, was a first-rate tennis player, and, coming from Poole on the Dorset coast, had inevitably become not only a leading light at Lake Kubaiyah, just to the south of the cantonment, where nautical-minded airmen ran a sailing club, but also nominal commander of the small marine craft section – those strange webfooted creatures who were neither airmen nor sailors – who existed to service and refuel the BOAC flying boats which landed there.

Since he still had energy to spare, he had acquired an old seaplane tender from Aden and started another small section on the river to the north of the cantonment where it was not unknown for students on their solo flights to run out of air and dunk their machines. When not on duty, this section became the Kubaiyah Cruising Club, which even made a profit for its members because from time to time it was hired out to the station catering officer to fetch limes, oranges, bananas and other produce from the village of Howeidi upriver or Sin-ad-Dhubban downriver to the east.

A man of everlasting curiosity, Boumphrey had also explored the long escarpment that ran to the south and east of the aerodrome, going on foot, alone except for the dog, Archie, through the wilderness of erosion and the gashes of rock. On horseback, he had covered the sandhills and valleys of the desert to the west, and the marshy area to the north of the river. Despite his languid appearance he was remarkably tough and in his way a bit of an inventor who had devised an additional cut-out system for the training machines that stopped the tail gunner shooting his tail off when the original system, sometimes old and none too reliable, failed to work. Because he was not considered by the chief flying instructor to be a great pilot, he had plenty of opportunity for his other interests and the war had made him a very useful asset to the station.

Flight Lieutenant Jenno was different. Ever since 1938 he had been cynically sure the politicians would make a cock-up of things and had taken the view that he might as well enjoy himself while he could because he might not get another chance. The vehicles of Number 5 Armoured Car Company, he considered, were as odd a group as Boumphrey's Belles. His one ambition was to return to flying but for the time being he was not unhappy. It was said that an independent command was always worth having, even if it were only a group of men under a corporal, and Jenno's *was* an independent command.

They carried fuel and water for four hundred miles and didn't worry about the lines of communication because, if they ran short, supplies could always be dropped to them by aircraft. Their job was to control the rebellious Kurds to the north who wanted to be independent, but they had a free hand to go where they pleased and were used to augment what few British troops were in Irazh and the groups of Assyrian and Arab levies who worked with them.

When the army had departed in 1922 and left the country to the RAF, they had also obligingly left their armoured cars, some of which had seen much service in the Egyptian desert, and everybody in the RAF in Irazh was expected to do some time with them so that they would know the tactics involved.

The work had originally been to guard the route across the desert, into Iraq, and as far as Baghdad, and the building of landing areas for aircraft carrying mail. The country was kept in order by what was known as 'Air Control', which meant bombing insurgent tribesmen in their villages and towns. But since this occurred only after the inhabitants had been warned to leave and because few lives were lost and the stone-and-mud houses were soon rebuilt, no real ill-feeling was created. Moreover, as the tribesmen no longer had columns of soldiers to ambush and plunder, many of them even lost interest – though occasionally there were serious raids across the desert by fanatical sects who, when chased, disappeared to safety beyond the border of Turkey.

For the most part they were intercepted before much damage was done because they were quickly identified by aircraft whose observers could note that they rode neither with the usual flocks of sheep and camels, nor the pack animals that meant women and children, and that their numbers had been kept to around two hundred, just sufficient for a *ghazzu*, a quick seizure of someone else's herd of camels. A short burst from one of Jenno's Vickers into the ground in front of the leaders always brought the whole body to a confused halt. Told to abandon the raid or risk being mown down by the machine guns, after a protracted altercation they all invariably swung round and set off for home with great reluctance. For the next few hours the cars followed slowly until the radiators began to boil and Jenno had to call a halt.

They had always managed to keep the Kurds under control but never quite as effectively as the Turks who had run the country before them and been utterly ruthless, because the British admired the tribesmen's independence and self-respect and, while squashing their disorders, even occasionally helped them. Jenno thought them a splendid body of men, despite the fanaticism which helped them believe they would go straight to heaven from a death in battle, and he always felt a twinge of sympathy for them at having to forego their loot after so long a journey. The raids, in fact, were a welcome change from normal patrolling – when there was nothing to do except shoot at an occasional gazelle, bustard or fox – and the established tribes were always so pleased to see the raiders turned back, the car crews were welcomed as saviours in the encampments of low black tents grouped round a water hole with their herds of camel, sheep and goats. The visits invariably ended in coffee with the leader of the tribe and sometimes even a ceremonial meal of steaming rice topped by a sheep's head, complete with teeth and eyeballs.

Despite the fact that their engines were five years old and in some cases their bodies twenty, the cars could tear effortlessly across the flat Irazhi desert at sixty miles an hour, in a series of manoeuvres designed so that the leader was always covered by the others. Unlike ordinary airmen, the crews didn't wear topees because they caught on doors and turrets and were difficult to keep on in the wind, and instead, like Boumphrey's Belles, wore keffiyehs – dyed khaki with coffee – which took up no room in the cars. They didn't catch the wind, and had a good flap over the neck and back that could be wound round the nose and mouth against the everlasting flying dust. All in all, Jenno had felt, it wasn't a bad life.

With the entry of the Italians into the war and the arrival of tension in the Middle East, however, things had changed. There was a far more dangerous enemy on the horizon now than raiding tribesmen and the natives were growing increasingly restless, inclined to take sides against the British on behalf of the Germans who – it had to be faced – looked at that moment like world-beaters.

2

The conference arranged to discuss the somewhat dubious future that had resulted from the disasters at home and in North Africa and the increasing interest in the area by the Axis powers, had been set up by Sir Wilmot Lyon, the ambassador to Irazh at RAF Kubaiyah, because he considered there could well be too many listening ears in his embassy in the capital, Mandadad.

The aerodrome lay alongside a tributary of the Euphrates where hangars gave way to the red roofs of bungalows and you arrived between pink flowering oleanders along a smooth metalled road that commenced with a whitewashed concrete block of stone on which someone with a sense of humour had placed a signpost. The eastward arm said 'Mandadad 55 miles', the westward arm 'London 3287 miles'.

In addition to workshops, an aircraft depot and a training school, RAF, Kubaiyah, also supported Air Headquarters for the area and as the ambassador arrived at the entrance to the building, a sentry of the Assyrian levies in a blue uniform shirt, bush hat and highly polished boots, the sling of his rifle blancoed dazzlingly white, slammed to attention and presented arms.

The ambassador was a career diplomat, a tall man with grey hair and intense intelligent eyes, and he acknowledged the sentry's salute with a nod and a flick of his hand. He was met just inside by an officer who led him through a courtyard with white verandahs that opened into cool shadowed offices filled with wall maps and filing cabinets. The air officer commanding,

Air Vice-Marshal Henry D'Alton, crossed to him at once. D'Alton was a dark suave man who had been an Oxford scholar in 1914 but had never taken up the scholarship because he had joined the army instead. Disliking the trenches, he had transferred to the Royal Flying Corps and, while he was not considered to be anything special as a flyer, he was acknowledged to be a man of great intelligence and ability and was considered to be in exactly the right place with the difficulties that lay ahead in Irazh.

The walls of the mess were hung with silky carpets from Shirhaz and Kirmanshah, and it was full of soft leather armchairs. There was an improvised bar with cool drinks, but most of the men gathered there were sipping coffee and nibbling Marie biscuits. Among them was Jenno, satanic-looking with his hawk nose and fierce dark eyes under heavy eyebrows, and Vizard, the group captain, thickset, fair-haired and pale-skinned because he had a complexion that burned easily and he kept out of the sun. He had been a famous fighter pilot in the earlier war and everybody credited him with the courage and the initiative to act decisively if anything happened.

Talking to the group captain was Colonel Craddock, of the Dragoons, whose headquarters had recently been moved from near the aerodrome to just outside the capital, in case it became necessary to protect the British residents there. Craddock was a man of medium height who liked to boast that he had the perfect build for a cavalryman, though it was a pointless boast these days because his men did most of their duties on foot or in lorries. He was a brisk man who always seemed to be playing the part of a brisk man. He had done well in the earlier war when he had won a DSO against the Turks in Egypt before being part of Allenby's great advance to Damascus, in which he had won considerable praise for his meticulous planning in an independent command which had led to a final tremendous charge. This had swept the Turks out of Assoum, opened the way north for the main army, and earned him a second DSO and the nickname 'Crasher'.

He had worked with Lawrence and his Arabs, and because he had never been able really to control them, he detested Lawrence, considered that all Arabs stank, had little time for Boumphrey and even less for his Bedou Legion. He had bitterly resisted the move to mount cavalry on wheels, arguing that it would turn them into lorried infantry and cause them to lose their cavalry panache. And now that, despite his protestations, his men had finally been given vehicles, he had somehow managed to retain the splendid hunters they had brought out from England and had taught them to regard their lorries merely as 'led horses'.

Sipping an iced drink at the bar was the chief flying instructor, Squadron Leader William Augustus Xavier Fogarty. He was an Irishman full of the joys of life who looked down on Craddock as a toy soldier and was detested in turn by the envious Craddock because he had once ridden in the Grand National and very nearly won it. He was a breezy man with a great love of life who somehow pushed his pupils through all their exercises and made them pilots, observers or air gunners without seeming to try.

With him was Verity, the major in command of the Assyrian levies, short, thickset and strong-looking, with a skin burned black by years in the Middle East. Like many other British officers, he had originally been attached to the army of some Middle East royalty to make sure their troops were properly trained and remained loyal to Britain; also like Jenno enjoying an independent command, he had remained there ever since. Alongside him was a thin-faced flying officer, who until eight months before, had been a civilian living in Mandadad with his French wife. He had never flown a plane in his life and never would because he had been a businessman before the war and was now responsible for Intelligence at headquarters. His name was the unlikely one of Osanna and the ambassador nodded warmly to him because Osanna knew the country inside-out and possessed all the right contacts, often

21

coming up with information the ambassador's own intelligence machine failed to produce. So far he had never been wrong, and, with the approval of both the ambassador and the air vice-marshal, was now being fed information from Middle East Headquarters in Cairo and from London.

The last man to arrive was Boumphrey, who was there solely as commander of the Mounted Legion. To the mess he was known as 'Ratter' because the splendid riding breeches he wore from time to time were known as his ratting suit. He was often ragged in a good-natured way since he was always a little detached. In the old days it had been because he was trying to work out why he was a failure as an airman. These days, he was trying to work out why he was such a success as a cavalryman. He arrived in a hurry, apologizing for being late, tripped over the edge of the carpet, blushed, and brought up in front of the air vice-marshal with another apology for his stumble.

'Hello there, Ratter,' Craddock said in his breezy booming voice. 'How're your dusky maidens and their donkeys today?'

Boumphrey's blush, which was just beginning to fade, flared up again. The AVM tried to make light of Craddock's scorn by making sure Boumphrey was given coffee and by taking him aside for a moment for a quick chat about his regiment. In the end Boumphrey finished up between Jenno and Verity, who he felt appreciated him because they, too, held the same strange sort of command he did.

'Donkeys!' he muttered angrily. 'Donkeys!'

There had always been a faint hostility between Craddock and Boumphrey. Craddock regarded Boumphrey's command as a Fred Karno outfit, while Boumphrey considered that if it came to an emergency, Craddock's great hunters would let the Dragoons down, if Craddock didn't let them down first by getting them all killed in a half-baked charge, which seemed to be his idea of how cavalry should be used.

'I think, gentlemen –' the AVM's voice cut across the chatter '– that we should perhaps get down to business.'

22

A room alongside the AVM's office had been set aside. There was a sentry outside the door – an RAF man, not an Assyrian – and as they approached, an officer wearing canvas webbing and revolver saluted.

'There's another man on the window at the other side,' the AVM said to the ambassador. 'There are a lot of natives here as mess servants et cetera and they've been warned to keep away. We'll not be overheard.'

The room had a large map of the area spread out on the table and, with the AVM's personal assistant to take notes, everybody stood facing it. The ambassador was the first to speak.

'We're here,' he said, 'to assess the situation and discuss what means we have of influencing the events that have arisen. I'll try to fill you in with what's happened, though I suppose you all already know most of it.' He paused, thinking, before continuing.

'This country,' he said, 'was formed from three former Turkish provinces after the last war and within its borders are many racial minorities and nomad tribes which have never been brought under control. It's filled with dynastic rivalries, local border disputes, political chess-players and unattached bandit chiefs who are always available to the highest bidder. Because there are no rivers or mountains to make natural barriers, boundaries are only lines on a map and are effective only in a legal sense.'

The ambassador paused. 'Neither the British, the French nor the Turks,' he went on, 'wanted the Germans or their jackals, the Italians, to disturb the equilibrium into which the Arab states in the Middle East had settled. Previously they had all been broadly in step and able to withstand all the intriguing of the German and Italian legations and the rebellion-mongering among the Arabs, but with the fall of France and the recent events in the Balkans things have changed.'

'Economically,' he continued, 'Irazh is in a feeble state of health, cursed by its geography, its climate and its reach-me-down communications. When we were given the mandate to run it, however, we were quite willing because we have an interest in the oilfields at Zuka. Since the Irazhis are drawing a large income from the oil subsidies, it was considered the advantages were equal.'

The ambassador paused again. 'As you know, under the 1930 treaty, the British are permitted one under-strength regiment to guard the embassy and British installations in the capital, and three RAF bases, one here, one in Iraq and one on the coast at Shaibah. Now –' he drew a deep breath '– as we all know, the Irazhi army leaders are fiercely nationalistic and anti-British, and at the moment the prime minister is a man who is opposed to the treaty and is, in fact, in touch with the Axis Powers, Germany and Italy, through the Italian minister here. For what follows I'll pass you over to Flying Officer Osanna.'

Osanna waited for a while in silence before speaking. It was as if he wanted to make sure they were all listening, and he gave them time to light cigarettes and clear their throats.

'We have definite information –' his accent was vaguely North of England '– that, although most Middle East countries have decided to declare their neutrality in the major conflict that involves us, in the case of Irazh a general uprising is to be started, supplied with arms by the Italians. It's believed this will tie down thirty to forty thousand British troops and relieve Italy's military position which, as you know, after the defeats in the Western Desert, is precarious.'

Osanna glanced up over his spectacles. He looked like a professor explaining a point to students. 'We have, of course, cracked the Italian code, so we knew about this in good time and decided to take a firm line. However, we have no troops to spare and strong diplomatic action and economic sanctions were relied on to do the trick.'

'Which,' the ambassador interrupted, 'is why I was sent to make these points clear to the regent, Prince Abdullah Illah, who is, as you know, the brother of the late king, who was killed in 1939 in a motor accident.'

'We were accused of assassinating him,' Osanna said and the ambassador agreed with a nod.

'The regent,' Osanna went on, 'runs the country and considers his best bet is to back Britain, though –' a faint smile seemed to crack his solemn face like old plaster '– since the defeats in the Western Desert he may be having second thoughts. Quite naturally, the Irazhis complain of interference in their affairs.'

There was a long silence. It was a complicated situation and they'd all been aware of the facts if not the details for some time.

'In Syria next door,' Osanna continued, 'the Vichy French commander is also having trouble with the Axis. But Vichy – have no doubt about it – is prepared to defend Syria against any British attempt to take the place over.'

There was another long pause. 'Now, as you know –' Osanna was at his most avuncular '– despite the regent the real power here is in the hands of one Ghaffer al Jesairi and two of his friends, enticingly known to us as the Golden Triangle. It's a group, formed with German help, of anti-British officers, and Ghaffer has asked the Italian minister – this we know – for immediate military aid in the form of four hundred light machine guns and ammunition, fifty light tanks, ten anti-aircraft batteries, with ammunition, high explosive, anti-tank weapons and – can you believe it? – 100,000 gas masks.' Osanna paused to let his words sink in. 'To say nothing of an Axis declaration of support for the Arab world against the British.'

Nobody spoke. Boumphrey was watching Osanna like a schoolboy attending a maths lesson he didn't really understand. Craddock looked bored. Verity and Jenno were listening with the earnestness of men who had known what was happening all along and were itching to say 'I told you so.'

Craddock lit a cigarette and the scrape of the match was loud in the stillness as Osanna continued.

'With the Italian defeats in the desert, of course,' he went on,

'Germany became the dominant partner and we know they've explored the possibility of supplying the arms the Irazhis want, to say nothing of money to Haj Amin, the Grand Mufti of Jerusalem and the leader of the Muslims in the Middle East, who's also believed to be here.'

Osanna smiled. 'The thought of power here must be intoxicating to Hitler. A German army in Asia, unlimited labour, food, oil, new bases for armies, new landing grounds. It would grip the windpipe of the British route to India. And it's not impracticable either, because there's been considerable penetration by German and Italian agents.'

There was a little restless movement but it died quickly and the ambassador took up the story. 'Irazhi ministers, traders, doctors and students have been invited to Germany and the Nazis have paid for a sports stadium in Mandadad, set up radio stations which they made sure could pick up Germany, and formed a youth society called the Ruftwah, after an ancient Irazhi order of chivalry. You'll have seen them. They wear a uniform not unlike the Hitler Youth and their programme includes military training. However, the German foreign minister felt Irazh should not declare war on us at this stage, because the Axis is unable at the moment to help.'

'Fortunately,' the ambassador went on, 'London was on to all this and pressure's been put on the Irazhi prime minister to take action against the Golden Triangle. We expect the Golden Triangle to retaliate by trying to use the army to overthrow the government.'

'When?' Craddock asked.

'We suspect not just yet because, before the Irazhis can move, the Germans have to have a base from which they can send help and so far, thank God, they haven't got Syria, which is the only possible place at the moment. However, they've sent men and machines there and, as we well know, the Vichy French were unable to prevent them. But, until they actually have Syria itself I think we're safe.'

There was a long silence as they digested what had been said

26

then Boumphrey blurted out his thoughts.

'It all seems a bit dirty to me,' he commented.

The ambassador smiled. 'It's what's called diplomacy,' he said. 'I don't have to remind you that Britain is fighting for her life and, knowing we're at bay with nothing much with which to defend ourselves except teeth and fingernails, we feel the Irazhis might well not wait to make their move. There's one other thing.' The ambassador allowed a long silence before he spoke again. 'Fawzi ali Khayyam.'

They'd all heard of Fawzi ali Khayyam. He had been an officer in the Turkish army in the days of the Ottoman Empire and a military leader in the Arab rebellion in Palestine in 1936. When that had failed, he had bolted to Mandadad where his activities had begun to alarm both the British in Palestine and the French in Syria. He had been on good terms with the Germans ever since they had helped him escape from the Turks during the first war, and the German minister in Mandadad had been supplying him with money and was known to have instructed him to raise a force of his A'Klab tribesmen to attack Irazhi pumping stations and pipelines. Frontiers meant nothing to him and his arms came from a variety of sources, and if he were around to complicate the issues they could well see why the ambassador had paused before speaking his name.

'Fawzi's a good soldier,' the ambassador pointed out. 'And at the moment he has no major project on, so that the devil may well find work for idle hands. We might even find grounds to employ him on our behalf.'

'I doubt if he's for sale,' Osanna said. 'Besides, at the moment he's receiving money, guns, lorries, even Irazhi soldiers, from Ghaffer.'

The ambassador gestured. 'Well, there you have it, gentlemen. All of it. Things are likely to erupt at any time and I've called you here to see what means we have at our disposal.'

He looked at the AVM who indicated Group Captain Vizard.

27

Vizard rubbed his nose and frowned. 'Means at our disposal,' he said slowly. 'Nothing. This aerodrome's not an operational one and our aeroplanes are all trainers. Biplane trainers for the most part, at that, and totally out of date.'

'Could we hold on to the place?'

Vizard managed a smile. 'We'd have to, wouldn't we? However, we have a few cards up our sleeves. Major Verity's levies, for instance, Flight Lieutenant Jenno's cars, Flying Officer Boumphrey's legion, and finally, Craddock's three squadrons of Dragoons.'

The ambassador turned to Jenno.

'Eighteen cars,' Jenno said. 'All old but all very robust. Three men to a car. Together with base details, mechanics and signallers.'

'Major Verity?'

'One thousand men. A few Kurds but mostly Assyrians. Unfortunately, the perimeter here's a long one and they've nothing but rifles and Lewis guns. No Brens or Bren carriers. And no mortars.'

'Boumphrey?'

Boumphrey blushed as he answered. 'Two hundred men. Well-mounted. Well-drilled.' Craddock smiled and Boumphrey's flush grew deeper. 'Armed with Lewis guns and rifles. They know their job.'

'Wouldn't be much good in a charge,' Craddock observed.

'I wouldn't use them in a charge,' Boumphrey said.

'You'd better not. Wouldn't they run?'

'No,' Boumphrey answered with spirit, 'they wouldn't. Would yours?'

Craddock's face grew red. 'Now look here Mr Damn Boumphrey —!'

As his voice rose the AVM jumped in. 'I'm afraid you rather asked for that, Craddock,' he said sharply. 'And as far as I'm concerned I didn't hear it. What about your own men?'

Craddock got control of himself. 'My men constitute the only British soldiers in the area,' he said stiffly. 'They're the only regular soldiers allowed under the treaty – to watch British interests in the capital. However, I have one troop near Bisha guarding the northern side of the aerodrome from across the river and keeping an eye on the oil pipeline to Haifa and Tripoli.'

Vizard turned to the ambassador. 'The pipelines are dotted with pumping stations but we make sure our training flights are directed along them to check no harm's come to them. At the moment there's a small party of Royal Engineers near the fort and oasis at Hatbah. They're working on the road there, between pumping stations K3 and K2. This base is their nearest friendly point. If trouble ever comes we shall all have our hands full.'

Boumphrey looked gloomy. 'And then some,' he muttered.

3

Mandadad, one of the famed cities of the *Arabian Nights*, had the sound of romantic history but inside it there was little romance. It was smelly, sordid, hot, parchingly dry, and consisted of a dusty, dirty mud–brick–and–reed–matting shambles with scarcely a mosque or a tomb in sight. The main street, ruthlessly cut through the city by the Turks during the previous war, was the only street wide enough to take three vehicles abreast, and then only just. It was lined for the most part with uninviting little grey shops set under curious arcade-type buildings which hung out over the entrances vaguely like Tudor streets in England. They were shabby and the dust lay thickly on the interstices of every brick or stone or piece of wood, flattening the colour to a uniform drabness.

The sukh area was fouled by the droppings of donkeys and mules and, under the overhanging windows of the pilgrims' caravanserais, the labyrinth of streets seemed to grow dirtier and dirtier the further you penetrated. But you could buy there magnificent carpets, trays and exquisite paintings on ivory, and mother-of-pearl to be made into bracelets. It was different from the main shopping area and the place was always crowded with people arguing over the price of Persian armour, in a friendly unhurried discussion, with Turkish coffee and cigarettes laid on and nobody minding whether you bought anything or not.

There were stalls – surrounded by women in their enveloping black *abbas* – containing melons, small oranges or sticky drinks, which the Europeans never bought for fear of cholera.

The taxis had a habit of falling to pieces as you rode in them, shedding a wheel or a mudguard or coming to a halt in a cloud of steam or smoke. Ragged Arabs rode side-saddle on limping donkeys, litter and refuse lay everywhere, and every building – even, for that matter, the RAF messes – was riddled with cockroaches. There was no air conditioning apart from ceiling fans. Where they weren't Irazhis, the inhabitants were desert Arabs, Jews, Christians, Persians, Iraqis, Syrians, Sabaeans and Kurds, who wore Arab or western clothes, or even both in the shape of shoes without socks or a European jacket over Arab robes. The river was crossed by ugly iron bridges and on the western bank there were a few old Turkish houses, built around tiled and mosaic courtyards where doves perched like fruit in the trees. It was never a good idea to go anywhere without arms – not even to the pathetic nightclubs that existed.

As Jenno drove in, the streets were almost empty save around the few hotels where the Europeans could gather for passable meals. Once the beer had been Japanese but now it was Canadian, and the Scotch, though it arrived in what appeared to be unopened bottles, was clearly watered. Most white people stayed on the main streets because on any of the others you were liable to get a knife in the back and robbed.

As the car headed down Muaddam Avenue, it passed a group of young men in sports jackets and flannels, all blond and pink-faced, a few of them with peeling noses.

'Germans,' Jenno said. 'Tourists, they call 'em.'

'Agents, I'd jolly well call 'em,' Boumphrey said indignantly. 'Why don't we kick 'em out?'

'No case to do so, Ratter, old lad,' Jenno smiled. 'This is a neutral country. We can't dictate who comes here and who doesn't. We can't even do a damn thing about the fact that there are German advisers behind old Ghaffer and his pals of the Golden Triangle. Nothing, that is, except be ready for when the bastards move. At the moment my job's simply to ensure that the out of bounds red light areas are proof against entry by the troops.'

Sitting alongside him, Archie, the dog, at his feet, Boumphrey nodded. 'Must be a touch embarrassing at times,' he suggested.

'Not at all,' Jenno said. 'They're better than those in Naples or Marseilles and they're managed with proper decorum. Most of the women are fat and frowsy and too heavily made up – perhaps that's how the Arabs like 'em – but I sometimes think the brothel area's the cleanest part of the city. Doesn't do much good, anyway. If a man wants a woman he'll always find one somehow and if government parsimony precludes married men having their wives with 'em, something's bound to go, isn't it? It means that the only white women here are the wives of civilians who are all members of the Lafwaiyah Club, and those are industriously chased when they're not too closely guarded.'

Boumphrey nodded solemnly. It was a fact that he well knew because the Lafwaiyah Club was where he had met Prudence Wood-Withnell, with whom he had what he liked to think of in the old-fashioned way as an understanding. But Boumphrey *was* old-fashioned, with old-fashioned manners, old-fashioned graciousness, old-fashioned shyness and morals – and an old-fashioned sense of honour. Jenno, he knew, didn't feel the same way and he'd heard that he'd been having an affair with Colonel Craddock's wife, a shapely blonde who somehow seemed to have slipped through the government restrictions on officers' wives by coming out to pay a visit to friends in Mandadad just before the war and then claiming it was impossible to get home. She had set up house there and was looked on with some alarm by the old inhabitants because, for the most part, with Craddock assiduous in his duties, she largely lived alone, something which was considered highly suspicious and was heartily disapproved of.

The Lafwaiyah Club – known somewhat smugly to its members as the Live Wire – was where the European residents of Mandadad liked to gather. It was surrounded by an iron fence, which had been put up in recent months as the anti-British feeling had begun to grow, and was close to the British embassy, a large white, two-storeyed building with a wide verandah running all the way round both floors. Hot water came through the taps, and there were English lawns, luxuriant trees and, at that time of the year, a tumult of flowers.

It was typical of all British clubs all over the Middle and Far East. There were wicker chairs and outside a Persian garden and a swimming pool surrounded by flowers. Inside there was a library, a billiard room, a bar, a wide verandah and a large reception room for dances and social evenings. Barefoot servants served whisky and soda and there were six-month old copies of *The Times* and English magazines. Launches could carry you there along the river and when you arrived you didn't use money but signed chits for everything.

The main hall and lounge were cool and bright with English chintzes, the settees and armchairs standing among potted palms and huge bowls of flowers prepared by silent Irazhi servants. There was an urgent buzz of conversation going as Jenno and Boumphrey entered – Boumphrey to find Prudence Wood-Withnell, Jenno to talk to her father. Colonel Wood-Withnell, formerly of the Indian Army Medical Corps, was now retired from the army but he had fought his way up the Euphrates through Iraq to the gates of Kut in the last war and had returned to Mesopotamia in the late twenties to get a job with one of the oil companies in Irazh. He had been due for return to England in 1939 but had been persuaded – without much effort – to stay on. He loved the desert and had forgotten what green fields looked like. Most of the Irazhis respected him as an honest man and, because of this, he insisted – mistakenly, Jenno thought – on continuing to live in a house on the Bandamar Road on the outskirts of the city well away from the rest of the British residents, most of whom tended to dwell in a narrow community near the embassy. He was an expert on Irazh by this time and had known Fawzi ali

Khayyam personally, which was why Jenno needed to see him. If anyone could tell him where the old rebel was, it was Colonel Wood-Withnell.

The colonel was standing near the bar, sipping a gin and smoking a pipe. He greeted Jenno with a smile, nodded at Boumphrey – none too encouragingly, Jenno thought – and jerked his head to draw Jenno to one side. As Jenno moved after him, he saw Wood-Withnell glance backwards to where Boumphrey was greeting his daughter, the dog wagging its tail expectantly. He ordered Jenno a drink, applied a match to his pipe, then sat back in one of the deep leather armchairs.

'Right,' he said without any preliminaries. 'What's on your mind?'

'Fawzi ali Khayyam.'

'That old bugger!'

Jenno grinned. The colonel's dislike of Fawzi was well known.

'He has a lot of supporters among the A'Klab tribe and he was always a superlative ruffian. But age hasn't improved his character and the old bugger's boasted of having sold himself in turn to the Turks, the British, the Arabs and the French. Now he's on the second time round. He'll always be for sale and as he's grown older he shouldn't be worth the price they offer but, with the situation as it is here, in fact it's probably gone up.'

'Know where he is?' Jenno asked.

'Why?'

'I suspect eventually it'll be my job to find him. No one's said so in so many words yet but I've been here long enough to know how things go.'

The colonel sucked at his pipe for a moment. 'He's not in Palestine,' he said. 'He may be in Transjordan or Iraq. But it's my bet he's here in this area somewhere.'

'Know where?'

'I could make a few guesses.'

'Try, sir.'

The colonel sucked his pipe for a moment, then he swallowed the remains of his gin, called a waiter over and reordered the drinks. This took several minutes during which he said nothing. Jenno didn't push him, knowing he was using the interval to think. Eventually, he sat back, sipped his second gin, relit his pipe and puffed for a few moments.

'Near Hatbah,' he said. 'That's one place he could be. It's halfway between here and Amman in Transjordan. It's roughly the same distance from Baghdad. In the hills in the Hatbah area he's out of sight but handy for any one of three places. Of course, he could also be in Iraq or at Ashuria, near the Saudi-Arabian border. He could also be somewhere along the Persian border or even in Syria, or he even might have crossed over into Turkey. He's no respecter of frontiers. It's my bet, though, that he's somewhere near Hatbah.'

'Why do you think that, sir?'

'Because this is where the trouble's going to come, isn't it? I hear the ambassador's been putting pressure on the prime minister to get rid of the Golden Triangle, and that the regent's been backing him up. I hope to God they know what they're doing because Ghaffer's got the army behind him and he might have something up his sleeve nobody's thought of. Are you watching Hatbah?'

'There's a group of Engineers near there working on the road. If they see anything I presume they'll bolt for the old fort.'

'I hope they don't get holed up there.'

'I think we could rescue them, sir.'

'Don't be too bloody sure.' The colonel's face grew grimmer. 'I was with that lot who tried to rescue Townshend when he got caught in Kut al Amara in the last bunfight. We never did save him. Longest siege in history, they say. I know we were at it a long time. And deserts don't change. They're as dusty and hot and difficult now as they were then.'

He paused, glanced across the room then turned again to Jenno. 'This feller Boumphrey?' he said. 'What's he like? As a man?'

'One of the best.'

The colonel didn't seem convinced.

'Just shy, sir, that's all. Blushes easily.'

'Looks a bit of a long streak of whitewash.'

'If I'm not mistaken, sir,' Jenno said gently, 'that was roughly the impression people had of General Wolfe, but he captured Quebec when it was considered to be impregnable. George III said he wished all his other generals were the same.'

Whatever Colonel Wood-Withnell thought of Boumphrey, his daughter, Prudence, had very different ideas. She was crouching to pat Boumphrey's dog, her own dog, an English fox terrier, sniffing suspiciously at it, its hackles rising aggressively.

'They like each other, Ratter,' she said.

'Not so sure,' Boumphrey replied doubtfully. 'Anything can happen with a dog like that. Fifty-seven varieties. Got a bit of dachshund in him somewhere. Accounts for the Queen Anne front legs.'

She laughed, then she paused before going on. 'They say there's going to be trouble, Ratter.'

'We'll be all right,' he reassured her. 'My chaps are ready for anything.' Boumphrey frowned. 'Colonel Craddock don't think much of 'em, though, and that's a fact.'

'Colonel Craddock's no one to talk,' she said firmly. 'He's not popular with his own men. Father says he's off his head.'

Boumphrey's eyebrows rose and she smiled.

'Not actually potty,' she explained. 'Although he has a dreadful temper and when he was younger he was twice reported for using his fists. He's supposed to be very strong physically – but he was badly injured twice in riding accidents so that, at one time, it was thought he'd never walk again, let alone ride.'

'Who told you this?'

'Father. There's another thing.' Prudence leaned closer. 'He's suffering from arteriosclerosis.'

'What's that?'

36

'Not sure. But it's incurable, isn't it? You end up so you can't move or something. Father says it's what makes him so choleric. You know what I mean. Goes off the deep end a bit quick.'

'He don't like me, and that's a fact.'

'Never mind, Ratter. Other people do. I know they do. They've told me so.' Prudence Wood-Withnell blushed. 'I do, too.'

Jenno wasn't listening much to the colonel now. He was going on about politicians and what a mess they'd got Britain into and Jenno was watching Boumphrey and the girl and wondering what her mother, now dead, had looked like. Because, though the colonel was thickset and sturdy with sharp clear features – distinctive colouring and black crisp hair only just beginning to turn grey – Prudence Wood-Withnell was tall, almost as gangling as Boumphrey and just as colourless. Her nose was too large while her eyes were as indistinctive as her hair which she wore in a nondescript style which was neither one thing nor another. She might, in fact, have been Boumphrey's sister.

'People keep insisting that Ghaffer al Jesairi's going to declare war on the British,' she was saying. 'Think he will?'

'Wouldn't dare.'

'Father thinks he would.' Prudence had kept house for her father ever since her mother had died and, because the old man no longer enjoyed entertaining or being entertained, she found herself listening a great deal to his opinions. It wasn't the most exciting life and there were few highlights beyond an occasional visit to the club. And there, only Boumphrey's appearances really pleased her because she was realist enough to be aware that most of the men just weren't interested in her while most of the women pitied her. Only Boumphrey seemed to enjoy her company.

'Well, he might,' Boumphrey admitted. 'But don't worry. You've always got the RAF on the doorstep. If it came to the worst, they'd evacuate you. We did the legation staff and their families from Kabul in 1929. Shifted over five hundred people. We've even got the same aeroplanes. Valentias are just an improvement on the Victorias they used then.'

'Wouldn't the Irazhis fire at them?'

'We've got a lot of chaps. They wouldn't get near enough.'

She didn't really believe him. She'd visited the aerodrome more than once and she knew what a vast perimeter it had. It would need a lot more men than those she knew were available.

'If it came to trouble,' she said. 'I'd have to see what I could do to help.'

'You'd be evacuated with the rest,' Boumphrey said firmly.

'Not jolly likely. If there were trouble, they'd need nurses. That's what I'd do. I'd be a nurse. Father wouldn't sit back and do nothing and neither would I. Nursing's the thing.'

'They'd have you doing all the dirty jobs.'

She thought about it for a moment with a shudder then braced her shoulders. 'It wouldn't matter. I wouldn't mind.'

'I think you're jolly brave.'

'Not as brave as you, Ratter. Why are you in Mandadad today?'

'Jenno wanted to see the colonel. About this feller Fawzi. It'll be me and Jenno who'll have to tangle with him if there's trouble and he thought your father might know where we could look for him. I just came with him.'

'Oh!'

Her face fell and Boumphrey hastened to reassure her. 'Also came to see you, of course. Bit worried under the circs that you live so far out of the city. Long way from help and all that. Worries me.'

'Does it really?'

' 'Course it does.' Boumphrey blushed again. 'Wouldn't like anything to happen to you.'

'Wouldn't you? Why not?'

Boumphrey's blush deepened and he became tongue-tied. 'Well –' he said '– you know.'

She stared at him, her eyes wide. For a brief moment she managed to look beautiful as her own cheeks grew pink and her smile returned.

'Oh, Ratter,' she said.

4

When Colonel Wood-Withnell had extracted his daughter, Jenno stood smoking by the bar for a while but never talking to anyone for long. Among the women was a statuesque blonde wearing a brilliant scarlet dress. She was Christine Craddock, Colonel Craddock's wife. With her pale hair, the dress drew all eyes to her.

Jenno watched her, his eyes never leaving her as he chatted to the other men at the bar.

'Crispy Christine's arrived,' one of them observed. 'On the look-out for prey.'

'RAF chap this time, I'm told,' Jenno's next-door neighbour said to him. 'One of your lot.'

'Really?' Jenno looked interested. 'Wonder who it is? Young Ratter perhaps?'

The man alongside him grinned. 'She'd eat Ratter alive.'

After a while, Mrs Craddock said her goodbyes and walked outside to her car. They heard the motor start.

'Entertainment over for tonight,' the man next to Jenno said. 'We can all go back to being normal. I often wonder what keeps those dresses of hers up.'

'Deep breathing, I expect,' Jenno said. 'And a lot of faith.'

'The women don't approve of her much.'

Jenno grinned. 'I suspect she doesn't approve of them much either.'

'The advantage's all on her side. She'd stir a bishop.'

It was noticeable that now that Christine Craddock had disappeared the remaining women in the club all seemed to relax. For some time, Jenno moved about among the men and spoke to a few of the women then he crossed over to Boumphrey.

'Pick you up in a couple of hours time,' he said. 'I've got to call on Ananda Patel, Queen of the Madames. Always well received there. Her place's one of the best in Mandadad and she likes to be told so. We usually talk about horse-racing. Been known to give me some useful tips.'

As he turned towards the door, one of the men he'd been speaking to grinned at him. 'Who is it tonight?'

'Ananda Patel, the queen of them all.'

'In need of an assistant?'

Jenno smiled. 'Would you include *me* next time *you* went?'

The grin died and the other man turned away hurriedly. Hypocritical bastard, Jenno thought.

Heading for the car, he drove away from the club down the road. The moon was low over the horizon like a great yellow orange in a pale sky. There were trees just beyond the club and, after a while, he swung the wheel and turned among them. A car was waiting in the shadows with its lights off. Slipping from his seat, he crossed to the other car and slid into the rear seat. A pair of arms went round his neck at once.

'What kept you?'

'Discretion chiefly.'

'I thought you'd never come.' Christine Craddock's voice was low and husky and as sexy as she could make it.

They made love hurriedly and not very satisfactorily then she sat up and lit a cigarette, the flaring match lighting their faces.

'For God's sake,' Jenno said. 'Keep that match down! You never know who's among the trees.'

'Irazhis, that's all.'

'That damn club's full of Brits,' Jenno pointed out. 'Some of them have their servants drive 'em here because they're often not capable of driving themselves when they go home. People talk.'

'Oh, for God's sake!' she snapped. 'Let them! What's the matter with you lately?'

Jenno frowned. 'The war's the matter with me. It's what's the matter with all of us. We all know we're living on top of a powder keg waiting for someone to light the fuse. If they do, we're in a hell of a place. Hundreds of miles from help and surrounded by a country full of Irazhis, all of whom would gladly cut our throats.'

'I get a bit sick of meeting like this,' she said after a while. 'It's all so unsatisfactory. We should find somewhere discreet we could go to. A house or something.'

'Here?' Jenno almost laughed. 'In Mandadad?'

She sounded petulant. 'Well, I don't like waiting like this in the dark. People are suspicious.'

'One chap in there got too close for comfort tonight. If your husband turned up occasionally it would help. Where is he this time?'

'Inspecting his bloody soldiers, I suspect. I'm not surprised they hate his guts. He never leaves them alone.'

'I think he's getting you down a bit.'

'Well *you* haven't been getting me down much. I wish to God you would. And preferably not in the back of a car.'

Jenno said nothing. He had got into the affair without thinking and there were times when her persistence bothered him. In the closed community of the Lafwaiyah Club eventually someone would catch on to what was happening.

'I wish to God something *would* happen,' she went on. 'Then he'd be so busy he couldn't stop me doing what I wanted. At a pinch I could start divorce proceedings.'

'Why?'

'So you could make me an honest woman.'

Again Jenno said nothing, suspecting she'd never been honest in her life. She was fifteen years younger than Craddock and the story went that, because he was wealthy, she'd been interested only in his money and had managed to seduce him when she was barely out of school. He wondered how he'd got involved with her, because she wasn't really Craddock's type. The place, he decided, and the climate. They said that the equator was the fornicating latitude, but Irazh was hot and people didn't wear enough clothes, and when a man and a woman danced together, as they sometimes did at the club, it was too easy to get ideas.

'Would he give you a divorce?' he asked.

'He'd be mortally wounded merely at the suggestion.'

'Don't you have any feelings for him any more?'

'Why should I have? There's nothing left between us. Not even sex.'

She quoted:

'His sporting days are over,
His little light is out.
What used to be his sex appeal
Is now his water spout.'

Jenno laughed and she giggled. Then she became silent.

'No,' she said. 'No divorce. But if I left him, that's how it would end up, isn't it?' She gave him a sharp suspicious look in the dark. 'And then what?' she asked.

'What do you mean – and then what?'

'What would *your* reaction be?'

'To what?'

'To the fact that I'd be free.'

Jenno gave a short bark of laughter. 'I suspect I'll be in no position to have a reaction,' he said. 'This war's heated up lately. Hitler's going to go into Greece and we know he has his eyes on Crete, and as far as I can see we can't stop him taking it. That would bring him a step nearer to us. The next place would be Syria and that would mean he'd got a foot in the door. There'd be nothing to stop him coming here.'

'He'd never do it.'

'Dammit,' Jenno snapped, 'the bloody place's already full of German tourists!'

'I've never seen any.'

43

'Then you must have had your eyes closed. They wear uniform.'

'Uniform?'

'Sports jackets and flannels. And they all carry cameras.'

'What's going to happen to us?' For the first time she sounded nervous. 'If things start, I mean.'

'I expect all the women and children would be gathered into the British embassy and all the men would dig around for what weapons they could find and would stand behind the gates with their teeth bared, ready to defend them to the last breath.'

'Sounds in the best tradition of the British Empire. Women and children cut off, defended by a gallant handful of males as they're besieged by hordes of hostile natives.'

'You sound as if you'd welcome it.'

'I'd welcome anything as a change. What about you? Where would you be?'

'Certainly not in the embassy. I'd be out in the desert, I expect, with my cars. And Boumphrey'd be out alongside me with his Belles.'

'A fat lot *he* could do.'

'You're the second person tonight who's underrated Ratter.'

She stirred irritably. 'God, you've only to look at him! And that half-witted girl who's drooling over him.'

Jenno didn't answer. Prudence Wood-Withnell was as shy as Boumphrey, just as awkward and, like him, apparently not very clever. But they seemed to complement each other and, though cynical himself, Jenno found himself hoping they'd eventually make a go of it. They'd be all right, he felt sure. They both had sunny natures and were the sort to put up with each other for fifty years without the slightest trouble, never complaining when things went wrong or they ran short of money. They were suited. They were even rather school-boyish and schoolgirlish in their conversation with each other but he had a feeling that Prudence Wood-Withnell, beneath her plain outward appearance, was as loyal and courageous as Boumphrey.

There was silence for a while then Christine spoke. 'Not much of a job for a man with your capabilities,' she said. 'Driving armoured cars around. In Britain your contemporaries have been fighting the Battle of Britain.'

'In which,' Jenno pointed out gently, 'most of them, according to the letters from home I've received, have ended up dead. They were flying obsolete machines thoughtfully provided by politicians more concerned with getting the vote than protecting the country.'

'You sound bitter.'

Jenno sighed. 'Friends dying make you a little bitter,' he said. 'People spend a lot of time sneering at soldiers, sailors and airmen, and a lot of clever people back home are now getting publicity because they've joined the forces. But they, my love, are the ones who'll survive. The ones who always end up dead are the regulars who are there when the shooting starts. Because it's a British tradition to make sure they haven't the proper means to protect themselves, they're always the ones who hold the dirty end of the stick.'

She gave him a long look. 'My,' she said, 'aren't we in a state?'

Jenno frowned. 'My cars,' he growled, 'are twenty years old.'

5

Number 5 Advanced Flying Training School at Kubaiyah was part of a scheme which had been set up in the twenties. Now that the war had started, a bigger scheme was being organized in Rhodesia, South Africa and Canada, even America, so that eventually, 5 AFTS would disappear. Of that no one had much doubt but, for the moment, there were still pupils there and they had to be trained. As Boumphrey put it, most of the pilots had already 'wrestled with a Tiger Moth for two falls or a submission' and were now getting acquainted with the more sophisticated machines which would lead them eventually on to front line aircraft. The air gunners were involved with ballistics – the Fraser-Nash turret and the Browning .303 – and were learning to strip weapons with their eyes shut, while the navigators struggled with drift, and the wireless operators with Morse code and the intricacies of service pattern receivers and transmitters.

Out of the uninviting terrain the RAF had created an oasis in the wilderness. A tall and – so they said – unclimbable steel fence, marked at intervals with concrete blockhouses, formed a perimeter almost eight miles in length alongside the river. Inside the enclosure had been built an airfield, half a dozen square blocks of hangars, a water tower, supply and fuel depots and ammunition dumps. There were quarters for the officers, men and pupils of the station, together with a number of civilian employees and their wives and families, and the battalion of Assyrian levies recruited for its protection. Above all and probably most useful, there were a large stock farm which kept it supplied with meat, vegetable plots and fruit trees.

Among the rectangles of mown grass that grew between the pattern of army huts, were beds of stocks, sweet peas and roses, always apparently in bloom. Since the airfield's establishment, the trees that had been planted had grown considerably and there was now a maze of shady avenues bearing homely English names familiar to everyone in the RAF – Halton, Uxbridge, Cardington – to say nothing of a nine-hole golf course – a little on the flat side, according to the padre, who was its most ardent habitué – a polo ground and a swimming pool. There was also the yacht club on the lake to the south – the whole eight hundred square miles of it – duck, pigeon and grouse shooting, and, this year as a bonus, because the area was on the migratory route of storks from Europe to Africa, a pair of storks with a nest on the wireless mast above Air Headquarters, complete with two nestlings.

Naturally there were drawbacks. The heat was like a blast from an open furnace door and the air pockets over the airfield had to be experienced to be believed. The temperatures could rise to 120 degrees in the shade and 112 degrees was considered cool. Chocolate could be spread on bread like fish paste and, since there were dust storms five days out of fifteen, when the sweat ran it made muddy rivulets on the skin. One unfortunate cook for whom it had been too much had stood under a shower all afternoon to cool himself, only to die as a result in the evening. In winter the storms of rain and flying dust could drag down tents, tear off iron roofs and leave great patches of flood water in the take-off area. In addition, the native labourers, never easy to train, occasionally drove trucks not through the gates but bull-headed through the fence like tanks; and it was always difficult to school the locals to leave things alone. They had different views of ownership from those commonly recommended in British establishments and considered it wasteful to leave around what appeared to be a superfluity of good things to the mercy of moths, rust and flying sand. Irazh

47

was the RAF's sackcloth and ashes and at some time or other in their careers almost everybody had to endure it.

Yet the place looked ideal and in peace time it was just bearable. Now, Group Captain Vizard had grave doubts. You couldn't fight a determined enemy with roses, stocks, sweet peas and acacias, and the aeroplanes under his command would have better graced an aeronautical museum than an operational station in a modern war – which Kubaiyah was likely to become if things took a turn for the worse.

He stood at the window of his office staring into the darkness while the chief flying instructor stood by his desk, listening as the group captain thought aloud.

'At the moment,' he was saying, 'less than one eighth of the aircraft available can be regarded as capable of serious operational work. Good God, Paddy, even a Gladiator or a Blenheim's no match for a Messerschmitt 109, and the ambassador has reports that there are 109s, 110s and Heinkels just over the border in Syria. Let's have the training stepped up, not merely in aircraft handling and navigation, but also in bomb-aiming and air gunnery. And put out a request for volunteers from the ground crews. Inform them that their training can be done here on this station and remind them that qualified air gunners now have the rank of sergeant. We'd also better inform Shaibah on the coast that we might have to call on their bomber squadron and that they're to be ready in every way.'

The group captain lit his pipe and drew a few puffs from it, deep in thought. 'And that,' he ended, 'is all that stands at the moment between the British Empire and an upheaval which threatens to throttle the flow of her oil supplies and cut her communications with India.'

For the first time people in Iraq were becoming aware of the faults in the Air Control System. When the enemy consisted only of raiders from the north, it was possible to keep things tidy with aircraft, dropped leaflets, and a few bombs and armoured cars. If the whole population were to turn against the British, however, the absence of a military force would be sorely missed because there were going to be precious few men to guard the installations and vital resources.

And Germany's resounding victories in Europe were beginning by now to take effect on the people of the Middle East. Victories were the most potent form of propaganda and the German broadcasting stations were never slow to announce them. The Japanese, still technically neutral, were also not behind in their efforts to undermine the British position.

Sooner or later trouble was inevitable. But the British were in a cleft stick. They dared not give up any of the treaty rights that had been granted to them, yet they were anxious to avoid any clash that might inflame the Arab world against them and involve their scanty forces – already under heavy pressure in Egypt, East Africa and the Balkans – in further military commitments.

Fogarty looked up. 'I take it Cairo and London have already been informed of the situation, sir.'

'They have,' Vizard said. 'But Cairo probably has other problems. German columns are reported to be massing on the Greek and Yugoslav borders and it looks as though Hitler intends to go into Greece. At the moment, I'm trying to keep my eye on the ball here. Against what we have, the Ghaffer can muster four infantry divisions –'

'Hardly of the best, sir.'

'They're supposed to be British-trained. One mechanized brigade –'

'Sixteen light tanks, sir, mainly Italian, which haven't exactly proved of great value in North Africa.'

'Tanks, nevertheless, Paddy. We have none. Fourteen armoured cars, mostly British, and two battalions of lorried infantry. The Iraqi navy –'

'A few river gunboats, sir. All old. All paddle-wheeled.'

'True enough.' Vizard smiled. 'Actually, it's their air force that worries me, Paddy. Sixty aircraft of various nationalities.

Italian Fiats, Bredas and Savoias; American Tomahawks and Northrops; and British Blenheims, Audaxes and Gladiators. Though they're probably not all serviceable, it's still quite a formidable force when you compare it with what we have. Taken as a whole, they're even more up to date.'

As they talked the telephone went. Vizard picked it up. Fogarty heard the instrument chattering quietly in his ear then Vizard's eyebrows shot up. 'What!' he barked. 'Are you sure?' He listened for a while longer then replaced the instrument and looked at Fogarty.

'That was the AVM, Paddy,' he said. 'What we've been fearing's already happened!'

'What, sir?'

'The guessing's come to an end and the fun's started.'

Jenno was silent on the way home. Boumphrey, the dog asleep by his feet, was chattering away most of the time but Jenno wasn't listening.

'Clever gel, Prudence,' he was saying. 'Wants to be a nurse.'

Jenno came to life. 'Wants to be a what?'

'Nurse. You know – Red Cross and all that.'

'Why?'

'In case of trouble here.'

'She'd be flown to the coast straight away. Like all the other women.'

'She says she won't go.'

'She might not be given any choice.'

The road out to the aerodrome was dead straight from the outskirts of the city, rising in slight waves to the shape of the desert. The river lay in the distance, sparkling in the cold light of the moon. As they reached the gates, they noticed there was a lot of activity at the guard house and the Assyrian levies who normally did the guard had been joined by RAF men, sweating in unaccustomed webbing harness. There was a great deal of fuss about identifying themselves and Jenno grew angry.

'You know very well who I am,' he snapped. 'What's going on?'

The airman he spoke to shrugged. 'Dunno, sir. We got orders. The guard's been doubled here and on the hangars.'

The mess was full of officers and there was a lot of chattering going on. Most of the younger men looked excited. The older ones who had already seen action were looking grave and concerned.

'What's happened?' Jenno demanded.

The adjutant looked up from the table where he was writing out a list of duties. 'We've been promoted from the Reserves to the First Division,' he said. 'The regent persuaded the prime minister to move against the Golden Triangle. All three of them were ordered to places where they couldn't do any harm – Ghaffer to Hil-Hafira, Tafas Raschid to Shah-Hiza, and Aziz el Dhiab to Ramitha.'

'Have they gone?'

'No, they haven't. And they're not intending to. Ghaffer's demanded that the orders be cancelled. It's mutiny, old boy, mutiny.'

By morning they learned more. Ghaffer had called a meeting of the National Assembly, packed it with his supporters and had then declared that the regent was working against the interests of national unity.

That evening the British colony kept to its own area because the natives in the city were truculent and the place had been brought to a standstill. Shops in the bazaar had been closed and there had been several shootings, while taxis and cars were being halted by the mobs, and the passengers persuaded, some of them none too gently, to walk. Meanwhile, a parade several thousand strong snaked its way with torches through the Agaba bin Naif area, shouting that it was time the British left. A few Europeans had had to take refuge in the United States and British embassies. The next morning they learned the result of it all. The regent had vanished.

He had never cut much of a figure and, with all the German and Italian agents surrounding him, hadn't really had much of a chance. It looked as if the trouble in the city was going to increase rather than die down.

There was a great deal of speculation at the aerodrome about what was going to happen, then, during the afternoon, a car belonging to the United States ambassador appeared down the road that led from the capital and swept in through the front gates to AHQ. Boumphrey, who happened to be passing, was startled to see a rug lifted in the rear of the car and a figure in woman's clothing climb out. His eyebrows rose – and he noticed the figure didn't walk with a female gait. Shortly afterwards, the British ambassador arrived in a hurry just as the American car left, and orders were given for one of the Vickers Valentias of the Communications Flight to be made ready for take-off.

There was considerable speculation as everybody asked what was going on and, later in the afternoon just before the Valentia left, it was noticed that – as Boumphrey had spotted – the figure that appeared from Air Headquarters was not that of a woman.

'It's the regent,' Boumphrey said.

As the Valentia disappeared southeastwards it became clear what was happening. The regent had escaped in the nick of time in clothes borrowed from one of his household's female staff and was now heading for Basra, from where he hoped to organize some resistance to the rebellion which had ousted him. Failing that, he intended to continue to Amman, the capital of Transjordan, where his uncle was the Emir.

'Well,' Jenno said. 'That seems to be that. The bloody situation's been threatening to erupt for months but now, when it has, it's caught everybody by surprise.'

The following day another conference was called. All the same people appeared, the ambassador's face more anguished than ever so that he looked like an elderly bloodhound.

'The German radio's joyful,' he said. 'And I gather the press is firmly in line. However, I think they're a little annoyed at the mistiming of Ghaffer's coup.'

'Mistiming?' Craddock said. 'I'd say they'd got away with it perfectly.'

'Not quite so perfectly as you might think,' Osanna commented. 'The Germans are poised to go into Yugoslavia and Greece. It won't be easy to give him any backing.'

'They'll try all the same,' the ambassador said. 'I expect German aircraft to arrive at any time.'

'And then –' Craddock snorted '– God help us! There isn't a single decent British soldier here except for my chaps. I take it we can expect some.'

'I've requested men,' the ambassador said, a shade warmly as he resented Craddock's suggestion that he didn't know his job. 'Indian Army Headquarters take the view that the sooner the situation's under control the better. However, London says that neither Germany nor Italy's anxious for a confrontation with us until they're certain they can profit from it and now isn't considered the time. Both sides have been caught on the wrong foot. The Germans because they've got their hands full in the Balkans. Us because we've got our hands full in the Western Desert. I learned this morning that the Afrika Korps has started an offensive in Cyrenaica and it looks bad. Middle East Command will be able to send us no help. Anything we receive will have to come from India.'

'And will amount to what?' the AVM asked.

'The matter's still being discussed. A brigade, together with artillery and Engineers, is about to embark at Karachi for Malaya – where, as you'll know, with the Japanese growing more difficult, another cloud's threatening – but it's been suggested that, since the emergency there doesn't yet actually exist while here it does, they should be diverted to Basra so they can be flown up here if necessary in Valentias. Under the treaty, we have a right to receive all possible assistance from the Irazhi government for the movement of troops, India's also offered four hundred men to secure the air base at

Shaibah, close to Basra, and is considering following up the first brigade with two more, so that eventually there'll be a full division in or around Basra. In the meantime, Ghaffer's been appointed head of the new government of national defence. He's declared the regent deposed.'

'It couldn't have come at a worse time,' the ambassador went on. 'Troops have had to be sent from the Middle East to Greece, together with units of the RAF, so that there'll be none to spare for us. Which means, until things resolve themselves, that we shall have to consider ways and means of taking care of ourselves. And that, chiefly, means aircraft.'

'Of which,' Vizard pointed out, 'excluding the Valentias, we have just forty that are capable of flying operationally. And they're really all training machines, and some are very old indeed. Hawker Audaxes and Harts, circa 1930, Fairey Gordons and Airspeed Oxfords. There are two Gladiators, of course, one Blenheim – at the moment grounded for lack of spares – and one DH Rapide. Most of them are biplanes. The Audax and the Hart are virtually the same machine, the only basic difference being that the Audax has been fitted with a device underneath for picking up messages from the ground. She's known –' he smiled faintly '– as the 'Art with the 'Ook.'

'What about the others?'

'The Oxfords – flimsy machines built of wood. Burn easily and very touchy on the controls. Gladiators – they were used in Norway where they proved that, while they're good machines they're no match for the German aircraft. The Blenheim – much the same. The Valentias are nothing but troop carriers and very vulnerable to anything fast and heavily armed. The Rapide's just a small transport fitted up for training wireless operators and observers. The Harts and Audaxes are for training air gunners, the Oxfords and the Blenheim for pilots moving on to dual-engined machines. The rest are for solos by pupils expected to fly single-seaters. What are left just happened to be here. A lot are unserviceable but, with the aid of the station engineer officer and the ground staff, we could doubtless make them serviceable.' Vizard paused. 'I wouldn't like to offer any of them against a German in a Messerschmitt or a Heinkel.'

6

There were sighs of relief all round when they heard of the departure of the Indian army brigade from Karachi and the readying of the four hundred infantrymen to fly to Shaibah to make the port of Basra safe for the arrival of the convoy.

It was expected that the outrage among the Irazhis would be loud and clear but, to everyone's surprise, the speeches in the Irazhi parliament were disconcertingly mild and Ghaffer's own speech even placatory.

Only Osanna wasn't fooled. 'Ghaffer's not ready,' he decided. 'And, because he's showing willing, I expect our people will start having second thoughts.'

Sure enough, two days later it was learned that it had been decided to hold up the departure of the airborne troops after all and to halt the convoy carrying the brigade at Bahrein.

'Ghaffer'll now request German support,' Jenno said to Boumphrey, 'and it'll all be over before they can arrive. We'll get nothing from Middle East Command. They're backtracking towards Cairo as fast as they can in front of the Afrika Korps, and the Germans have gone into Greece. Osanna's just heard.'

The tension in Mandadad increased and there was considerable unrest in the labyrinth of narrow streets among the ill-lit houses, shops and bazaars. The teeming, gesticulating people seemed noisier than ever and the British colony kept well out of the way. A fine dust filled the air and overhead the kites wheeled and the vultures watched blank-faced from vantage points on roofs and in trees.

It was well known that agitators were at work, and not the normal agitators either. These were two champions of the local people, a doctor who had been educated at Cambridge, and the newspaper editor, but neither of them was particularly against the British. Now the secret agents who supplied Osanna with his information were reporting other men, new men, who had been seen talking to the grey-flannelled German tourists. It was quite obvious what was going on. The place was being set up for a take over.

There had already been terrorism, bombs, shooting, arson and sabotage. Though, so far, it had not affected the British – only those Irazhis who were considered to favour the British – nobody was in any doubt that the opposition was in fact *against the British*. Messages written on scarves and inciting action had been passed from hand to hand, and there had been a strike which had brought the city to a standstill.

Colonel Wood-Withnell was in no doubt about what was happening and he didn't hesitate to say so at the Lafwaiyah Club. 'There's a rising in the offing,' he said, 'and the Germans are behind it. And if they chose to start something we wouldn't have enough men here to defend even the railway station. We'd have to give up nine-tenths of the city and retire to the RAF at Kubaiyah.'

Those people not in the know who felt that membership of the club gave them security, didn't believe him. 'It'll be nothing worse than the usual noisy picnic,' they said.

Nevertheless it was with some relief that they heard that Delhi had changed its mind again and that the troops were on their way once more from India. To keep things calm, the ambassador sought an audience with Ghaffer al Jesairi and pointed out gently that if there were no trouble when they arrived London might see its way clear to recognize the new government. The following day it was learned that the convoy had arrived at Basra and the men were already disembarking and that the airborne troops were due to follow at any moment. The dock area, the civil airport and the RAF cantonment at Shaibah had been secured and, according to the BBC, which was blatantly dispensing propaganda, the reinforcements had been welcomed with open arms. Ghaffer issued a statement to the effect that Axis claims to the contrary were unfounded and all seemed set fair again, because even the Turks to the north felt that the arrival of British troops in an area seething with discontent would at least keep open their own communications southwards.

The following days were punishing in the heat. Kubaiyah was as pleasant a place as it was possible to find in Irazh. There were not only green lawns, native palms and cactus, but also clematis, jasmine, lilac, honeysuckle and other English shrubs, while among the fruits that were growing were apple, pear, peach, plum, lime, orange, banana, pomegranate and zizyphus jujuba, known to the airmen as the Tree of Knowledge.

But, despite all these delights, despite the swimming pool, the gymnasium, the golf links, the riding stables, the polo ground-cum-racecourse, and the sailing dinghies on Lake Kubaiyah, the place was still a prison. In the middle of the summer it was cooler to stifle with the windows shut than open them to the oven-like breeze from the desert, and there was nothing outside the station apart from occasional visits to the overpriced delights of Mandadad – now for the moment out of bounds, anyway, because of the unrest.

It was no wonder that the favourite songs were 'You'll get no promotion this side of the ocean', and Kubaiyah's very own song:

> Sweet music rising to the sky
> In tune with songbirds fluttering by,
> A garden fair where all is bliss,
> A place the Air Force would not miss.
> To passers-by it thus appears.
> To us inside – two bloody years!

Nevertheless, with things as they were, being in prison seemed to be the worst they were going to have to endure as the four hundred airborne troops arrived in Shaibah. Shaibah was 450 miles to the south but it was within easy reach by air and it was a comforting thought that reinforcements were handy, especially as no one was certain how much the Assyrian levies could be trusted.

The talking continued between Ghaffer al Jesairi and the ambassador, but it was well known to Osanna that the meetings were all being reported to Berlin, and the following morning Kubaiyah learned what the talking had been about. Ghaffer al Jesairi and the Golden Triangle had informed the ambassador that the troops which had arrived at Shaibah should be moved at once to Palestine – which was where it had been claimed they were heading – and that, despite the treaty rights which allowed the British to move troops through Irazh, before any more landed the ones who had already arrived must move out, while future troops were to be allowed to pass through the country only in small units.

'So they can be mopped up more easily,' Jenno growled.

The ambassador fell back on the claim that the annual flooding of the roads after the seasonal rains – and they could all see the great sheets of steely water on either side of the road between Kubaiyah and Mandadad – made the movement of troops impossible, but every single man in Kubaiyah knew that they didn't and, moreover, that Ghaffer knew they didn't.

'He also knows we haven't enough troops here to stop them taking over if they wish,' Jenno said. 'And that with every day he delays we could grow stronger. He's bound to move before long.'

It was clear that Air Headquarters had the same feeling because that day Group Captain Vizard was instructed that nothing was to stop him turning out pilots, navigators and gunners.

*

To Vizard it seemed that while it was essential to continue training – if only to show the Irazhi government that nothing could disturb the icy calm of the Royal Air Force – it was going to have to be speeded up. The courses, he decided, must become crash courses and all training flights would take place over Irazhi bases and installations while, just in case, a mosaic of air photographs would be prepared of all routes between the airfield and the capital.

'All of which,' he observed to the chief flying instructor, Squadron Leader Fogarty, 'isn't really a great deal of help, though, because, although we've got the bombs, we haven't got the aircraft to carry 'em. The Audaxes could carry two 250-pound bombs instead of the official load of 20-pounders, but the Oxfords aren't supposed to carry bombs of any kind and that's a pity because we've got more than our share of those. And that raises another question. What crews could we raise?'

Fogarty frowned. 'We have a few instructors, sir,' he said. 'Most have operational training but there are some who are unsuitable for combat at the moment and are supposed to be here as a rest from ops.'

'Then we must push the pupils.'

'Most of the flying here's only circuits and bumps, sir.'

'I think we'll find there are a few who would have the skill and nerve to fly an aeroplane straight and level over a target and drop a bomb if they had to.' Vizard shrugged. 'And we can probably raise a few other pilots among AHQ staff and our own staff, a few from the aircraft depot and one or two from the Military Mission in Mandadad. They're all out of practice but, all told, we could probably manage about thirty-five.'

'I made it thirty-two, sir.'

'You've forgotten Jenno and his second in command. If it becomes necessary, they can be pulled in. They're both pilots. We can leave the cars to the sergeants.'

'That makes thirty-four, sir. Who's the other?'

'Boumphrey. After that, we shall have to promote the more promising pupils who've finished initial flying training. They'll learn quickly enough under combat conditions. What about the rest?'

'They've all already volunteered to act as observers or gunners.'

Vizard frowned. 'It's a good job they have,' he said. 'Because we've only four experienced men in that category.'

The following day it was learned that the British government had turned down the Irazhi government's requests that no more troops should be sent from India, and the ambassador told the air vice-marshal that he had better be prepared.

Tension was increasing and Jenno and Boumphrey found themselves doing longer and longer patrols towards the north where troop movements had been reported, or towards Hatbah where the Engineers were busy on the road. The fort looked like something out of *Beau Geste*, solid white walls with firing slits and a gate of heavy timber. Despite its imposing looks, however, it would be useless against artillery or bombs.

Barber, the Engineer colonel in command there, was far from happy. 'Still,' he admitted, 'we could take off at a minute's notice for Transjordan. Who are you expecting? Fawzi ali Khayyam?'

'It could be,' Jenno admitted. 'On the other hand, it could be straightforward Irazhi regulars.'

While Jenno moved north and west, Boumphrey's Belles kept up a constant patrol towards Mandadad. The ground on either side of the road was flat and low and, after the rains, was so flooded it was impossible for vehicles to move away from it. The ponies the legion rode *could* move off the road, though, and since most of the riders knew the dry patches, they managed to pick their way through and Boumphrey was able to report that Irazhi police seemed to be increasing in numbers at the village of Sin-ad-Dhubban and at Fullajah, even at the iron bridge across the canal at Shawah just outside the capital – facts which even the aircraft crews had not produced, because the positions had been reinforced at night and the lorries had disappeared before daylight the following day. Vizard immediately contacted Fogarty and from then on the aircraft on training flights were instructed to practice their S-turns to the east over the villages, and both pupils and instructors were to keep their eyes peeled.

Practically every European in Mandadad knew that more troops would be sent in if the situation deteriorated, and that, they knew, would cause riot and civil commotion, and they were all – every one of them – out on a limb.

'Don't you know anyone who lives nearer the embassy you could stay with, old thing?' Boumphrey asked Prudence Wood-Withnell when he met her at the club that evening.

'Of course. But they're as scared as anybody else. And you know Father. He's been here so long, he's convinced nobody will harm him. He thinks he's a father-figure to the Irazhis because he's always treated Europeans and Irazhi patients alike.'

'There are a lot of people in Mandadad who *aren't* his patients,' Boumphrey pointed out realistically. 'And politicians aren't inclined to deal with individuals, anyway. He might find he was wrong.'

Prudence stroked Archie and looked fondly at Boumphrey. At the moment he seemed brisker than normal, his thoughts more carefully collated, and she had a suspicion he had put his finger on the truth.

'All the same,' he went on. 'Don't worry. If it's in my power, I'll be there if trouble starts, to make sure you're all right.'

'Oh, Ratter,' she said. 'You mustn't take risks for me.'

Boumphrey blushed. 'I can't think of anyone I'd rather take risks for,' he said.

The following day they heard that more troops *were* to be sent from India to Basra and almost at once they learned that there had been trouble in the oilfields in the north round Zuka. Anglo-Irazhi Oil Company employees had been roughly handled and the Irazhis had closed the pipeline across the desert to Haifa on the Mediterranean coast. Jenno was already on his way with half a dozen lorries escorted by his armoured cars to bring the Europeans to the safer area of Mandadad.

Everybody turned out to see the cars leave. They were ugly vehicles, despite their 40–50 horsepower Rolls-Royce engines. They carried Vickers guns and were ugly chiefly because they had been built in the days before anyone had thought of streamlining. They had steel cylinders mounted on them fitted with revolving turrets and their bonnets and the flaps covering the radiator and other important points were of specially toughened $\frac{3}{8}$ inch armour plate. As they disappeared northwards in a cloud of dust, everybody knew they were an inch or two nearer a crisis.

They were right. Late in the day they heard that as a further gesture of protest Irazhis who had been imprisoned two years before for an attack on the British consulate at Musol had been released with a considerable amount of ostentation. What was more, Ghaffer al Jesairi had learned of the impending arrival of more British troops and had made it clear that there would be no question of them passing through the country.

'He's elected for war,' the ambassador told air vice-marshal D'Alton. 'He must be expecting German help.'

'Doubtless,' D'Alton said dryly, 'in the form of the Luft-waffe.'

There was a buzz of consternation at the club and a few remembered what had been said only a week or two before.

'That picnic everybody said it was going to be,' Christine Craddock observed, 'is turning out to have terrifying proportions.'

April was a punishing month in and around Mandadad. The working day, governed by the sun not the hands of the clock, began early and ended early. The glare turned the dusty city into a smelting house, coating everything with a shimmer of heat that dulled the capacity for clear thinking. For most people the day ended at noon when the British headed home to change from sweat-stained clothes and even the local Irazhis sought what shade there was.

The political parades started around lunch time. Normally, the British watched them, enjoying the colour, the noise and the enthusiasm, but this time there was a perceptible current of unease and they kept away. They went on all day, growing noisier all the time, and Osanna reported that an agitator whom he knew to be in the pay of the Italians had called a meeting in the great square of the Place Habib abi Chahla for two days ahead, had sent telegrams to people he hoped would speak at it, and had been going about the city in a hired horse-drawn carriage encouraging people to attend. Stones had been thrown at Craddock's Dragoons near the British embassy.

At Hatbah, Lieutenant Colonel Barber of the Engineers was handed a radio message from Mandadad. It came from the Military Mission based on the embassy and it warned him to be ready for trouble. He immediately alerted his men and they checked to make sure their lorries were loaded and ready. A culvert ran underneath the road where they had been working, to carry away the water that ran off the hills in the rainy season. It was a big culvert because a lot of water came from the hills and that night, Barber and his men stuffed explosives inside it, ran a wire to a car battery, and packed the explosives with stones and soil to contain the blast and increase the power of the explosion.

As the last shovelful of earth was tossed into the culvert and tamped down tight, the Engineers climbed out, sweating. Dawn was just breaking and alongside the road a stove was roaring to provide breakfast. They were just standing in a group drinking mugs of tea when a crackle of rifle fire sent them bolting to the safe side of the lorries. Two men were yelling with wounds.

As they dragged the injured men to shelter, it was difficult to see where the firing was coming from, then Barber realized it was from a gulley just to the north. The stove was put out and shoved aboard one of the lorries, and the last of their tools were tossed after it, with the generator and the lights they'd been using. Two men were running out a reel of wire to a point in a rainwater gulley twenty yards away where they could shelter behind a pile of sand-coloured rocks. There was nothing about the hills surrounding them to indicate they were full of eyes but Barber knew they were being watched.

The sun rose higher and the jade green of the dawn became lemon yellow, then the heavens were tinged with a bright brassiness which told Barber they were in for another scorcher. It was ghostly in the silence as they waited. A sergeant came running from the direction of the radio van.

'A message's gone through to Mandadad, sir,' he said. 'They know we've been fired on.'

'Good show, Sergeant,' Barber said. 'And just keep your head down –'

Even as he spoke there was a rifle shot and the sergeant, his face bloody, tottered away and fell into a ditch. As men ran to him Barber concentrated his gaze on the hills. He could see movement and was able to place where the shot had come from.

A corporal appeared beside him, clutching the earth.

'Sergeant Selfridge, sir –'

'How is he?'

'He ought to be all right if we can get him to the doctor.'

'We shall, Corporal, we shall,' Barber said. 'We shan't be staying here. I'd just like to know what the opposition is.'

Still studying the hills, he decided the best thing they could do was bolt as fast as they could down the pipeline to safety in Transjordan.

'What about the oil dump?'

'All ready, sir.'

'Right. Stand by to fire it.'

A vast column of black smoke began to rise and at once they heard yells from the cluster of rocks.

'Right,' Barber shouted. 'Mount!'

The men scrambled into the lorries and they began to move off at speed along the road west. Immediately the firing increased.

Driving a scout car, Barber was the last to leave. Stopping at the far side of the culvert where they had been working, he climbed out. The two men there, hiding behind the cluster of rocks, looked up. Little puffs of dust showed where the bullets were striking.

'Let it go,' Barber said, and the men behind the rocks touched a wire to the terminal of the car battery.

There was a tremendous roar and the road above the culvert seemed to bulge, then it disintegrated into a lifting fountain of dirt, dust and stones. As the rocks came down, bouncing on the dusty earth, Barber turned to the car. The two men were already running to it with the battery.

Barber began to walk slowly to the car. As he climbed into it, one of the men looked at him.

'Who was it, sir? Old Fawzi ali Khayyam?'

'No,' Barber said. 'Not this time.'

7

'The Royal Engineers working party near Hatbah has been fired on,' the ambassador said. 'Barber managed to get in a signal after he left. He said they were Irazhi police.'

'Irazhi police?' Colonel Craddock's red face grew darker. 'That's an act of war. They wouldn't do that without prior instructions. Where's Barber now?'

'Holed up in the fort at Hatbah. It was his intention to head for the border and cross into Transjordan but he found his way blocked and he had no option but to go into the fort and prepare for a siege.'

'And now?'

'We're in touch by radio. He's safe enough for the time being but he can't get out. He's well armed and has plenty of supplies, but we can't leave him there.'

'No, by God, we can't,' Craddock snorted. 'I'd better get along there and fish him out.'

'Wouldn't the RAF armoured cars do the job more quickly?' the ambassador asked.

'The RAF armoured cars are no damn good. Anyway, they're all up in the north fishing the oil company employees out of Zuka. What are left are needed to watch the perimeter of the aerodrome.'

'I thought there was a ten-foot fence. Isn't it supposed to be unclimbable?'

'All it does is keep the camp population in and the jackals out.'

'If you disappear to Hatbah, what happens here?' The

ambassador gazed at his military commander, wondering how much he could trust him. 'Wouldn't it be better if we sent the Irazhi Legion?'

'Boumphrey's Belles?' Craddock snorted his scorn. 'That lot couldn't rescue a drunk from drowning. I'll do it with my people in lorries and be back in two days. I'll leave two squadrons here and take the other one to Hatbah. It should be enough. Dammit, Ambassador, the Irazhi regulars aren't very hot and these are only police!'

Unfortunately for Craddock, his departure happened to coincide with the great meeting which had been organized in the Place Habib abi Chahla. The German and Italian-paid agents had been hard at work ever since the idea had been put into their heads in the Italian embassy.

Concerned with details, Craddock didn't move terribly fast either. He occupied the rest of the night preparing his men for the move, and, in the end, decided it might be wiser to take two squadrons and leave one to guard the embassy. There was a great deal of confusion as the second squadron was alerted and finally he also changed his mind about using lorries and there was a last-minute scramble because the big horses he used didn't like the heat much – and some of them had fallen off in health, so that the weaker animals had to be changed for the stronger ones belonging to the squadron that was to remain behind. His officers and NCOs were nagged until they were worn out but when dawn came the two squadrons were lined up alongside their mounts on the sandy square of the parade ground.

Craddock looked on them with enthusiasm. During the great debates that had taken place in cavalry barracks and in parliament during the thirties he had always advocated retaining the horse.

'The horse,' he had heard Colonel Wood-Withnell say more than once, 'pulls things, you can ride it, it raises the ego, takes the weight off your feet and allows you to go to war sitting down. When it's cold you can borrow its warmth and when it's dead you can even eat it. But it has no place whatsoever on a modern battlefield. In the last war the movement of the armies was halted time and time again by the fodder they had to bring up for them, and outside Kut all the bloody things did was die on us.'

Craddock had never been convinced. Horses, he felt, were needed for shock action. Charging cavalry had a demoralizing effect on infantry and he could just imagine what effect it would have on Irazhi policemen.

As the horsemen left the city their route passed near the Place Habib abi Chahla. The streets were jammed with people and, as the horsemen clattered past, they started to shout insults.

Craddock ignored the yells and the stale rubbish that was thrown at them. The opposition was stronger than he had expected, but it was none of his business to deal with it. But, then at the end of the Bab el Wastani, he ran into the crowd trying to get into the Place Habib abi Chahla. It was an immense crowd. The Italian-paid agents had worked well and the Habib abi Chahla was a popular place. It was little more than an open space surrounded by buildings and devoid of greenery, but to the people of the poor quarter of Mandadad it was a park and they had been arriving ever since the previous afternoon. The Italian agent had spread it around that the British were to make concessions and they were anxious to hear them but, because there *were* concessions, none of them was really particularly opposed to the British. According to what they had heard, the British were even due to leave.

Those who had arrived the previous night had slept on the dusty ground, pi-dogs scavenging for food around the muttering groups. Most of the people had gathered near a large tree in a corner of the ground where there was a little shade. Among the innocent and unconcerned, however, there were others who had heard different stories. The story *they'd* heard was not that the British were leaving but that they were being

69

thrown out, and some of them had come from outside the city with carts because there had been talk of loot.

Many of the people in the Place Habib abi Chahla weren't even aware of Craddock's approach. They had drifted inside, seeking the shade of the few trees and, although speeches had started, most of them weren't listening. Some were playing cards or dice, some were sleeping or gossiping, some merely guarding the shoes or sandals of friends who were in the nearby mosque. It was only slowly that they became aware of the growing disturbance outside the square and rose to their feet to see what was happening.

In the Bab el Wastani, Craddock had suddenly realized that he was facing a solid wall of people. Most of them weren't looking at him, but were moving across his front, blocking the road. Then a few of the paid agitators became aware of the approaching horsemen and began to shout. Immediately, the moving crowd turned to their left and found themselves staring at a column of men mounted on huge foreign horses.

With Craddock was an interpreter on a white mount. He was an Irazhi and, because Craddock had never mastered the language, he went everywhere Craddock went when he was likely to be confronted by locals.

Craddock lifted his arm and the column halted. An officer cantered up to him then Craddock's hand gestured to the interpreter to join him.

'I want these people out of the way,' he said. 'They're blocking our route. Tell them to move. I'll have the trumpeter sound to attract their attention.'

The high notes of the instrument stopped the shouting and there was an abrupt silence which, to the trumpeter, the interpreter, the officer and every man in the column of horsemen, suddenly seemed ominous. Only Craddock appeared not to notice it.

'Tell them what I want,' he said.

The interpreter swallowed, knowing perfectly well that his

association with foreign troops had damned him forever. He had fallen into the job quite by accident, simply as a means of earning money, because he had once been employed at the oil depot on the coast and spoke English. Now he was wishing he'd never heard of England.

'Go on,' Craddock said calmly.

The interpreter swallowed again and started to shout the instructions on a high note, trying to keep his voice steady when it threatened to slide off into a nervous quaver. As he finished, there was a long silence and for a moment he thought he had done the trick. But the yells started again, at first in patches, then the noise grew in volume and it became clear that the agitators in the crowd had no intention of clearing the route.

'Warn them,' Craddock said, 'that if they don't clear the road I shall make it my business to clear it.'

The announcement only brought more yelling and the first of the stones. There must have been several thousand people now milling about at the end of the street, and as the stones began to rain on them, Craddock and his group retreated to the main body of the squadron. He gestured at his second in command.

'Have the men dismount.'

'Dismount, sir?' The officer stared at him as if he were mad.

'I said "Dismount!" Horse-holders to the rear. The men are to line up in front of me armed with their rifles.'

The officer looked at Craddock. His face was uplifted.

Colonel Wood-Withnell was occupied with his surgery at the British hospital when he learned what was happening. One of the young doctors appeared in front of him, his expression excited and shocked, his breath coming in pants.

'They say *what*?' Wood-Withnell asked.

'They say Colonel Craddock is facing the mob by the Place Habib abi Chahla and that his men have dismounted and have rifles. It looks as if there's going to be trouble.'

'Good God!' Wood-Withnell tossed down his stethoscope with a clatter. 'I've always said that madman would start something if he got a chance. Have my car brought to the door. I'll be there in a moment.'

But when Colonel Wood-Withnell left the hospital and approached the centre of the town, he found it impossible to get through. The news of trouble had spread quickly and the streets had filled up rapidly so that he was quite unable to push towards the Place Habib abi Chahla.

By this time, Craddock's men were facing a mob that had grown to the region of fifty thousand. They were yelling 'Down with the British' and the Italian agent was urging them to stand fast. It was his job to see that they didn't move and if he could create a situation where the crowd was fired on so much the better.

'They'll never shoot,' he was yelling from behind the safety of a stone pillar. 'They'll never shoot! They wouldn't dare to shoot Irazhis!'

The Irazhi interpreter with Craddock wasn't so sure and was already looking about him for a nearby hole into which he could bolt.

'Tell them again,' Craddock said. 'Tell them I wish to go about my task. I mean them no harm but I will not have them stop me from doing my duty.'

Again the interpreter tried but the agitators drowned his shouts with their insistence that the British soldiers wouldn't dare shoot.

'Very well,' Craddock said in a flat voice. 'A Squadron left. B Squadron right. Prepare to fire.'

A few people ran for safety as the rifles were raised, but the agitators were still yelling from behind the thick ranks of the mob. 'Ignore them! They've only got blanks in the guns!'

Craddock looked at his watch, took out a cigarette and lit it, then looked at his watch again.

'Right,' he said. 'Fire!'

'Over their heads, sir?'

'No, dammit! Into 'em.'

At the command, the soldiers fired a volley into the heart of the crowd. As a wail of horror rose, people began to run, yelling, and there was a flurry of white garments as the crowd crumbled and began to stream away. Deciding their job was done, the agitators were already disappearing.

'Again,' Craddock said quite calmly. 'Rapid fire.'

The officer gave him a shocked look but passed on the order, and the soldiers reloaded and fired again. The crash of musketry came like the roar of cannon, then it died to a steady crackle. Eventually it stopped and there was an eerie silence.

'That ought to shift 'em,' Craddock said. 'Have the men mount.'

Looking a little shocked, the soldiers lowered their rifles and the horse-holders ran up holding the reins of the horses. Ahead of them, the walls of the houses were pockmarked and the shuttered windows were splintered. Several of the soldiers, unable to bring themselves to fire directly into the crowd, had aimed high. Ahead of them there was a litter of white-clothed bodies and dust stained red in the sun. A few figures were crawling away like wounded animals.

Craddock stared ahead and now even he seemed to have doubts. 'We'll about turn,' he announced, 'and leave by the south gate. Have a messenger sent to the barracks to warn Major Johns with C Squadron that he might be needed but that I expect to be back by this time the day after to-morrow.'

There was a creak of leather and a jingle of equipment as the soldiers settled in their saddles. Followed by his second in command and the shaking interpreter, Craddock turned his horse and rode back alongside the ranks, each file turning after him to follow.

By the time Colonel Wood-Withnell arrived, Irazhi doctors had begun to appear on the scene and, hearing the yelling and then the firing, people had arrived to search for relatives.

'Good God Almighty,' the old man said. 'What on earth has that idiot been up to?'

The cries of protest and horror were being drowned by the wails of the injured. The wounded were being hurried away and overhead the vultures, aware of blood, began to gather. Suddenly the whole of the poor quarter of the city seemed to be sending up a single wail of misery and protest. A sixteen-year-old boy was sitting with his back against a wall, trying to hold his entrails in. Alongside him a man was crawling away on hands and knees, his jaw shot away, his tongue flopping out, pink and obscene. By this time the bodies of the dead were being taken to the mosques where crowds were gathering, yelling their fury. One of the Irazhi doctors, seeing Colonel Wood-Withnell bent over a dying woman, moved quietly to his side.

'Colonel Pasha!' he said. 'I would advise you to go home. Soon there will be trouble.'

Wood-Withnell looked up, his leathery face indignant. The cries of the mob in the distance were chilling. 'My place's here,' he said.

'Sir!' The Irazhi doctor was adamant. 'You are a good man. I know that. I have known you a long time. But I say "Go". Soon you'll not be able to go. I beg you – leave.'

The colonel stared at him, his face expressionless, then he wiped his bloody hands on his khaki trousers and straightened up. 'Very well,' he said quietly. 'I'll go.'

From his window, squinting against the sun, Group Captain Vizard was watching the descent of an Audax trainer, wondering just how good the pupil pilot was and if he'd be able to use him in an emergency.

Apart from the freeing of the Irazhi prisoners at Musol and the rough handling of the British employees at Zuka, so far there had been no further move from the Irazhi authorities. A good forty-eight hours had elapsed and, though air recon-naissance near the Irazhi airfields had reported that there were

74

the expected Irazhi Gladiators, Audaxes, Northrops, Bredas and Savoias, there was so far no sign of anything more up to date and no sign of German machines.

He decided that perhaps they were going to get away with it after all. He'd heard of the Royal Engineers being fired on, on the road towards the Transjordan frontier at Hatbah, but that was not being allowed to go unanswered and he'd heard that the ambassador had agreed to Craddock and a squadron of his dragoons in lorries going out to rescue them.

The shrilling of the telephone made him turn. The air vice-marshal's voice spoke as he picked it up.

'Get over here, Tom,' it said. 'Quickly! We have trouble.'

By the time he reached the air vice-marshal's office, the place was full of officers. The AVM filled him in at once.

'That damn fool Craddock fired on the mob in Mandadad,' he said. 'Two hundred dead, I understand, though that seems a lot and may be exaggerated.'

'Where's Craddock now?'

'On the way to Hatbah,' the AVM said. 'On horses! Horses, for God's sake! He said he was taking one squadron in lorries but during the night he changed his mind and instead he's taken two – on horses! What's more, he's picked up the troop from Bisha, so that now there's nothing to stop the Irazhis occupying the place and threatening the north side of the camp from across the river. The man must be off his head.'

It had long been Vizard's belief that Craddock going round the bend was an event they could all expect sooner or later, but he said nothing. The AVM had plenty on his plate already.

'Rioting's started,' the AVM said. 'One of the banks has been attacked and a British official has been beaten to death. It wasn't even a British bank but, because a British national was there in an advisory capacity, they set it on fire. It's already burned out and the mob's now raiding the store next door. What's more, it's spreading. The one squadron Craddock left to handle the mess he created just isn't enough. They turned out under Craddock's second in command and tried to bar the way to the station but the crowd was around forty thousand strong and they were forced to retreat to their barracks. Major Johns thinks he can hold the barracks but already he's getting people in, scared stiff and seeking safety. They're also turning up at the embassy and the ambassador's sufficiently alarmed to ask if British women and children can be evacuated from Kubaiyah.'

'The Valentias can move some of them, sir. But there won't be enough.'

The AVM gestured. 'I've been in touch with Shaibah,' he said. 'They've agreed to send Dakotas up to help. They'll be bringing extra troops and weapons for the defence of this place, but the ambassador's clearly worried and half-expecting a siege of the embassy and he's asking if we can supply a few extra weapons, supplies and sandbags. What can you do?'

8

Boumphrey was caught out of touch by the rioting.

By this time, with the troops in the capital insufficient to deal with the crisis and with the Irazhi government and army affecting not to have noticed what was going on, incident had piled on incident and the air was filled with shouts of revenge. A British corporal sent some time before to the post office on behalf of Major Johns was caught outside by the mob. Backing up against a wall, with only a little of the Irazhi language at his command, he was set upon and beaten to death. He didn't even have the pleasure of knowing why, because the shooting at the Place Habib abi Chahla had occurred far enough away not to be heard. A British telegraph office was set on fire and the telegraph master, an Irazhi who worked for the British, was torn limb from limb. The goods yard was attacked and British equipment there, which had come up on the single line from Basra at great expense, was covered with kerosene and set on fire. A British bank was attacked and the manager and his assistant, normally both popular men who had had many dealings with the Irazhi businessmen, were murdered and their bodies thrown onto the pile of furniture from their office which was then set on fire with the building.

The rioting had started so quickly and spread so rapidly after the shooting, many people were caught unawares. A woman missionary was dragged from her bicycle and, though she managed to escape to the home of a local family who knew her, she was dragged out again and savagely beaten. Left for dead, she was rescued once more by the Irazhi family who placed her in a cart, covered her with a blanket and took her to the embassy, more dead than alive. A British electrician working at the power station had his skull smashed in, again – like the soldier at the post office – without even knowing why.

By this time the news was spreading and British homes were being evacuated, the families who occupied them leaving with only what they could carry. Some fled without even packing the bare essentials and made their way to an old stone barracks used by Craddock's troops as a fodder store. As they gathered behind the line of British soldiers who held the gate, more news of burnings and killings came in. The heat was appalling because the day was windless and stifling and there was an acute shortage of fans. Realizing that, with only one squadron, he couldn't hold the larger new barracks, Major Johns had occupied the smaller old ones which, though they were stronger and of stone and couldn't be set on fire, were dirty, lacked proper sanitation and were short of mosquito nets. To the perspiring British women and children, used to being waited on hand and foot, the conditions were agonizing.

News came in dribs and drabs. The Christian church had been burned down and the Missionary Society's school had been destroyed, the four women who normally occupied it rescued by a squad of men sent by Major Johns. It was quite clear the Mandadad police were making no attempt to help and small groups of Europeans prayed for darkness so they could sneak across the railway lines past the mob and make their way either to the barracks or to the embassy which was already surrounded and in a state of siege.

In the old barracks and in spare quarters at the embassy the wilting women and children were being packed in sixteen to a room and already there was a case of typhoid among the children. They all had horrifying tales of the mob yelling for British blood. Those who could understand Arabic knew what they were saying: 'Rise! Murder the Europeans!'

With dark, the rioting died down and the streets became deserted. But the uncanny silence was perhaps even more unnerving than the din. There was debris everywhere and every now and then flickering flames where some house or building had been set on fire. Discarded plunder from British-owned warehouses was scattered among the gutted buildings, and telegraph wires hung in festoons to the road where British motorcars still burned.

Uncertain what was happening fifty-five miles away, the RAF had nevertheless not been idle. They had been on the alert for some time and reconnaissances were being made by the remaining armoured cars, and by aircraft – still trying to maintain the fiction of training – over the neighbouring villages. They had confirmed that Irazhi troops had picketed the bridge at Fullajah and the iron bridge at Shawah over the canal leading into Mandadad; and that Howeidi, a village fourteen miles to the west along the trans-desert road from Palestine to Mandadad, had been occupied by what appeared to be a whole brigade of Irazhi troops soon after Craddock and his squadrons had trotted through on their way to Hatbah, so that now they would be unable to get back. Aircraft flying over the fort had found him and his two squadrons inside. They had evidently reached the Engineers but were now sealed up with them, and the fort was surrounded by Irazhi police and regular soldiers, together with a few robed horsemen who had been identified as belonging to Fawzi ali Khayyam.

'So he's turned up at last,' Osanna said dryly. 'At least we now know where he is.'

The ambassador, in touch with Kubaiyah by radio now that the telephone link had been cut, had informed AVM D'Alton that attempts were to be made to bring help with a column of men in lorries from Palestine under a Brigadier Lindley and other troops were to be flown in from Basra as soon as possible. In the meantime, it was virtually impossible for traffic to move between Kubaiyah and the embassy in Mandadad because of Irazhi army vehicles filling the road. Even as he made a strong protest to the Irazhi authorities, the ambassador was aware that Craddock's action had made it nothing more than a cynical gesture.

Boumphrey and his Belles were camped for the night to the north of the Mandadad road when they spotted one of Jenno's armoured cars approaching. It came rocketing across the flat landscape trailing a vast cloud of red-brown dust behind it. It was Flight Sergeant Madoc and he brought them the first news of the rioting in Mandadad and informed Boumphrey that he was to take his men to the iron bridge at Shawah and wait there.

'They're going to allow a convoy of lorries through to the embassy to evacuate the women and children,' Madoc said. 'An attempt's to be made to fly them out. You're to wait for the convoy, sir. It'll be accompanied by the armoured cars, and there'll be aircraft overhead.'

As he gave the necessary orders and watched his men swing round and head for the road from Kubaiyah to Mandadad, Boumphrey found himself thinking of Prudence Wood-Withnell. He'd given his word he would make sure she was safe and he was now trying to work out just how to set about it.

Boumphrey's Belles were waiting just to the west of the iron bridge when the RAF lorries appeared. Officially they contained food, medicines and water-purifying tablets because the embassy was full of refugees from the rioting. Under the food they carried barbed wire, sandbags for the defence, and rifles in case it came to an attack. They came slowly from the west, moving along the dusty road in single file, twelve of them, one behind the other. There was no sign of weapons but every cabin contained an extra man and Boumphrey had no doubt they were all armed, even if their weapons were discreetly out of sight.

As they appeared, escorted front and rear by armoured cars, Boumphrey saw one of the cars break away and head towards him at speed. He glanced at his men, a colourful bunch of ruffians with their pink keffiyehs, white robes and bandoleers of ammunition. They were muttering among themselves and he knew they were itching to do something. His mind was still busy with the problem of Prudence Wood-Withnell and her father, but nothing in the way of a plan had emerged.

The lorries were eyed by Irazhi soldiers who had set up machine guns near the bridge. They were an unprepossessing lot on the whole, conscripts from the hills and northern plains, dark-skinned and long-legged and wearing mustard-coloured khaki tunics and shorts, their legs bound with puttees. Many of them didn't wear boots and on their heads they wore a khaki cloth cap with earflaps and a pointed crown such as had been worn by Bolsheviks after the war of 1918. Some of the caps still had a red star on them, in fact. A few of them rode donkeys, their long legs trailing almost to the dusty surface of the earth.

Though the officers in the better regiments had sometimes been trained at Sandhurst, which had left its mark firmly on them, those of the reserve regiments wore hybrid uniforms which seemed to have been bought as a job lot from the Germans after the first war. Many of them unshaven, they wore German-type harness and weapons over khaki jackets with, as often as not, a field-grey cap of the peaked, high-crowned type favoured by the Kaiser's generals, some still even carrying the badge of the German Imperial armies. But despite their looks they were dangerous, if only because of their number.

As the armoured car slid to a stop, Boumphrey saw that the man alongside the driver was Jenno, his dark hawk features sardonic.

'Hello, Ratter,' he said. 'You genned up on what's happening?'

'Not entirely,' Boumphrey admitted. 'Gather there's been rioting in Mandadad and a few casualties.'

'A nasty night, I gather. That bloody dimwit, Craddock's

left us sitting on a wasps' nest without a swatter. There've been burnings and killings.'

'Got any names?' Boumphrey spoke casually but Jenno knew he was thinking of the Wood-Withnells.

'Expect we shall hear 'em when we get there.'

'I shall go and look for Prudence,' Boumphrey said.

'You're sticking your neck out, old man.'

'It's a tougher neck than it looks.'

'You'll be in trouble.'

Boumphrey looked worried. 'Suppose I will. But you didn't think I'd let old Prue down, did you.'

Jenno smiled. 'Not really.'

More than that, he thought: Not for a moment. Boumphrey was the sort of man to whom a promise was a promise and honour was honour. Towards the end of the previous century, people like Boumphrey had died in dozens, their eyes blazing, saving the flag, or defending their womenfolk against mutinous natives. These days they were regarded with derision as muscular Christians – well brought up in the belief of honour, duty and the principles of Jesus Christ, but not afraid to poke someone in the eye if he spoke a woman's name in the mess, insulted the Empire or spat at the flag. The idea amused the cynical Jenno. Boumphrey would have done well in Victoria's Happy and Glorious, at the siege of Lucknow, saving the women after the disaster at Kabul, charging with the Light Brigade, or stopping the bung-nosed Boers at Spion Kop. There'd still been a lot left even in 1914 and they'd gone to war with their eyes bright and a song in their hearts to defend the Empire against Kaiser Bill and German Kultur. There were still a few even now, but Nazism and the disasters in France had got rid of most of them. Those who'd managed to survive had changed their views rather sharply, yet Boumphrey had remained exactly as he was – as out of date as the brontosaurus but still curiously admirable.

By this time the lorry convoy had reached the bridge and an Irazh officer was demanding the right to inspect their loads. Jenno joined in the discussion with a will, insisting that, because they were heading for the British embassy, they had the same rights as a diplomatic bag. It developed into a noisy argument but Jenno managed to shout the louder and in the end the Irazhi agreed to let them pass without an inspection. Boumphrey separated his force and half of them moved ahead and spread out on either side of the road on the other bank. Jenno's armoured cars followed, then the convoy, then more armoured cars and finally the remaining half of Boumphrey's Belles. The Irazhis didn't move and, apart from the rumble of the lorries, the convoy crossed the bridge in dead silence.

They were soon in the outskirts of the city. The streets were still full of smoke and ashes and a few shop owners whose premises had been caught up in the conflagration were picking over the charred remnants of their properties. Sheepish Irazhis moved about in the rubbish-littered alleys and there were yelling defiant groups on the corners. Telegraph wires looped above pavements strewn with broken glass, stones, paper and blowing chaff. Here and there a burnt-out car still smoked.

There was silence at first but eventually, as if the word had passed round the city what was happening, the crowds began to appear and they found themselves passing through jeering throngs. The embassy gates were closed but they had been spotted moving down the Sa'adoun Parade where it was situated. There was a mob outside and a lot of yelling, and swastikas and 'Go home, English' had been daubed in several places on the walls.

'Not hard to see who's behind this lot,' Jenno said.

They drew up outside, Jenno's machine guns turned towards the crowds as the lorries moved inside to be unloaded. All the embassy staff, together with the male refugees, joined in the unloading and even a few women gave a hand. Jenno remained outside with his cars, Boumphrey's Belles just behind them.

'I'm going inside,' Boumphrey said. 'I've got to find out.'

The embassy was full of women and children and the noise

83

was a shock after the silence Boumphrey remembered from his previous visits. The ambassador bumped into him as he sought information. He looked tired and strained but he was surprisingly optimistic.

'We've lost wireless contact with Kubaiyah,' he said. 'But I expect we'll pick it up again. I have messages. I'll hand them over before you leave. Could you do with a drink of something?'

'No, sir. I'm just seeking information about someone.'

'My deputy has all the names. Is it anyone special?'

'Colonel Wood-Withnell, sir. And his daughter.'

The ambassador's face fell. 'Ah!' he said. 'We've been trying to contact everybody, of course, to bring them in to the embassy or to the old barracks. Some we've managed to contact by telephone and a few of them have been able to give information about others. But about the colonel I have to admit I know nothing.'

'Not at the hospital, sir?'

'Afraid not. There are no Europeans left there. They're all here. They'd expected to be safe there but the mob got in and the matron and two of the sisters had to be smuggled out in Irazhi clothes with their faces and hands darkened. They took refuge for the night in the home of one of the Irazhi doctors who, thank God, was more aware of what they'd done for the place than the mob was. I've talked to them but they know nothing of the colonel. It seems that when the rioting started someone came to tell him what was happening and he immediately left in his car. He's not been heard of since.'

'With your permission, sir, I'm going to look for him.'

'I'm afraid I've got a job for you before that, my boy. I have to ask you to bring in all the people who've taken refuge in the old barracks, together with Major Johns and his men. He sent one of his officers disguised as an Irazhi to ask for help. He couldn't hold the new barracks against a determined attack and the old barracks aren't suitable for a crowd of women and children. In addition, I have to admit we need his men here in case we have trouble.'

84

9

It was well into the afternoon before the lorries were unloaded, then the armoured cars and Boumphrey's Belles
headed with them down the wide Sa'adoun Parade towards
the old barracks.

The crowd seemed to have dispersed but in no time they
were back, shouting insults and hurling rubbish at the vehicles. Noticeably little was thrown at Boumphrey's Belles. It
puzzled Jenno at first why it should all be reserved for him
when the Belles were clearly more vulnerable, then he realized
that, while the Europeans in the armoured cars and lorries
couldn't retaliate without stopping the whole convoy, any one
of the Belles could simply spur his pony out of line and react in
any way that pleased him. None of them did because Boumphrey had been haranguing them on the necessity of keeping
their tempers, but that was something the crowd wasn't aware
of and they were being careful.

Johns was waiting for them. He had his lorries in the
courtyard of the old barracks, laden with anything that was
considered necessary. They were piled high with ammunition, weapons, barbed wire, radios and every other necessity
for making war. Six of them were crammed with women,
who filed out of the old barracks carrying bundles and drag-
ging unwilling children. They were pushed aboard, then,
with soldiers manning machine guns on accompanying lorries, and with the armoured cars and Boumphrey's Belles
forming an escort on either side, they prepared to head for the
embassy.

'What's happened to the nags?' Boumphrey asked.

Johns gave him a bitter look. 'Gave 'em away,' he said. 'We can't handle fifty-odd horses and this lot as well. They're no damn good anyway. Everybody but Craddock knew that. We gave 'em to the native grooms, and they disappeared with 'em during the night. All but three, one sick and two injured. They're still in the stables. I expect when we've gone the mob will come in. They'll probably kill them out of spite. Probably even eat 'em. The rest will be out of the city by now. We'll probably get a few of 'em back when the trouble's over but I bet not all of them. I expect I shall be court-martialled when Craddock comes back.'

He moved down the line of lorries and the tailgates were slammed home. As Jenno climbed into his car, Boumphrey was studying a list of names.

'I'm going to look for Prue,' he said.

'Do you know where she is?'

'No. But I expect I shall find her.'

'For God's sake, don't hang about.'

As the lorries moved off, Boumphrey called his senior NCO, Ghadbhbhan, to him.

'We're going to take a look along the Bandamar Road,' he said.

They reached the Wood-Withnell house within a quarter of an hour. It was a squarely built place with a verandah that ran round the whole of the second floor, giving a distant view of the desert. There were a few trees to give the place shade but in the dusty garden the bushes and flowers had been trampled down, and Boumphrey's heart sank at the desolation. His men dismounted under the trees and began to water their ponies in groups at the fountain still playing under the trees. Slapping at his boots with his riding whip, Boumphrey walked into the house. The front door was scarred as though someone had hacked at it with a sword. Inside, the hall was full of wreckage. It had contained all the things the Colonel had acquired in his years in the east, but the pictures were slashed, the chandelier was a wreck and the floor was covered with the remains of the statues he'd collected.

Boumphrey's yells echoed from the silent rooms as he moved through the house. Glasses, plates and china lay in shards, and swathes of wreckage were strewn across the floor. Persian carpets had been kicked into heaps and slashed like the furniture and the pictures. On the verandah a native cart stood, its rear end half through the doors, as though the mob had used it to break their way in. Boumphrey felt his eyes prickle with tears.

'Prue!' he called. 'Prue, are you there!'

His voice came back to him, echoing past the torn curtains and smashed windows. Just inside the kitchen he found her dog. It had had its throat cut and lay in a pool of dried blood.

He was just about to continue his search upstairs when he heard a footstep and, swinging round, he found himself face to face with a small dark-visaged man in a crumpled linen suit. His hand went immediately to the revolver he wore but the newcomer held up his hand.

'Please, sir,' he said in English. 'There's no need for that. I am unarmed.'

'Who are you?' Boumphrey demanded.

'I am Doctor Amad. I worked at the hospital with the colonel.'

'Where are they? Do you know?'

Amad nodded vigorously. 'I know, sir. I found him in the street when the shooting took place and warned him to go before the mob turned on him.'

'Where is he now?'

'He's at my home. I heard the mob coming down the road here and I heard them going through the house. When they'd gone I came to look for the colonel. I found him and his daughter hiding in the stables and took them to my home until I could get in touch with someone. I had just returned to look for food.' He held up a sack. 'Tinned food, sir. It will help. Have you come to take them away?'

87

'Yes, I have,' Boumphrey said. 'And I can't express my thanks sufficiently to you for what you've done. Are they unhurt?'

'Well –' Doctor Amad hesitated '– the colonel has a bad cut on his head. After he left the scene of the shooting, his car was attacked and set on fire and he was beaten. But he's all right and in good heart.'

Two hours later an old car left Doctor Amad's house. In the rear seat were two dark-skinned people in white robes, one of whom limped badly. The car was driven off hurriedly.

Meanwhile, Boumphrey had sent a troop of his best men to the old barracks. There were people in there by this time, looking for loot. Some of them were carrying away chests and abandoned army blankets, plates and clothing, some merely fodder for their animals. There were men in the stables arguing about the sick horse; others had harnessed one of the other animals to a cart which it was trying to kick to pieces. Seeing Boumphrey's men, their dark kohl-rimmed eyes gleaming at them over the barrels of their rifles, they bolted as fast as they could. Boumphrey went to the trembling animal in the cart and calmed it.

None of the three horses which had been left behind was in good condition. Two were limping badly and the third had a staring coat and a wild eye. It was decided to leave the sick animal and take the two lame ones – and they clattered off again back to the Wood-Withnells' home with the horses on leading reins.

By the time the car arrived from Doctor Amad's house, they were saddled and hitched to trees, surrounded by the smaller animals of Boumphrey's Belles. The soldiers were waiting quietly, all of them armed and alert, their eyes watchful. As the car appeared, there was a stir in their ranks, and they pressed forward to watch it drive round to the back of the house.

Boumphrey was waiting by the rear entrance when the car

stopped. First to appear was Doctor Amad who climbed the three steps to where Boumphrey was waiting.

'All is well, sir?'

'All's well,' Boumphrey said.

Ghadbhbhan turned and gestured to the car. Doctor Amad's wife climbed out and opened the rear door. Prudence Wood-Withnell appeared, angular even in the Irazhi robes she was wearing. Turning, she helped her father out as Boumphrey came down the steps towards them. The colonel looked old and his moustache had been shaved off. With his dark leathery skin he could pass as an Irazhi from the northern hills without difficulty.

Muttering to himself, he was helped into the house by Amad and his wife. Inside, he turned and grasped Amad's hand while Prudence threw her arms round the doctor's wife. 'How can we thank you enough?' she said.

'Better go now, Doctor,' Boumphrey advised. 'Best not to stay here too long. Will you be all right?'

Amad gestured. '*Ishu Allah*,' he said. 'If Allah so wills.'

As the car drove off, Prudence turned towards Boumphrey.

'Oh, Ratter,' she said. 'What can I say?'

'Don't say a word, old thing. Bit of a shaky do, what?'

'I felt sure you'd come. Because you promised. They killed my dog.'

'I saw. I'll get you another. Perhaps not just yet, though. Later. When things have settled down a bit.'

Faintly embarrassed, Boumphrey turned away to complete the arrangements. 'Couldn't use the doctor's car,' he said. 'It would have made it difficult for him. Couldn't raise one of our own either. But there are lorries at the embassy if we can get you there.' He looked at the colonel. 'Can you ride a horse, sir?' he asked.

'Injuries largely on me head,' Wood-Withnell growled. 'Nothing wrong with me bum.'

Boumphrey produced robes and keffiyehs. 'Better put these on,' he said. 'Then you'll look like my people. They won't attack us. And the horses won't bolt. They're lame.'

The robes and keffiyehs were slipped on, then Boumphrey helped them into bandoleers of ammunition. Calmly and with no sign of panic, Prudence pushed her father into the saddle and made him comfortable, then she turned to Boumphrey with shining eyes. 'How super, Ratter,' she said. 'You've thought of everything.'

It didn't turn out quite as Boumphrey had expected. By the time they had gone a quarter of a mile down the road towards the city, the colonel and Prudence lost in the centre of the Belles, an Irazhi ran out and stopped them.

As the little column halted, a car appeared from around the back of the Irazhi's house. It had obviously been hidden under hay because wisps of it were still jammed between the bonnet and the front mudguard. A white man was at the wheel and the rest of the car was packed with his family and luggage.

'We heard from Doctor Amad that you were going to the embassy,' he said. 'Can we join you?'

The car was fitted into the column and they set off again. A mile further on another car joined them, then a family on foot carrying what possessions they could. By the time they reached the city outskirts, they had acquired five more families and by the time they halted outside the embassy another three, all of them exhausted, frightened and in need of help. They were spotted some time before the embassy came in sight and two of Jenno's cars under Flight Sergeant Madoc roared towards them, circling behind them and taking up positions at either end of the column, their machine guns a threat against any attempt to interfere. His eyes alert, his face set and strained, Boumphrey raised a hand to Madoc but didn't halt the column. When they reached the embassy, the gates opened and they all swept inside the wide courtyard.

As Boumphrey climbed from the saddle, he found himself facing Prudence. Her eyes shining, she flung her arms round him, and hugged him.

'Oh, Ratter,' she said. 'You were quite splendid!'

'Steady on, old thing,' he said. 'Can't go off like that.'

The ambassador appeared on the steps to greet them. Behind him were Johns and a few white men, and every window seemed to be packed with faces of women and children.

'I'm delighted you found them, Boumphrey,' the ambassador said. 'I was worried about you but it seems to have been worth it. I've been given permission by the Irazhi government for all the women and children to leave. I've also been in touch with the air vice-marshal and he's arranging to fly them to the coast. The first batch will leave for Kubaiyah as soon as possible tomorrow.'

'Well,' Boumphrey said, 'that appears to be the end of that.'

'Is it?' Jenno said cynically. 'I'd say this was just the beginning.'

10

'Due to unforeseen circumstances,' the ambassador said, 'the crisis we feared seems to have arrived rather sooner than expected.'

The conference was being held while the new arrivals were being found places in the billiard room and settled in. In the ambassador's office were Johns, Jenno and Boumphrey, together with the ambassador's aides.

'I'm in constant touch by wireless with Kubaiyah,' the ambassador went on. 'But the situation's worsening hourly. Ghaffer's agreed not to interfere with the evacuation of the women and children but I've heard from Flying Officer Osanna that Irazhi troops are being assembled to the north of the city and it seems clear that, after the evacuation of women and children, they intend to stop all movement to or from the airfield.'

'Who's behind it?' Johns asked.

'The Italians,' the ambassador said bluntly. 'And doubtless the Germans. The army in Greece is in trouble and will doubtless eventually have to be evacuated to Crete, where inevitably there'll be another attack because it's another stepping stone to the Middle East. I don't think this coup was engineered on Axis instructions, but I think Ghaffer's confident of Axis support. Rommel's advanced to the border of Egypt and I expect Ghaffer feels a decisive stage of the war's been reached and that his coup's come at exactly the right moment. They expect Axis forces to arrive very soon and that the decisive battle of the Middle East will be fought here. They will naturally expect a reward.'

'Can they get away with it?' Jenno asked.

The ambassador pulled a face. 'We know that Mussolini's now totally dependent on Germany but we think Hitler regards this area merely as a sideshow. However, though direct intervention by the Luftwaffe is out of the question at the moment because we're out of range, it's possible to fly arms in, in individual aircraft, providing they stop to refuel in Syria.'

'Won't that require clearance by the Syrian authorities?'

'Syria is Vichy-controlled,' the ambassador said gently. 'And Vichy is controlled by Hitler.'

There was silence for a while then the ambassador spoke again. 'Without doubt, the Axis will endeavour to get aircraft here to neutralize Kubaiyah. Which is why I'm anxious to have all the women and children away as soon as possible. We now have around three hundred and fifty people here, and the United States ambassador has another one hundred and fifty. The children must go first. The men will remain until the end, especially the fit, in case this place needs defending.'

'Will it?' Johns asked.

'Embassies have not been sacred cows for a long time.' The ambassador gave a wry smile but he seemed quite calm. 'However, I suspect that any fighting that takes place will be at Kubaiyah because if Kubaiyah were to surrender, Ghaffer would have all its aircraft, all its fitments and workshops and a good landing ground where the Germans could fly in from Syria. I've therefore decided to send most of the British doctors and nurses there and keep here only sufficient to look after ourselves and any refugees who might turn up.'

The gates of the embassy were opened early the following morning and Boumphrey's Belles, whose horses had been quartered in the embassy gardens during the night, clattered out and took up positions in the road.

A few Irazhis appeared to watch the proceedings, and there were a few jeers and a little half-hearted stone-throwing, but it soon stopped. The women and children began to climb into the back of the lorries. Including Wood-Withnell, there were three doctors spread through the convoy. There were also seven British nurses and the remaining lorries included among their passengers those women with a knowledge of first aid – among them Prudence Wood-Withnell, who had lied like a trooper to be included.

'Father says he doesn't intend to be trapped in the embassy,' she explained to Boumphrey. 'I think he smells battle.'

As the ambassador took up a position on the steps, Christine Craddock was talking to Jenno.

'Why can't I come in one of your cars?' she was asking in a low voice.

'Because if there's trouble,' Jenno said. 'I'd just have to dump you on the pavement and get on with the job, I can't fight off a mob with you aboard.'

She glanced up at the people in the lorry waiting patiently for her to make up her mind. 'Well, I'm not going to ride with that lot,' she said. 'Half of them are tradesmen. They're not my type. I'll stay at the embassy. It'll be safer and a lot more comfortable.'

The convoy left the city in silence, led by the armoured cars, with Boumphrey's horsemen trotting in single file on either side. There was a distinct sense of unrest as they headed through streets heavy with resentment and teeming with gesticulating people.

They began to meet Irazhi troops as soon as they left the city, and as they approached the iron bridge at Shawah the convoy had to halt because of Irazhi vehicles filling the road. Soldiers in mustard-coloured khaki waited by the roadside, loaded down with equipment and weapons. Nearby, mule-hauled carts piled high with equipment had become entangled with a span of oxen hauling a gun.

As the convoy halted, Boumphrey moved ahead to stop alongside Jenno's car. 'Something's up,' he said. 'Where are they off to?'

'They say they're on manoeuvres,' Jenno explained. 'I expect that's a euphemism for taking up positions in case hostilities commence. It can't be that idiot, Craddock, holed up at Hatbah with the Engineers. Two men and a boy on a donkey could handle that.'

The wait to cross the bridge was a long one and as the people in the lorries, stifling in the heat, began to feel distressed, an elderly man collapsed. Jenno approached the officer in command of the bridge and started a long argument, but the officer insisted that Irazhi troops must be allowed to cross before the refugees. No matter how Jenno argued about the women and children, he refused to be moved and they had to wait for two hours as the gun and the mule carts were sorted out and the movement began again.

Waiting in the baking heat, listening to the rumble of wheels and the thump of feet crossing the bridge, Jenno was aware of hostility in the watching black eyes. There were a few shouts of 'Britons go home' as the Irazhi troops tramped past the halted vehicles but, despite the resentment, no hostile move was made.

Eventually, the road cleared and, aware that more troops were coming up behind, Jenno quickly moved the armoured cars into the gap, and waved the lorries on, nose-to-tail so that none of the Irazhi units could be interposed.

'Close up,' he kept shouting. 'Close up! Don't open out, for God's sake, or we'll be split up!'

Every now and again a gap opened because of some squad of marching men moving between the lorries. It happened so often it was clear it was deliberate. Then Boumphrey hit on the idea of hindering the movement of the marching men before they could hinder the movement of the lorries. Keeping his horsemen ready, he moved them up the minute he saw a gap opening and the jostling ponies effectively prevented the infantry from halting the lorries by getting between them.

Across the bridge at last, they began to speed along the narrow strip of black asphalt shimmering in the sun. By this time the heat was fiery and the asphalt was beginning to bubble. As they left the canal behind, however, they ran into another jam and had to halt again. Children began to cry and distraught mothers attempted to shield them from the sun. The nurses were fully occupied and Boumphrey saw Prudence Wood-Withnell and a doctor attending a figure in one of the lorries.

An Irazhi lorry ahead had broken down and, as with all military columns, vehicles had piled up behind it, so close to each other it was impossible to move them in any direction. Angry officers were shouting at each other, and vehicles at the tail of the column were trying to reverse. As soon as the jam was cleared, Jenno pushed in, stationing his cars and Boumphrey's horsemen along the sides of the road so that their convoy couldn't be interrupted.

Eventually they came to Fullajah, a little town of mud brick houses. It had been an international halting place in the days of Xenophon and Alexander the Great but, despite the trans-desert highway that ran through it from Palestine, its streets were narrow, its houses of yellowish brick and corrugated iron. It was a shoddy, ugly place, and round it the land was as flat as a plate, stretching away for ever, it seemed, vast, desolate, pallid, the pale bulrush stubble of the river standing in water that reflected the vast blue sky.

Palms fringed the river bank and on the surface of the water were all sorts of craft – Arab trading boats rigged for full sail, primitive bitumen canoes from the marshes upstream, launches, steamers, even circular rafts of reed matting. In the shallows, water buffaloes moved, slow, shaggy and enduring, voicing their protests not with a moo but with a groan that seemed to come straight from the heart. Standing on the raised bund that held the river in check, the villagers watched them pass, robes and headcloths flapping in the wind, among them young girls with eyes like gazelles. The place was full of troops and once again they were held down to a crawl. The Irazhi officer in command was making things as difficult as possible, and it was now approaching midday with the sun at its hottest and the wind rising to scatter the dust.

There was an ominous number of guns about the streets – 4.5 field guns, 3.7 howitzers, two anti-tank guns, Bren guns and machine guns of other types; armoured cars, a light tank and several gun-towing lorries. The Irazhi soldiers stood along the roadside, their faces expressionless and impassive, their unshaven faces dark with hostility.

Kubaiyah came in sight at last and the view of the hangars gave way to leafy avenues and the red roofs of bungalows. Aircraft were dispersed about the landing area, the air above them shimmering as the sun struck their metal parts. The convoy drove in between pink flowering oleanders. At the entrance to headquarters a sentry of the Assyrian levies saluted Jenno. The air vice-marshal had arrived from Air Headquarters to welcome the women and children and with him were Group Captain Vizard, Chief Flying Instructor Fogarty, and a few other officers. The lorries drew to a stop with their occupants bravely singing 'Rule Britannia' and, as they halted, one of the women shouted for three cheers in a high-pitched voice.

The air vice-marshal called for silence and announced that a meal would be served within half an hour and that quarters had been prepared.

'We're going to fly you out to Basra just as soon as possible,' he said. 'You'll find it cooler there. The troop carriers are being prepared now.'

Jenno edged towards Boumphrey. 'There's what looks like a new flight of Gladiators,' he murmured. 'It must have arrived while we've been away. And I also thought I saw a new Blenheim.'

They learned what had happened when the air vice-marshal called a conference later in the day.

'We've received one Blenheim and five Gladiators from the Middle East,' he pointed out. 'However, I'm under no delusions but that they were sent here because they're considered

97

to be of little use there, so you can draw your own conclusions about their value. And, with things developing as they are there, I think we can expect little likelihood of any more.'

He made no bones about the deepening seriousness of the crisis. 'Still,' he went on, 'another squadron of Wellingtons is being flown to Shaibah and, if necessary, we can use them as reinforcements here. The Dakotas bringing in troops and supplies will be used to fly out more women and children. When the Valentias return, they'll be bringing arms, ammunition and food supplies. They'll also be bringing in four hundred men of the Loyals who've arrived at Basra from Karachi. With the six companies of the Assyrians and our own people, that gives us around two thousand men for the defence – if it comes to a defence – of a perimeter of nearly eight miles. Unfortunately, we also have, plus the civilians who have just arrived, the families of the levies, the station bearers, Indian laundry hands, labourers and other workers, so that the total of people inside the perimeter is around nine thousand. I don't have to tell you that number is far too many if we're to be besieged.'

The AVM paused. 'However,' he continued, 'on the credit side we have eighteen elderly but still robust armoured cars, the Irazhi Mounted Legion, and a force of all arms is now assembling in Palestine under Brigadier Lindley to come to our relief. But they're separated from us by four hundred miles of desert and a lot of flooding and we're not over-supplied with weapons.'

The station armament officer spoke. 'We have two 4.5 howitzers, sir.'

The AVM looked as if he didn't believe him and the armament officer explained with a grin. 'The ones used as ornaments on the lawn outside, sir,' he pointed out.

The AVM's eyebrows rose. The two old guns, which had last seen service in the first war, had stood outside Air Head-quarters so long no one noticed them any longer. 'Will they work?' he asked.

'I've examined them, sir,' the armament officer said. 'And they appear to be in good order. Fortunately, the climate here precludes rusting or deterioration of that sort and I've learned that the breechblocks have been discovered in the stores of the Aircraft Depot. They should be a help.'

11

Not for one day had the flying training ceased. Every morning the field emptied of aeroplanes until five minutes to midday when it was filled with returning machines, each trying to get in first so that the pupil pilots would be at the head of the queue for lunch. After lunch they all took off again and the aerodrome was quiet once more until the stroke of four when they all arrived back, like pupils summoned to their classroom by the pealing of the school bell.

The Valentias of the Communications Flight, enormous ugly biplanes, were wheeled forward late in the afternoon, and the whole aerodrome turned out to see them leave.

The first batch of women and children were hurried to the airfield. They were a pathetic-looking lot, wearing everything they could because they were allowed only what they could carry. Despite the growing heat, some of the women wore two coats and children were complaining about the weight of two sweaters. They were all borne down with suitcases and packages and they all looked tired, unwashed and exhausted.

As the Valentias took off, the AVM gave a sigh of relief. As he turned away he glanced at the ridge of high ground overlooking the aerodrome and his eye caught a flash of light. He knew exactly what it meant. Irazhi soldiers were up there.

That evening there was another of the interminable conferences. By this time there wasn't a man at Kubaiyah who wasn't expecting the Irazhis to attack and only Osanna had much to say that was encouraging.

'We understand,' he pointed out, 'that Hitler believes –

erroneously – that there are 14,000 British troops in Irazh and another 14,000 on the way.'

'I wish there were,' the AVM said.

'Besides –' Osanna continued '– we know that now the fighting in Greece is reaching its climax Hitler's occupied with the invasion of Crete. It's obvious that will come next because the German airborne general, Student, is in Athens. For us, if not for the men in Crete, that's an advantage. Thank God it doesn't seem to have occurred to Hitler that he could use his aircraft here to greater effect.'

As the talking went on, discussions were also taking place in the hangars. They had been going on ever since they had realized Kubaiyah could be in danger of attack but now, with the knowledge that the Irazhis were taking up positions on ground overlooking the cantonment, an extra urgency had entered them. The Fairey Gordons, which could do only eighty miles an hour and were normally used only for target towing, had been fitted up to carry bombs, which meant that twelve of their aircraft could now carry 250-pound missiles. The increase in their strength, however, only served to make Fogarty dissatisfied with the Audaxes which were supposed to have only two light racks for 20-pound Cooper bombs.

'If the Gordons can carry two 250-pounders,' he said, 'then the Audaxes can, too. And if *they* can, so can the Harts. They're virtually the same aircraft. And if we can make 'em do so, then we'll be able to treble the weight of bombs we could drop if we have to. What about the Oxfords?'

'They can't be adapted.' The station engineering officer was in no doubt. 'The Oxford's a very delicate aircraft and the disturbance caused by bombs or a bomb rack could make it hard to handle.'

Among the listening officers, Boumphrey frowned, and, soon afterwards, while the matter was being debated in Group Captain Vizard's office, he set off for Workshops, with the dog, Archie, at his heels. He had always been good with his hands and, during his pupil training at Cranwell, had done very well in the essential metalwork tests. Jenno found him bent over a vice with a file, his face set in a frown of concentration. The dog, asleep nearby inside a coil of wire, opened one eye.

'What's on, Ratter?' he asked.

'The engineering officer insists the Oxfords can't carry bombs,' Boumphrey explained. 'He sounded as if he were explaining the thing to a lot of delinquent children. But that's a pity, because we have more Oxfords than anything else. I'm trying to make a bomb rack for 'em.'

'Think you can do it?'

'I was always a dab hand with Meccano.' Boumphrey bent over his task, the perspiration dripping off the end of his nose. 'And engineering officers are noted for their resistance to the obvious. In France, they refused back armour to Number One Squadron's Hurricanes because they said it would affect the flying qualities. Number One didn't agree and took some off crashed Battles and it made no difference at all.'

'What's Groupy say?'

'He's not keen if Workshops aren't keen. I think we ought to suck it and see. With a bit of one-eighth mild steel sheet, a hacksaw, a file, a drill, a bench and a vice, I reckon we ought to be able to come up with something.' Boumphrey's head lifted and he gazed at Jenno with his gentle blue eyes. 'I reckon we've got to, in fact, don't you?'

By afternoon, with the help of a flight sergeant fitter, he had made a bomb rack which could be fitted to an Oxford. Jenno stared at it.

'The bomb's tail fins will stick out beneath the fuselage,' he pointed out.

'The group captain'll never wear it, sir,' the flight sergeant agreed.

When the engineering officer was consulted, he immediately refused to permit the rack to be fitted. 'I can't allow an aircraft to be flown with irregular additions to it,' he insisted.

'I'll have a go,' Boumphrey said. 'If it doesn't come off, nobody'll miss me. I'll sign a blood chit. Every civilian we fly has to sign one when we take him up, to show the RAF can't be held responsible. If I state that I'm prepared to fly an aircraft not cleared as serviceable, that covers everybody.'

The engineering officer remained unhappy, but he wasn't so rigid he couldn't see the advantages if it worked, and he suggested the matter should be put before the chief flying instructor.

Unfortunately, Fogarty was with Group Captain Vizard in the air vice-marshal's office discussing what could be done, and wasn't available.

'Four bombing flights have been formed,' he was pointing out. 'Together with one fighter flight of Gladiators. I've taken command and the Kubaiyah Air Striking Force is ready.'

There were a few smiles but they soon died. 'If the Irazhis come,' the AVM pointed out, 'we would expect them in numbers on the escarpment. There are already a few in position. It's a hundred feet high and a rifleman could put a bullet through any window in the camp from up there. It provides a magnificent view of the hangars and the water tank, on which, I might add, we depend because it not only keeps the trees and flowers alive, it keeps *us* alive.'

'Let's not shout "All is lost" until the ship starts to sink, sir,' Vizard said. 'It's true, *if* the Irazhis do appear on the escarpment in numbers, the main airfield's going to be completely under their domination. But the repair shops and the aircraft aren't.' He paused. 'There's one other thing in our favour. The hangars mask the polo ground and, by combining it with the golf course, we can make a small landing ground there for the Audaxes and Harts. Works and Bricks have already started, in fact. The trees between have been felled, the road taken out and the golf course levelled.'

'Oh, woe!' mourned the padre.

'The remaining trees have been left because they obscure the view of the landing ground from the plateau. Meanwhile, pupils have been set in their spare time to belting ammunition for the Gladiators. I hope there isn't too much demand on them, though, because the belts can only be filled at a rate of twenty-five rounds a minute while the guns can empty them at a rate of eighty.'

During the night the sound of traffic to the east and south of the aerodrome was heard. Before dawn the following morning a cipher message from the embassy in Mandadad informed them that, due to the large bodies of troops on the road towards Kubaiyah, no more women and children would be sent for the time being, and the RAF lorries which were to have left for them were to remain inside the fence because the Irazhi forces now blocking the road were quite clearly intended to threaten Kubaiyah.

The orderly officer, a very young pilot, was informed and the alarm was sounded on a bugle. Heads appeared from windows because, although many of the men in Kubaiyah had been in the RAF for some time, none of them had ever heard that particular bugle call before. Those who had could only assume it was a practice.

The information was passed on to the group captain and the chief flying instructor. Fogarty hauled himself from his bed and headed for his office. As the crimson sky paled to yellow, it was immediately possible to see Irazhis along the edge of the escarpment digging trenches and erecting what appeared to be fortifications. He reached for the telephone.

'Let's have the first training flight of the day away,' he instructed. 'It will be crewed by two experienced pilots and they will pretend to do S-turns along the edge of the escarpment. They're to report what they see.'

The machine roared off within minutes. When it landed the crew confirmed that the Irazhis had indeed arrived.

'The buggers are there all right,' the observer said. 'They're setting up gun positions. They're not much more than a thousand yards from the perimeter fence.'

Well, now they knew.

Kubaiyah was being threatened and – exposed to attack on two sides and dominated by the guns moving into position on the plateau – seemed to be at the Irazhis' mercy.

Flying that morning didn't follow the usual pattern. The aircraft that took off from the airfield all carried experienced crews because every NCO, airman and anybody else who could be spared was digging trenches, setting up blockhouses and gun positions and manning the weapons they had installed.

'Which means,' Fogarty said flatly, 'that the only people left to move, bomb up and arm the aircraft – forty-six of 'em now – are the pilots. However –' he pulled a sheet of paper towards him '– since the crisis has finally arrived, under the prevailing conditions, the following circumstances will prevail: The Oxfords and Gladiators will be moved as far as possible out of the sight of the guns on the plateau behind the hangars. The Harts and Audaxes will go to the polo field where they will be dispersed under the trees. The Gordons get the sticky wicket nearest to the plateau.' He looked at his sergeant clerk. 'What about an operations room?'

'Set up, sir,' the sergeant clerk said. 'In the flight office in B hangar. We've cleared everything out and maps and telephones have been installed.'

The aircraft started moving, the pilots taxiing where possible, pushing where taxiing wasn't possible. In the meantime, everybody began to find excuses for why they shouldn't be digging trenches. Digging trenches in the heat of the Irazhi noon was not the sort of thing most people enjoyed and it was amazing how many fitters, riggers and flight mechanics found there were unfinished jobs on aircraft to be completed. There was a tremendous new interest in the Form 700, the air serviceability form, in daily inspections, and the Q Form, which was the aircraft unserviceability sheet; and it was amazing how many machines suddenly developed mag drops, loss of revs and unexpected engine temperatures, and had to be put right.

Soon after midday a string of cars and lorries arrived at the main gate, filled with civilians who turned out to be the engineers from the pumping station at Dhubban village just to the east of the cantonment. They had not been harmed but there had been no mistaking the Irazhis' intentions.

'The buggers have taken over the whole works,' they announced.

Kubaiyah was one of the few places in Irazh that had its own sanitary system. The sewage was pumped into the river, whose fast-flowing current dispersed it rapidly, but it was clear that in the event of trouble the occupation of the pumping station was going to be a problem. With the refugees, there could well be as many as 10,000 people at Kubaiyah and the effects if the Irazhis switched off the pumps could be disastrous.

As the news flew round the cantonment, an old popular service song could be heard in the billets, workshops, hangars, stores and trenches.

Sweet vi–o–lets,
Sweeter than all the roses,
Covered all over from head to foot,
Covered all over in –
Sweet vi–o–lets . . .

Two hours later, the station orderly officer appeared at the group captain's door. Things were always done properly in the RAF and when an incident occurred at the main gate, the corporal of the guard called the orderly sergeant who called the orderly officer, who was now handing a note to the group captain.

'Delivered at the main gate, sir,' he said. 'By an Irazhi

106

colonel. He was accompanied by a captain and a sergeant carrying a white flag.'

'A white flag?' The group captain's eyebrows shot up. 'Why? We're not at war.'

'Perhaps we're about to be, sir.'

The group captain lit a cigarette. 'I can guess what this is,' he said. 'It's a request to hand the place over to the Irazhi Air Force. I suspect it'll get a dusty answer. Very well, I'll deliver it to the air vice-marshal. In the meantime, go back to the Irazhi gentlemen at the gate. Tell them that the air vice-marshal will have to be informed but that it will be done at once. However, show them every courtesy. Tell them – regretfully – they can't be allowed inside but that we'll deliver a reply as soon as possible. In the meantime, tell the adjutant to contact the chief flying instructor, the chief engineer and everybody else and tell them to get things moving. Because this very much seems to be *it*.'

While the message was delivered to the gate and the Irazhi colonel, a smart man wearing a pith helmet with a khaki neckcloth, climbed with his captain and his sergeant into his car to wait, things began to be stepped up. Trenches were now being dug at a remarkable speed and machine gun positions, surrounded by sandbags – there was never any shortage of sand at Kubaiyah – were going up.

When the news reached the chief flying instructor he was in the middle of an argument which included the chief engineering officer and Boumphrey.

'It'll play the very devil with the behaviour of the Oxford,' the engineering officer was saying. 'We know the characteristics of the machine. It could become catastrophically unstable on the final approach.'

'Nobody's tried yet,' Boumphrey said again. 'I'm willing to have a go.'

'I'm not very happy,' the engineering officer persisted.

Fogarty looked from one to the other before giving his

opinion. 'When I was on the North-West Frontier in 1930,' he said, 'flying from Peshawar, I had to make a forced landing in a Bristol fighter and it played hell with the tail skid and broke several cross-members at the rear of the fuselage. There was a distinct list to the tail, but we got the local carpenter to patch it up with the leg of a chair and a few bits of wood. In addition we were in a small depression. So we unloaded everything we could, worked out just how much petrol we needed to get out, pushed her up the slope at one end, paid several villagers to sit on the tail, and decided to take a chance. We knew we couldn't stay where we were because the tribesmen had heard about us and were on their way, and you know what they do to your private parts. We buried the machine guns and gave away everything else, then I took off, sitting on the knees of the observer who was in the front cockpit to make the tail lighter. I revved the engine, the chaps on the tail let go, and away we went. The tail skid made a hell of a row and eventually there was a colossal bang. But we'd just about reached flying speed so I shoved the stick forward and we came unstuck and just made it out of the depression. When I landed at Peshawar the Engineering Officer said the tail ought to have fallen off. But it didn't.' He gestured. 'Sign the blood chit, Ratter, and have a go.'

The bomb rack was fitted and the practice bombs hoisted into place. Normally the Oxford carried only an 8-pound training bomb but Boumphrey was carrying eight 20-pounders, and half the Workshop force turned out to watch what happened. At the last minute, Jenno decided to fly as second pilot.

As they climbed aboard, the dog, Archie, jumped in with them. It went everywhere Boumphrey went and when Boumphrey flew Archie also flew. Whenever it saw Boumphrey reach for his flying helmet the dog ran ahead of him, watching which aircraft he was heading for and waiting alongside it until he arrived. As they turned from the hangars and taxied to the gate that led on to the flying field, it stood with its Queen Anne front legs up against the Plexiglass bomb-aimer's window and watched the movements on the ground with approval.

They taxied onto the take-off and landing area and swung to face the length of the field. Watched by Jenno, Boumphrey did his checks carefully and professionally then he turned and smiled. It was a strangely attractive smile.

'Here goes nothing,' he said.

Opening the throttle, he released the brakes and the Oxford began to move forward, slowly at first, then swiftly gathering speed. Lifting the tail to a flying attitude, Boumphrey allowed the speed to increase further, then very gently began to lift the machine off the ground. He wasn't sure what he had been expecting but, whatever it was, it didn't happen. The Oxford lifted slowly, even a little sluggishly – and, holding it level for a while to build up the speed, Boumphrey pulled gently back on the stick and the machine began to climb in a slow right-hand turn.

Having supervised the lift-off, the dog, which had watched every movement below as they roared into the air, climbed down and chose a spot near Boumphrey and went to sleep. Jenno had long since noticed that no amount of manoeuvring disturbed the dog, but when Boumphrey throttled back for his final approach, it would be back at the front dome to supervise the landing and at the doors as they rolled to a stop, waiting to be let out.

'Bang on,' Boumphrey said cheerfully. 'It flies. That means that if they're needed we have twenty-seven more aggressive aircraft. Let's nip along the edge of the plateau and see what's happening there.'

Flying at two hundred and fifty feet, a hundred feet above the highest part of the plateau, the turbulence started, the instrument panel dancing on its mountings, and as they drew nearer the machine began to drop and flounder so that Boumphrey had to work hard at the controls to contain the fluctuating airspeed within a safe range. But it was possible to see everything that was happening. The escarpment was like an ants' nest and swarming with men. They appeared to be all over the high ground and batteries were already in position, the gun barrels pointing towards the landing field. They could see lorries, cars, carts, Bren carriers, batteries and machine gun posts all being set up and trenches being dug along the edge of the plateau. Hundreds of faces lifted as the Oxford passed over.

'Bit like walking down Piccadilly with no clothes on,' Boumphrey observed. 'Everybody's interested.'

He took another look through the window and started a gentle turn to the right. 'Well,' he said. 'Here we go. Now to see if the bombs will come unstuck when I pull the string. It's a good job they're unprimed. I should hate to drop one on the air vice-marshal's office.'

A deep dry ditch ran along the far end of the landing field and Boumphrey indicated it. 'How about that?' he said. 'I'll pop 'em in between the trees there and the pile of mud they took out last time they did the spring clean.'

Jenno said nothing. Boumphrey seemed to be managing very well. He turned over the hangars and, flying south along the ditch, pressed the tit of the bomb release. As they pulled up in a climbing turn, through the Plexiglass Jenno saw three puffs of dust in the ditch and one on the bank.

'That was a pretty good try, Ratter,' he said.

'Luck' Boumphrey shrugged. 'Well, at least the bombs drop. Let's try the other four.'

They came round again and this time Boumphrey dropped two of the bombs in the ditch.

'At nought feet, mind.' Boumphrey sounded self-deprecatory. 'Might be different a bit higher up – and with chaps shooting at me.'

A lorry was speeding across the airfield as they turned for their final approach over the escarpment, Jenno holding his breath as Boumphrey skimmed the edge so low he could see Irazhi soldiers lighting fires.

As the engineering officer had warned, the stability of the

aircraft on the final approach wasn't all it was intended to be but it also wasn't as bad as they'd expected and, since they were up and had to get down, it was something they were going to have to cope with.

'Watch the port wing,' Jenno said quietly. 'If you're not careful it'll drop and you'll be in a spin.'

'Bit touchy on the controls,' Boumphrey admitted. 'But nothing that can't be handled.'

The dog awake and checking the landing, the propeller wind-milling, the machine making a whirring noise in the silence, they skated over the perimeter fence and a second or two later the wheels were rumbling along the ground. As they turned at the far end, the lorry they'd seen racing across the field appeared alongside and a flight sergeant stuck his hand out, his thumb up, his face covered in smiles.

'Five out of eight, sir,' he yelled. 'And three near misses.'

Boumphrey smiled. 'Wizard,' he said. 'Ten for effort at least.'

12

The air vice-marshal was just considering the contents of the note delivered by the Irazhi colonel when the telephone rang.

The note informed him that the Irazhi army had occupied the Kubish ridge to the south and east of the airfield for the purposes of manoeuvres and requested that all flying should stop.

As the telephone shrilled, the air vice-marshal picked it up, reaching out one hand without looking. It was the group captain.

'We've just flown an Oxford loaded with eight 20-pound practice bombs,' he said. 'And dropped them onto a chosen target at the end of the airfield. That gives us twenty-seven more aircraft, sir, a total of seventy-three instead of the forty-six we had with the new arrivals.'

'Thank you,' the air vice-marshal said. 'I'm glad to hear it, because we've just learned officially that the Irazhi army's occupied Dhubban village and the plateau overlooking the airfield and that all flying is to cease forthwith. I shall be able to refuse with greater confidence.'

As the reply was sent off in the AVM's car, carried by a squadron leader, accompanied for the look of the thing by a flight lieutenant and a flight sergeant carrying a white flag, another of the interminable discussions began, this time in the office behind the main hangar which had become the operations room.

'Though they've collared the pumping station for the sewage system,' the Works and Bricks representative announced, 'the clots don't seem to have had the wits to switch off the pumps.'

'And a damn good job, too,' Vizard remarked. 'With 10,000 people dependent on them.'

With this information and Boumphrey's successful experiment, they could now reconsider their position.

'Leaving out the troop carriers which are not only slow but practically prehistoric,' Fogarty said, 'we can now conceive five squadrons in the event we shall need them.'

There was one squadron of Audaxes, each carrying eight 20-pound bombs; one of Audaxes carrying two 250-pounders; one of Harts; twenty-seven Oxfords now fitted to carry eight 20-pounders; and one flight of Gladiator fighters. Unfortunately, not one of the flights had a sufficient number of pilots and there was an even greater shortage of observers and gunners. For the Gordons there were no pilots at all.

'Though I expect we could raise one or two more at a pinch,' Fogarty said. 'There are also the Blenheims, one still unserviceable until spare parts can be flown in, and the Rapide. The Blenheims could be flown by any of the old hands and the Rapide could be flown if necessary by a man with no hands.'

Vizard said nothing and Fogarty continued. 'That uses up every man on the station who can fly, whether he's experienced in operations or not, and every bomb rack and every front gun. For bomb-aimers and rear gunners we shall have to use pupils and anyone else who's willing to have a go.' He drew a deep breath. 'It's not exactly a formidable force, is it?'

The second Irazhi attempt to stop flying took place later in the morning. The Irazhi colonel was as polite as before but his note was more peremptory this time.

'No aircraft or armoured cars are to leave the compound,' the note stated. 'Otherwise artillery will be obliged to fire on them – if necessarily heavily. Irazhi troops are digging trenches and installing anti-aircraft guns, and armoured cars will be patrolling towards the airfield.'

113

The air vice-marshal read the note carefully, studied it and digested it, and wrote his reply in exactly the same terms as before, with the suggestion that the Irazhi manoeuvres take place elsewhere. He could not agree with the demand and it was refused.

He had decided that he must strike first. A British colonel was on the way to command the ground forces but they still possessed no artillery. However, he had Audaxes and Harts, both of which had been developed with a view to using them as dive bombers after it had been discovered in the twenties that an aircraft could hit a target more often by diving low on to it at an angle of forty-five degrees. The technique had been discovered by the Americans and developed to perfection in Poland and France by the Germans, and while Harts and Audaxes were hardly Stukas they had been built for the job and now looked like having to do it.

The AVM lit his pipe and sucked at it for a while. He still wasn't certain of the Assyrian levies on whom the defence was largely based and, if the Irazhis put in their attack after dark, they would be helpless because they couldn't mount any kind of air defence after daylight had gone.

He decided to temporize for as long as possible and to obtain via the embassy some general diplomatic advice from the Foreign Office on what line to follow. It was obvious the Irazhi commander wasn't going to rush things. Perhaps he was in doubt about what retaliation he might expect and how much he could trust his peasant soldiers. Perhaps, even, he was one of the Sandhurst-trained officers in the Irazhi army and had no wish to go to war against his mentors. The AVM had already been in touch with Cairo and he had been told to retaliate if the Irazhis opened fire, but if the Irazhis opened fire first he could well lose his only weapon, his aircraft, before they had had time to do anything for their own protection.

He looked at Flying Officer Osanna. 'Would you say it was permitted to punch in the nose a man who's holding a club to your head, Osanna?' he asked.

114

Osanna smiled. 'In my view, sir, it is, but I'm only Intelligence and that would seem to be a decision for a diplomat. Perhaps we should ask the ambassador.'

The AVM called for the signals officer and told him to get in contact with the embassy. 'I want authorization to take what measures I consider necessary,' he said. 'And at once.'

Communications with the embassy had been restored and the ambassador didn't hesitate. His view was that it *was* permissible to throw the first punch if you felt threatened.

'Twice blessed, sir,' Osanna said, 'is he whose cause is just. Thrice blest he who gets his blow in fust.'

The Valentias returned towards the end of the day. As they taxied towards the hangars and rolled to a stop, the doors opened and men began to pour out, heavily loaded infantrymen in shorts and topees and carrying rifles. Someone raised a cheer and the native workers clapped politely. As the soldiers began to line up, the air vice-marshal's car arrived and swung round to a stop as a man wearing the crown and star of a lieutenant colonel stepped out.

'Ballantine,' he said. 'GSO1 to the C-in-C at Basra. I've come to look after the ground defence.'

'Glad to see you,' the AVM said. 'It looks very much as though we're going to need you. I think the Irazhis mean business. We've just learned that they've not only occupied the heights over there but Howeidi, a few miles upriver from us, as well. With Dhubban and Fullajah to the east also occupied, it looks very much as though we're cut off.'

Almost as the first two Valentias discharged their cargoes, the next two arrived. Somebody somewhere had pulled their fingers out and had organized the thing, and at Kubaiyah the AVM's staff were responding in the same way. As soon as the aircraft were seen approaching, vehicles left headquarters for the airfield and were alongside even as the machines drew to a stop. There wasn't even the need to switch off the engines and the machines were away again almost immediately. The

AVM had no intention of having the Irazhis opening fire and catching them at their most vulnerable on the ground while surrounded by women and children.

Ballantine brought news that the solitary bomber squadron stationed at Shaibah was to be reinforced by ten Wellingtons, two-engined heavies from the Middle East, on which the AVM could draw if necessary. It was heartening news, as also was the information that the polo field/golf course airstrip was now ready for use, that the gun positions were finished and the trench digging was progressing favourably.

As the Valentias came and went, the numbers of civilians, both white and Asian, began to dwindle. But there was still a great number of them and the AVM called in the catering officer. 'We shall have to start thinking of supplies,' he said. 'What can you suggest?'

The catering officer had already given it some thought.

'Normally, sir,' he said, 'the Asian families live almost entirely on mutton and we've been requiring as many as a hundred and fifty sheep a day. However, I've had a word with their leaders and I know they'll waive their scruples if necessary and be prepared to eat tinned beef. So there'll be no starving. However, it's going to require a lot of tins and I suggest that someone – me, for instance, since I know more about it than anyone and can also urge the necessity for speed – should fly off with one of the Valentias and arrange to purchase food at the coast, which I can bring back tomorrow.'

The AVM frowned. 'There might not be a tomorrow if they start firing on us,' he pointed out.

Despite the AVM's defiant message, there had still been no move from the Irazhis on the escarpment and the Valentias were still coming in and taking off – bringing in supplies, weapons, ammunition and bombs and taking away the women and children. They also, to the AVM's delight, brought an artificer from the Royal Artillery, a stumpy leather-faced sergeant called Porlock who immediately set

116

about examining the two howitzers in front of the head-quarters building.

'Around thirty-two coats of paint on 'em,' he announced in disgust. 'You buggers believe in keeping things pretty, don't you?'

The two guns were unshackled from their concrete plinths, hitched to a tractor and towed round to Workshops where a space had been cleared for the sergeant and a small army of native labourers who were to work with him. He peered at the breeches lying on a bench, sniffed at them, ran his hand over them, and pronounced his opinion.

'Looked after these a bit better than the pieces themselves,' he announced. 'Nice and shiny. Clean, bright and lightly oiled. A bit pitted here and there, but at least you 'aven't painted the buggers.'

During the afternoon, a message was received from the Foreign Office in London via the embassy in Mandadad, saying the position must be restored at all costs and the Irazhis moved from their threatening stance. The AVM didn't require instructions to realize how the minds in London were working. With the whole of the Middle East in the balance, with Greece and the Balkans on the point of falling and Crete threatened, with Rommel running riot in North Africa and Vichy more than willing to allow Luftwaffe machines to pass through their territory in Syria to help the Irazhis, the best defence was attack while the Germans were tied up with their plans for Crete. He sat at his desk, his fingers tapping its surface, his mind working swiftly. Then he called in Osanna and his signals officer and arranged for a new message to be sent under a white flag to the Irazhi commander on the escarpment.

'Inform him that his people must be gone by 0500 hours tomorrow,' he said. 'If they're still there then, we shall take steps to make them go.'

As Osanna and the signals officer went about their business, the AVM called in his chief staff officer and arranged to call another conference. The departmental officers gathered quickly, all of them sober and thoughtful, and the AVM put the position to them quickly.

'We have permission to do what we think necessary to protect ourselves,' he pointed out. 'We have even been told that if we have to strike, we must strike hard. I gather Churchill himself is right behind us. The question is "When?" and still of course, "What with?" '

The figures were trotted out again and the AVM listened in silence. All the Oxfords were being fitted with Boumphrey's amateur bomb rack which, now that it had been proved successful, carried the august approval of the engineering officer, and to the extra machines now available they could also add the ten new Wellingtons in Shaibah, which could be called upon if necessary.

'They *will* be necessary,' the AVM said. 'What about the Irazhis?'

'Crews doing their S-turns over the escarpment report an additional twenty-seven guns,' Fogarty reported. 'Together with more vehicles and more men. It would be fatal to allow them to get in the first blow.'

'I don't intend to,' the AVM said sharply. 'However, it's too late to do anything today because when we start we must make it as heavy a blow as we can and I want the bombing attack to go on the whole day from dawn until darkness. I want every available aircraft in the air by first light ready to bomb as soon as the crews can see their targets. I've warned Shaibah not to send in any more Valentias for the moment. We don't want them getting mixed up with our machines. Ground crews and those pupils not in the air will remain in the trenches.'

'That'll leave nobody to move the aircraft, sir,' Fogarty pointed out.

'That can't be helped. The air crews and ground crews must do it. I want nobody about except the air crews, ground crews, armourers and refuellers. At last light tonight we'll send up a machine on a provocative flight to see how the Irazhis react. All civilians must remain out of sight.' He glanced at Colonel Ballantine. 'You have your men deployed, Colonel?'

'I have.' Ballantine was a short brisk man not unlike Sergeant Porlock, the Royal Artillery artificer, and, like the sergeant, clearly didn't think much of the casual ways of the junior service.

'You'll have the support of the levies.' The AVM glanced at Verity, the commander of the levies. 'What about them? Can you trust them?'

'We have to, sir, don't we?' Verity said.

The station armaments officer spoke. 'We have plenty of ammunition, sir, and we've had every spare man belting ammunition since the crisis started. I've also had a word with Sergeant Porlock. He claims he *can* make the two howitzers usable, but not immediately.'

'Ask him to move as fast as possible.' The AVM looked at Jenno. 'Armoured cars: These will be kept out of sight where possible but the perimeter must be patrolled constantly.'

'I'll see to that, sir.'

The AVM cleared his throat. 'Not you, Jenno. You're a pilot and you and your second in command are going to be needed.'

Jenno looked startled, then his expression changed. 'I'm pleased to hear it, sir.'

The AVM looked at Boumphrey who sat up straight. As the junior officer at the conference, only there on sufferance as the nominal leader of the suddenly important Mounted Legion, he was always on his best behaviour.

'How about your people, Boumphrey? Are they ready in every way?'

'In every way, sir. Camped under the trees round the polo ground.'

'They know what to do?'

'Yes, sir.'

'Can you trust them?'

'Absolutely, sir. They'll fight anything. Even their own side.'

'What about your second in command?'

'Ghadbhbhan's entirely trustworthy.'

'Then they're going to have to do it without you, Boumphrey. You're a pilot, too.'

13

The evening came in a satin sunset of oyster and duck egg blue, against which could be seen a long skein of flighting ibis heading for the marshes further south. Slowly the sky turned yellow then salmon pink, one grey streak of cloud cutting across it like a sword stroke. The wind had dropped to nothing.

His dog at his heels, Boumphrey stood on the airfield as the last of the parked aeroplanes were pushed through the gate into the compound and out of sight behind the hangars. The take-off area stood empty except for the solitary Audax which was to make the reconnaissance flight over the escarpment the AVM had ordered. It was to be flown by Fogarty and Flight Sergeant Waldo, who was one of the most experienced observers at Kubaiyah.

The Audax was giving trouble. To start the engine, the ground crew had to wind a large handle pushed into the side and they were cursing as the effort made them break into a sweat. The sergeant removed the side panel from the engine, put his arm in and made an adjustment, then he replaced the panel and turned to the men on the handle.

'Give it another go,' he said.

This time the engine crackled into life, spluttered and settled down to a steady roar. Fogarty shuffled himself to comfort in his seat and Waldo in the rear cockpit arranged his maps. They were already marked with the gun positions and lorry parks on the plateau.

'All right!' Fogarty lifted his gloved hand. As he held up his thumb the mechanics hauled away the chocks.

The engine's roar increased, and the aeroplane began to move slowly forward, throwing up an enormous cloud of gritty dust which made the ground crew and the few watchers close their eyes and turn their backs until the machine was far enough away for it to start settling.

They watched the aircraft thunder down the airfield towards the ditch at the end, then they saw it, a moving shadow against the horizon, start to lift until it was a sharply etched shape against the glow in the sky. It climbed steadily to a height of five hundred feet then turned and headed back towards the plateau. As it roared over them, their heads turned with it as if they were all attached to a string.

The flight sergeant in charge of the ground crew turned to his men. 'Right, lads,' he said. 'You know what to do. Got your torches?'

The flight mechanics nodded and the flight sergeant indicated the nearby gate that led from the airfield to the space beyond the hangars. 'When he lands he's going to come straight across here and straight through that gate there. Got it?'

More nods.

'Just in case them guns on the hill there wade in, see? We want him behind the hangars in double-quick time where they can't hit him. Got it? I want one man either side of the gate with his torch making circles so he can see where it is and the other thirty feet inside, dead centre for him to aim at. If the upsadaisy starts, we might be doing it all the time.'

'That'll be the day,' one of the mechanics observed. 'Especially with the pupil pilots.'

The machine was up for no more than an hour, and they watched it making provocative runs only a hundred feet above the line of the escarpment. Every moment they expected firing to start, but nothing happened. They could see lights up there and a few fires and an occasional lifting column of dark smoke, but there was absolute silence.

The Audax came in quickly, making a perfect three-point landing and heading straight for the gate where the flight mechanics with the torches were waiting. As it went through the gate, it swung left and disappeared behind the hangars.

Osanna was waiting as the crew climbed out. Alongside him was Boumphrey. He was getting the feel of an aircraft again and that morning's flight had set him thinking. Despite his fondness for his dark-skinned legionnaires, there was something about flying that got hold of you. It made you feel as if you were one of God's chosen few, able to feel the sun before it touched lesser mortals chained to the ground. It gave you a vision of God, able to see whole countrysides when the normal eye could carry only as far as an earthbound horizon. He suddenly found himself itching to have another go.

Leaving the tarmac outside the hangars, Boumphrey headed for the hospital. With the fun about to start, it was time he saw Colonel Wood-Withnell to make sure his daughter had got away safely to the coast. He had been occupied during most of the day but he knew her name had been on the list for one of the earlier flights.

In the growing darkness there was movement everywhere near the hangars. The Audax which had just landed was being pushed slowly towards the trees that grew round what had once been the golf course and the polo ground. There were other Audaxes there, parked with the Harts in the shadows, and he could see lights where men tinkered with engines and airframes. Outside the hangars, the Oxfords were parked haphazardly, fitters putting the finishing touches to them, all talking a little more loudly than normal with the excitement. What was going to happen to them the following day none of them knew, but they'd all guessed it wasn't going to be pleasant. The solitary serviceable Blenheim was still inside the open doors of the main hangar because it had been decided to keep it as a reserve to be used only after finding out what happened with the older aircraft. The seven Gladiators were parked in a line, compact and workmanlike but since 1939 well out of date. The last biplane fighters produced for the RAF, they were only a step in what had been a ridiculously long-delayed change to monoplanes. Nevertheless they had been well conceived and, despite their drawbacks against more modern machines, were remarkably manoeuvrable.

The Fairey Gordons, with their two-bay biplane wings and their huge Panther radials, looked lonely, parked away from the other machines by the end of the hangars nearest to the escarpment. They were slow, and had been placed there where they were likely to become the first casualties because they were considered to be the most expendable.

There was activity everywhere as Boumphrey moved from the airfield to the main complex of buildings where the hospital was situated. A large Red Cross flag had already been erected above it and ambulances stood ready outside. A petrol bowser growled past to refuel one of the Oxfords. It was followed by an armoury truck. Inside, beyond the open tailgate he could see belts of shining ammunition. Boards had been erected with arrows indicating the route to the shelters and the trenches.

He wondered if it would work. Fogarty had given him a group of Oxfords, all flown by pupil pilots whom he suspected he'd have to lead by the hand.

'Show 'em how to do it, Boumphrey,' Fogarty had said.

It had crossed Boumphrey's mind that Fogarty was being kind and, because he had done so little flying at Kubaiyah and was a bit of an unknown quantity, had deliberately given him an easy job. He felt no qualms, however, and was quite certain he was capable of doing anything that was asked of him. Boastfulness was not one of Boumphrey's vices but, despite his retiring manner, he also didn't suffer a great deal from false modesty.

There was a lot of surreptitious movement round the hangars. With the ground personnel ordered to remain in trenches and the only people left to refuel, arm and move the aircraft the crews themselves, they had already started clandestinely tackling odd airmen and getting their promise to ignore the order. The pupils were more than willing and had no intention, if a battle started, to spend it all with their heads down.

'We're supposed to be the cream of the younger generation,' one of them said, not entirely jokingly.

'Jesus,' someone replied, 'if we're the cream the future's far from certain.'

The hospital showed the same signs of activity as the rest of the station. Sandbags had been erected at all the doors and windows of the low, single-storey building and every patient who could be moved out had been discharged, to leave the beds empty for casualties when the fun started.

The entrance hall was covered with the RAF's favourite brown linoleum and smelled of floor polish, ether and Dettol. Colonel Wood-Withnell was sitting at the station medical officer's desk, going through a pile of papers. There was still a sticking plaster on his head, his hands were bandaged, and there was a livid bruise on his face, but he seemed alert enough and to be relishing the thought of action.

'Hello,' he said, his view of Boumphrey considerably changed since his rescue. 'You involved in the bunfight tomorrow?'

'Yes, sir. But they've taken the legion away from me temporarily.'

As Wood-Withnell's eyebrows lifted, Boumphrey explained. 'Thought I'd be more use as a pilot,' he said. 'We're a bit short and we need to give those clots on the escarpment what for. All at once. One big bang sort of thing, to make 'em think. I'm to go back to the legion when things settle down. That's if I want to.'

Suddenly he wondered if he did. Another step up in rank, he decided, and he could start thinking of applying for staff college.

'Prue get away all right?' he asked.

Wood-Withnell stared at him for a moment, frowning. 'She wouldn't go,' he said.

Boumphrey's dismal expression lifted. 'She wouldn't?'

'No. Dammit, it made nonsense of all that effort you put into getting us out of Mandadad!'

'Why wouldn't she go?'

'Because *I* wouldn't go. They're going to need every experienced pair of hands they can get here in the next few days. I said they could use another doctor and the station medical officer agreed. So when I said I wasn't going, Prue said she wasn't going either. I couldn't make her change her mind. Several of the nurses volunteered to stay and she said if they could, she could. God knows what she'll do. She knows nothing about it.'

'I expect she'll learn, sir.'

The old man shook his head. 'Shouldn't think so,' he said. 'Not very bright, Prue. Never did very well at school. Nervous type. Unreliable.'

Considering how calmly Prudence had behaved during Boumphrey's rescue of her and her father from Mandadad and during the long slow trip from the city to Kubaiyah, Boumphrey was inclined to doubt it.

'You can never tell, sir.' Prudence had once told Boumphrey that she had hated the boarding school to which she had had to go while her father was serving abroad in the army. Since Boumphrey had also hated boarding school, it gave them a lot in common. 'Where is she now, sir?'

His head down again, the colonel waved his hand vaguely without bothering to look up. 'Somewhere about. The station medical officer found her a job.'

Boumphrey found Prudence in a room off one of the wards. With her were two other white women and several Asians, the wives of the Indian staff. She jumped as Boumphrey spoke her name and he apologized sheepishly.

'Sorry, old thing,' he said. 'Shouldn't have come on you suddenly out of the sun like that.'

'No, no, Ratter,' she said, bending to acknowledge the wriggling dog at his feet. 'I'm delighted. How super! Though you ought not to be here. They'll kick you out if they see you.'

She gestured to the other women to carry on with what they were doing and led him into the corridor.

'They tried to shove me on the aeroplanes,' she said. 'I wasn't having that.'

'It's going to be sticky here,' Boumphrey pointed out. 'Aren't there medical orderlies?'

'They're going to be busy if it turns out the way everybody says it will. They've given me the job of looking after linen, towels, utensils and so on. They've even given me a staff because they've also added the job of making sure that as soon as any of the water containers is emptied it's refilled immediately. Everything's to be kept filled in case the water tower's hit and the supply runs out.'

Boumphrey said nothing because they all knew the water tower was their most vulnerable point. It rose above the surrounding buildings in clear view from the escarpment and if it were destroyed – or even if the pumps which kept it filled were smashed – the water supply on which they all depended would dry up. They'd been filling baths, sinks, jugs, basins, and every empty bottle in the officers', sergeants', airmen's and workers' messes with water, and instructions had gone round to the effect that they were to be kept full as long as the water tank could supply water.

'They can't fire at that,' he said as cheerfully as he could. 'They might hit the radio mast at AHQ and that's got storks nesting there with a couple of young.'

She wasn't deluded. She knew he was being cheerful for her sake.

'What about you?' she asked. 'Is your legion ready?'

'My legion,' Boumphrey said, 'is being taken into action, if that's what it comes to, by Sergeant Major Ghadbhbhan.'

'Is he the good-looking one who was there when you fished us out of Mandadad?'

'Yes. He was once an actor. Clever chap. Remarkable mimic.'

'But, Ratter, why have they taken them away from you?'

'They've given me an aeroplane instead.'

For a brief moment concern showed in her face. Ground duties would probably mean sitting with your head down in a trench, while flying was a considerably more dangerous sport. She'd had two cousins killed already in the Royal Air Force, one of them flying a Blenheim, who'd been shot down trying to stop the Germans in France, and one flying a Hurricane who hadn't survived more than the first few passes during the Battle of Britain. And both of them had been flying better machines than Boumphrey was likely to fly in Kubaiyah. But she had long since learned that one didn't show fear or apprehension to a man about to go into action and she tried to look cheerful. To her surprise, Boumphrey also looked cheerful.

'Never thought they'd suggest it,' he admitted. 'But they've decided to take a chance. Have to make sure I live up to their view of me.'

'Oh, Ratter, you will take care?'

Boumphrey smiled reassuringly. The one thing that was wanted, it seemed, was that he should *not* take care. The first briefing they'd had, had indicated that every possible risk within reason was to be taken, the object being to do as much damage as quickly as possible in the hope of discouraging the Irazhis.

'Piece of cake really,' he said lightly. 'Not much for us to do. I've been given an Oxford and they're not bombers really so we'll just be stooging about beyond gun range dropping our eggs where we can.'

She tried to push her fears to the back of her mind and managed a bright smile. 'And you came to see me, Ratter, before it all started! How splendid!'

'Thought you'd be gone, as a matter of fact,' he admitted. 'Then I heard you hadn't. Thought I'd better look you up.'

She gave him a fond look. She was well aware that he wasn't the handsomest of men, with his pale hair and his long thin body. But she was aware of her own failings in that department, too, and the lack of interest most men showed in her, so she was happy to ignore Boumphrey's looks for the fact that he was loyal and pleased to be in her company.

And at the moment, in fact, he seemed vaguely like a knight in armour about to gallop off to war. He'd already rescued her once and here he was about to rescue her again; she felt he should be carrying her favour on his helmet – a scarf or a handkerchief or something of that sort. But people these days didn't wear their lady's favours on their helmets, especially not on flying helmets, and she knew he'd be embarrassed if she suggested anything so silly.

Instead she took his hand and squeezed it. 'Best of luck, Ratter,' she said. 'I'll pray for you.'

He was probably going to need more than prayer, Boumphrey thought as he headed away from the hospital. As the beseeching words went up, he could only hope the Almighty would be handy and that the prayers would be loud enough to attract His attention.

The camp cinema had been set aside for the briefing and when Boumphrey arrived the aircrews were gathering. Among them were what by RAF standards were elderly officers who hadn't flown for some time, and office wallahs who were more at home flying a desk. There were also the younger men, of course, the flying instructors, the sergeants, the people who towed drogues, a flying officer observer whose normal job was running classes for navigators, and Flight Sergeant Waldo, whose job was to dispense information on the bomb sight and teach the pupil air gunners how to fire their Vickers K guns, Lewis guns and Brownings. He had been an observer in Blenheims in France the year before and had emerged from the slaughter there wounded and badly shaken, because you rarely got out of a stricken Blenheim and, when you did, it was said, you were often decapitated by the aerial that ran from above the pilot's cockpit to the tail. Flight Sergeant Waldo had managed it but it had left him unfit for flying for some time, but here he was, in Kubaiyah for a rest, offering himself as aircrew once more.

The final move before the briefing was to make up the aircrews. Normally new crews flew together for a while to get used to each other before facing the enemy. In Kubaiyah there was going to be no chance of that and they were going to have to do their best without, so that whom you chose could be very important indeed. But when they got down to it, re-markably little effort was needed and it took place in the usual casual RAF manner. It had always been casual. On operational training units in England, pilots, observers, wireless operators and gunners were all thrown into the crew room together and told to sort themselves out. It invariably ended up with 'We've got a couple of pilots and a gunner. Fancy joining us as observer?' and it was the same here.

The more senior officers had naturally acquired the more experienced crew members but, since there weren't many of these, most were having to accept pupils. Boumphrey had no idea where to start. He could see a lot of faces, none of which he knew and none of which he appeared to have come across before because of his absorption with the legion. In the end he picked on one of the pupils for the simple reason that he looked a little like himself. He was tall and thin and fair-haired, though in no department as pronounced as Boumphrey.

'Who're you?' Boumphrey asked.

'Aircraftman Second Class Darling, sir. Observer under training. AC2/Obs/UT.'

Boumphrey smiled. 'Sounds like a chemical formula, doesn't it?'

Darling seemed to be struggling with a confession. 'Most people call me "Sweetheart," sir,' he admitted with a grin.

Boumphrey smiled back. 'My name's Boumphrey. Pro-nounced Bum-free.'

'Delighted to meet you, sir.'

'What's your bomb-aiming like?'

'Not bad, sir.'

'They've given me a bunch of Oxfords to look after. Mostly pupil pilots. So you'll probably be called on to show them how to do it.'

There were a few catcalls and remarks as they settled into their seats for the briefing, but not many because none of them had any idea of what they were facing. The group captain appeared on the platform in front of the screen. At the table with him were the chief flying instructor and Flying Officer Osanna, who was handling Intelligence. In England they had meteorologists and other experts to tell them what to expect. Kubaiyah was different.

The group captain held up his hand and the catcalls died away abruptly.

'Normally,' the group captain said, 'at this stage of a briefing in England, the senior officer drags back a curtain showing the Continent, and all is revealed, with routes and targets marked for everybody to see. All very dramatic. Here, we don't have that because we're not going very far.'

He spoke about the need for courage and self-sacrifice and the need to keep the flag flying. He didn't believe his own rhetoric any more than the people listening to him did, but it was a simplistic form of address and they all knew what he meant. If Kubaiyah fell to the enemy, the whole Middle East could fall and, with it India, and eventually the United Kingdom.

As he sat down, Fogarty rose and the screen above the men at the table became bright with a map of the edge of the airfield and the escarpment. Someone had photographed a large-scale map and blown it up and Photography had made a slide of it.

'It's all there,' Fogarty said. 'Mark it on your own maps, those of you who have them. Gun positions are marked in red, and lorry parks in green. Your orders are very simple. You are to drive the Irazhis beyond artillery range – in other words, off

131

the escarpment. Targets: Guns, armoured fighting vehicles, by which I mean tanks if there are any, armoured cars, transport columns, and troops. There'll be plenty to go for and I don't have to tell you that guns are the most important. There are plenty for everybody and I don't think you'll have difficulty seeing them, because they'll all be pointing at you. The Wellingtons from Basra will start the ball rolling, followed by the Harts, the Audaxes and the Gordons, with the Oxfords picking up the bits.'

There was some comment about numbers and a lot of scribbling as the positions were marked off on maps.

'Details,' Fogarty continued. 'The escarpment is one hundred feet high at its southern end and around one hundred and fifty feet towards Dhubban village. However, I don't have to tell you that, because you know it already and won't need to be advised not to fly below that height.'

There was a murmur of laughter and Fogarty went on. 'Weather: This is normally a meteorologist's job but we've been able to dispense with him here because it's not likely to change. Wind: West to east and as usual full of sand. Temperature: Too high. Skies: Cloudless. You needn't take the weather too much into your calculations. I suspect,' he added, 'that calculations won't enter into the thing overmuch at all, in fact. It's going to be a case of getting in close and doing as much damage as you can.'

There was a murmur of approval and Fogarty continued bluntly. 'We've heard nothing further from the Irazhis so we can assume that they haven't moved and don't intend to. They hadn't at last light, so anything you see will be a legitimate target and you needn't worry that you'll be bombing civilians because there aren't any up there. Every aircraft that can get off the ground is to be in the air by daylight and you will bomb as soon as you can see your targets. Try not to be in too much of a rush and all bomb the first target you see. We have a limited number of aircraft and a limited number of bombs, so, if someone else's hammering something, leave it to him and go for something else. Our chance of success depends about 25 per cent on matériel and 75 per cent on a confident spirit. In fact, it's going to be a case of colossal cheek and unflagging labour, and it's going to mean intensive flying, doubtless for several days, to reduce the odds against us. We have to smash their firepower before they can smash ours.'

'Or before they hit the water tower,' someone at the back called out.

Someone flourished a couple of Irazhi notes. 'Two fils on them hitting that first.'

There was a laugh but they all knew that the unseen speakers had hit the nail on the head. As Prudence Wood-Withnell had noticed, although every bath and every vessel on the station had been filled, if the water tower was hit that was that and it would be only a matter of time before the station fell.

Fogarty was talking again. 'Details: Aircraft will be re-fuelled, loaded and started up behind the hangars where they're out of sight. As soon as they're ready they will taxi round the corner, through the gate, and on to the runway. You'll be taking off under the enemy's nose, so don't waste time. The first take-off will be the most difficult because you'll be stepping on each other's heels to be up before daylight. As you return, you will taxi back behind the hangars where the ground crews will be waiting. Try not to hit each other. There'll be a man at the gate to warn you, so don't ignore his instructions. If you have any wounded or are in trouble, fire a red Very as you come in and you'll be helped. That's about it. I suggest now that you try to get some sleep. Reveille will be at 0245 hours. Assembly at your aircraft at 0315 hours.'

As Fogarty turned away, they rose. It hadn't been a briefing such as was being given these days in England to bomber crews or the pilots of intruding fighters; it wasn't even the sort of briefing some of those who had experienced action at the beginning of the war had been given. But its point was clear and it was sufficient and faces were set and thoughtful.

133

Part Two

1

The first machine moved off at 0430 hours. It was one of the Oxfords and it moved slowly round from the hangars to the gate that led to the airfield.

There had been a constant sound through the night of revving engines as machines were tested and checked. The noise was partly deliberate. Petrol wasn't a problem and ever since the previous noon engines had kept starting and stopping to keep the Irazhi commanders on the escarpment guessing. Since engines had been roaring on and off throughout the afternoon, evening and night, it was hoped the noise in the early hours of the morning would not raise any alarm.

It was just possible to see the gates as the pilot of the Oxford turned and taxied onto the airfield. He moved slowly across to the south western corner, closely followed by another Oxford and another and another. Aircraft were also moving on the polo field as the Harts and Audaxes headed for the perimeter to make the most of their run, the motors revving in short bursts as the pilots, watching either side of their uptilted noses, zigzagged into place. The machines were painted in a variety of colours, from the green and brown of normal ground camouflage, through the sandy ochre of desert war paint, to the yellow of trainers. A strong breeze had got up.

This was going to be the tricky bit, Boumphrey decided. The aircraft were at their most vulnerable as they jockeyed for position, one behind the other, ready for the take-off. If the batteries on the escarpment chose to fire while they were all crowded together at the end of the runway and were lucky enough to drop their shells through the darkness into their midst they could destroy the only weapon they possessed in the first minutes. There was no flare path, so they were going to be taking off by instruments alone. All the leading planes were in the hands of experienced pilots. Those pupils who had been selected to fly would be taking off later when it was growing light.

The first faint suggestion of daylight was colouring the landscape as the last engines of the first wave of aircraft fired. By now the peace of the early morning was completely shattered. Blue tongues of exhaust flames were visible in the grey light, smoke curled up and there was a tang of high octane fuel. As the propellers turned the air became murky with rising dust as pilots checked cylinder head and oil temperatures, opening the throttles so that their aircraft bounced against the chocks.

The constant pounding roar as engine after engine crackled and rumbled in violent metallic life filled the heavens, and more and more machines surged forward to the edges of the airfield and the polo ground. A car containing Fogarty roared across to the first machine in the line. Fogarty climbed out and clambered on to the wing of the Audax to speak to the pilot.

'Whenever you like,' he said. 'The Wellingtons have indicated that they'll be overhead and in position to start at 0500 hours. Bombing will start as soon as they go in. You and the Harts will go in after them, followed by the Gordons and the Oxfords.'

As the car drew away, the pilot of the Audax lifted his hand and, as the chocks were removed, he opened the throttle and the machine began to move. As it raced forward, the tail lifted to a flying attitude and it gathered speed, continuing low above the ground until it had built up speed to climb. It was out of sight now from the watchers and the pilot was flying by instruments, lifting into the dark sky. He was followed almost immediately by another and then another.

With the rising sun behind them, they were taking off away

from the escarpment into the darkness and were hard to see, but as the light increased it was possible to pick out the dwindling specks against the lightening sky. They were a queer assortment, arranged in four squadrons, three of them bombers, one of fighters. Fortunately no one collided.

His dog – disgusted at being left behind – clutched by Ghadbhbhan, Boumphrey was well to the rear of the line, leading the second string of Oxfords. Still dazzling in its yellow paint, the Oxford had been considered in England the ideal vehicle for visiting friends on other stations, and it was difficult to accept that here it had become a frontline machine. One of the flight mechanics appeared, eyeing it sullenly over the starting handle he was clutching. The handle had to be inserted through the inboard engine cowling and not only did the effort of grinding it round and round until the revolving cylinders fired produce an unwanted amount of perspiration, but to most people it also seemed a highly dangerous pastime because it meant taking up a squatting position by the leading edge of the wing. When the starter dogs automatically disengaged, if you didn't watch what you were doing there was a nasty tendency to pitch forward into the whirling propeller. Ground crews always had a habit of disappearing when the call came to start an Oxford.

The engine crackled to life and the puce-faced mechanic thankfully disappeared, streaming sweat. Roaring down the field after the other machines, Boumphrey climbed to get as much height as he could so he could see what was going on below him. As he felt the excitement quicken inside him, he felt elated as never since his first operations in 1939 against the Germans. His hands were busy, checking and rechecking, his practised eyes on the temperatures, the oil pressure gauges, the artificial horizon, the air speed indicator. As he did so, his thoughts were busy. The Oxford was not everybody's favourite machine because, in addition to its built-in instability and the fact that it burned only too easily, it was difficult to get out of in an emergency. The roof exit was not directly above the pilot and was difficult to release, and it was something he'd always had trouble with. Because of the problems it raised, it left only the door down the fuselage, which was difficult to reach while wearing a seat parachute. The main spar, covered with plywood, went through the centre of the fuselage and had to be scrambled over to reach the door, and on the only occasion when he'd practised getting out in calm weather, before he'd even reached the door the port wing had gone over, the nose had dropped and he'd had to scramble hastily to his seat to right the machine before it fell into a spin.

As they climbed, Boumphrey's eyes searched the sky both ahead and behind and after a while he spotted a line of dots over his shoulder and slightly above. He recognized them at once as Wellingtons and wondered how long it would take Darling to see them. It didn't take as long as he expected and Darling thumped Boumphrey's shoulder and pointed.

'Use the intercom, old son,' Boumphrey said calmly, showing no annoyance.

Darling yelled into his microphone and as Boumphrey shook his head he began to yell louder, his words quite unheard above the roar of the engines. He was still yelling as Boumphrey tapped his earphones to indicate he should switch the microphone on, and then his words almost deafened Boumphrey.

Boumphrey's hand went to his own mike. 'Steady on, Darling,' he said, his voice unruffled. 'I can hear. No need to shout. Let's start again, shall we, and take it calmly. You've got something to report?'

There was a second's pause then Darling's voice came. 'The Wimpeys, sir.' He pointed vaguely.

Boumphrey nodded amiably, a note of academic interest seeping into his voice. 'There's a right and a wrong way to do it, old son. Let's do it the right way, shall we? Makes things easier. Try again.'

'Over on the right. Up a bit.'

Boumphrey glanced at the Wellingtons. They were still a

long way away and there was plenty of time for a little instruction. Might as well get it right, he thought. It could save a lot of trouble if the fun came thick and fast.

'Got 'em,' he said calmly, pretending to see them for the first time. 'But there's a proper way to deliver your message. First of all, you say who you are. *I* know, of course, because there's only you and me. But if you go from here to a Wellington like those chaps over there, you'll find there are five other chaps in the crew and the pilot will want to know which one you are. So, first of all, you say "Observer to captain", "Gunner to captain", "Copilot to skipper". Whatever happens to have been decided. Then he knows who you are and what part of the aircraft you occupy and in what direction you're looking. That immediately tells *him* roughly where to look, so he's ready for your next line. Which will be "port" or "starboard" or "red" or "green" – whichever you use. If it's off the starboard bow, it's "green bow" or the number of degrees. If it's off the other bow, it'll be red. If they're behind where those chaps are, it's "red quarter". That makes it spot-on, see? Then instead of saying "up a bit", you say "high" or "low" and, finding the rough position, the pilot then lifts or lowers his eyes until he sees 'em. Amazin' how important it is when the other chaps are enemies and you need to spot 'em quickly. Let's have another go, shall we?'

'Yes, sir. Sorry, sir.'

'Don't worry. Don't get excited and certainly don't panic. Just report it calmly – and, if your mike's working, without shouting. Right?'

He heard Darling swallow then his voice came quite calmly. 'Observer to skipper. Aircraft bearing red quarter high. I – I think they're Wellingtons.'

'Splendid,' Boumphrey said and, turning his head, gave the nervous Darling a beaming encouraging smile. Darling would willingly have died for him.

'You're quite right,' Boumphrey went on. 'They *are* the Wimpeys and I'm going to turn behind them and watch them

141

go in, then we'll let the Audaxes and the other gentry go down, then we'll sail across after 'em and drop our lot.'

In the scramble to take off, the flights had got themselves all over the sky and the different machines were now jockeying to get into position for their run in.

The Wellingtons, big, two-engined, geodetic-airframed machines, their round Hercules engines thundering, came in one behind the other in immaculate formation. They were at 2000 feet, moving very precisely, and Boumphrey saw their bomb doors open. Then they all dropped their bombs at once with a great air of pomposity.

'Daredevils,' he said and Darling grinned.

As the big bombers sailed over the plateau, tracer went down from the front and rear turrets and almost immediately they saw it start to come up in return. The Wellingtons seemed to be swallowing it.

The flashes as the bombs exploded were quite visible. Boumphrey glanced at the watch on his bare brown wrist. 'Oh-five hundred hours exactly,' he said.

Down on the ground, the men watching from the control tower could see the machines manoeuvring like dark birds along the edge of the escarpment. The larger shapes of the Wellingtons were beginning to move away now and the second wave of aircraft, Audaxes and Harts, began to drop down.

As they watched the smoke rising they heard the first shell coming. It screamed towards them, sounding like an express train, and exploded on the edge of the airfield. The officers ducked instinctively. The accounts officer, a precise man used to exactness, glanced at his watch. 'Oh-five hundred and fifty-five seconds,' he said. 'It didn't take them long to hoist in the idea and get cracking.'

The shells were beginning to fall faster now and a lorry moving from the hangars towards the polo ground disappeared in a flash and a puff of smoke and dust. From the control tower, they saw the bonnet cover, a wheel and what might have been a man flung out of the centre of it; then, as the dust settled and the smoke lifted, they saw only smouldering wreckage and a man with his clothes on fire running wildly, his mouth open, screaming. Another man appeared from the trees, knocked him over and rolled him in the dust. The flames disappeared and they saw the wretched man squirming on the ground, his clothes smoking. Within a minute an ambulance had roared up and the crew were lifting him through the open rear doors.

The next salvo of shells dropped nearer to the control tower and a group of men moving towards one of the aircraft began to run, their khaki stockings falling round their ankles as they scuttled for shelter. From one of the trenches a head popped up and they heard the iron voice of the station warrant officer. 'That man! Pull up your stockings and don't run so slovenly!' Then a machine gun opened up from the plateau and, as a line of spurts of dust ran along the ground, the head disappeared as abruptly as it had appeared.

Sitting up above the fight, watching what was happening, Boumphrey manoeuvred himself for his run in. The plateau was like an ants' nest now with men running in all directions. Lorries had started up and were lurching jerkily away. He could see the flashes of guns and the dark puffballs of smoke as the shells exploded. Then, as an Audax went rocketing past them at a crazy angle that almost gave him heart failure and left the Oxford bucketing in its slipstream, his full attention was occupied by the controls.

They seemed to be doing quite well so far but it was a crazy sort of affair, without much order and people dropping bombs and firing at anything that moved. Boumphrey could see the flashes from the guns as they sailed over at 1000 feet, Darling frantic with excitement, as though he were afraid the war would be over before he could do anything to affect it. He was jumping about excitedly in the nose of the Oxford, peering through the Plexiglass, and Boumphrey spoke quietly to him to calm him.

'Steady on, Darling,' he said. 'Take your time. Make a good job of it.'

'Yes, sir.' Darling managed to quieten down, then, as Boumphrey nodded, began to direct him on to his course.

'Left, sir. Left a bit more. Too much. Right a bit. That's it. Hold it. Hold – it. That's it, sir. I can see them going down. Christ almighty, sir, it's the whole bloody lot!'

With the weight gone, the Oxford lifted in a huge swoop and wavered until Boumphrey adjusted the trim.

'All the lot?' he asked as he regained control.

'Yes, sir.'

'Your fault, Darling? Panic a bit?'

'No, sir. I selected half. I think there must be a fault in the bomb rack electrics.'

'More than likely,' Boumphrey agreed, 'considering the speed they were pushed together. But never mind. On the whole it works and the armourers can have a look at it. Did we hit anything?'

'One of 'em seemed to go straight in, sir. T'others missed, I'm afraid.'

'One ought to be enough to do the job,' Boumphrey said. 'And you'll do better with practice. Well done. Give yourself a chocolate bar. Just one thing: In future, let's have your report properly, old son. The correct method is to say "Bombs gone" or "Bombs away". It don't matter much. It don't worry me particularly either but if you've got a nervous chap at the controls he might get confused with all that chatter. "Bombs gone" is just enough to tell him the machine will need a little trimming and that, if the nonsense is coming up at him fast and furious, he can push off for home. Next time, can we do it that way?'

'Yes, sir.' Darling sounded suitably crushed.

'No need to be downhearted though,' Boumphrey assured

him. 'It was a good show for a first try. Ten for effort, Darling.'

For a while longer, they sat above the fight. Boumphrey knew he ought to head for home but for a moment the sight of the swarming aircraft fascinated him. Then he realized that, despite the damage they were doing, RAF, Kubaiyah, didn't have a thing which could stop one of the Irazhi tanks driving, if it chose to, right up to the door of Air Headquarters. Nothing except bombs. They had to fly, fly, fly, knocking out anything that moved, bombing and gunning, finding new targets as fast as they destroyed the old ones. The best thing he could do, he decided, was land, pick up more explosives and get ready for another go.

At least in Darling he seemed to have picked a good partner. Despite his understandable excitement, the boy seemed to be good at his job. He was unafraid and even appeared to have an eye like a hawk, and he was keeping up a running commentary on what was happening as Boumphrey concentrated on picking his way through the whirling machines back to the airfield. They'd all read reports of the dogfights over southern England during the Battle of Britain and he supposed this was what it must have been like – except that back home there wasn't such a hairy mixture of obsolete biplanes as there was here.

Just ahead of him he saw a Gordon waver and part of the starboard wing fall off as it was hit. It went into a spin and dropped away, but the pilot managed to regain control and put it down on the edge of the field. As he passed overhead, Boumphrey saw two figures scrambling clear and the machine spread flatly on the ground like a dead bird.

Another Oxford was landing ahead of him, just settling for its touchdown. It was doing it neatly and cleanly; the wheels had just contacted the earth and it was just beginning to slow down when it received a direct hit from a shell. Boumphrey flew through the lifting cloud of black smoke and flame, and put the machine down on the other side, almost hitting the fire engine and the ambulance as they hurtled across the field.

There was a short queue of aircraft waiting to go through the gate from the airfield into the enclosure behind the hangars and, rather than stop and present a target for the Irazhi gunners, he swung the machine round in a large circle. He had to do it twice before the gate was clear and he could sweep through to the shelter of the hangars.

Immediately he stopped, fitters and riggers swarmed over the machine and the armourers arrived within seconds. They hadn't enough bomb trolleys and everything was being man-handled from lorries. Aircrew and pupils who were not flying started to bomb up at once. Engines were shut off and by the grace of God none of the running men was hit by a whirling propeller.

'Take any hits, sir?' A sweating flight sergeant appeared at the window alongside Boumphrey.

'None I know of, Flight. I think we came through untouched. Who was that who blew up just ahead of me?'

'Mr De Sousa, sir. With two pupils.'

'And the Gordon at the other side of the field?'

'Sergeant Chapman. He's all right. So's his observer.'

'How're we doing?'

'Not bad, sir. But the shells are doing a bit of damage. There've been casualties. What's it like up there?'

'More danger from our own side than the Irazhis, I reckon. And we're going to have to improve this business of getting to shelter, Flight. It leaves us on the field in full view and sitting ducks for the guns up there. When I go out again, I'm going out at full speed and I shall come back the same way.'

Apart from the two machines he had seen hit, there had been no other casualties in the air, but one of the parked Gordons, waiting for a pilot, had been destroyed. There was only one way to prevent them all from being destroyed and that was to keep up the nonstop bombing and gunning to keep the Irazhi heads down and prevent them bombarding the aerodrome as they undoubtedly would now.

The AVM had grasped the nettle and, no matter what they called it in diplomatic circles, the truth was that hostilities had commenced and Britain was at war with Irazh.

An Indian bearer, his face grey with fear, came hurrying up with a tall metal container of coffee balanced on his head. Heading for the hangar he put the container down and vanished inside. One of the ground staff, stripped to his shorts in the heat, appeared alongside Boumphrey and handed him a chipped tin mug.

'Fancy a swig, sir?'

'Thanks. No end kind of you.'

Boumphrey hadn't left his seat when the flight sergeant lifted his thumb. 'OK, sir. Off you go!'

'Right, Flight. Just make sure that bloody gate's clear, because I'm going through it at top speed.'

Pausing behind the hangars to complete his pre-flight checks out of sight of the plateau, Boumphrey lifted his head to see the flight sergeant waving at him to indicate there was no aircraft on its way in through the gate.

'Hold your hat on, Darling!'

With a judicious use of the throttle and brakes and a great deal of luck, Boumphrey turned the corner to face the gate in the fence that led to the airfield, then he opened the throttles and shot past the startled flight sergeant at forty miles an hour to lift off as soon as he was clear in a steep climbing turn away from the plateau.

Darling looked startled. 'My God, sir! That was fast! We nearly hit the post!'

'Never mind.' Boumphrey gave a self-deprecatory smile. 'Next time I expect we will.'

2

By the time they took off for the fourth time that day, everybody was trying Boumphrey's method. While the trees round the polo ground hid the Harts and the Audaxes until they were actually lifting into the air, the Oxfords, Gladiators and Gordons were in full view the minute they were on the airfield. So, as Boumphrey had done out of sheer necessity, they all started doing.

They completed their pre-flight checks behind the hangars, and one of the ground crew moved out, hidden by the hangars from the plateau and gave the signal that nothing was on the way in; then, with the engine roaring and the brakes squealing, the aircraft lurched, zigzagging at speed through the gate straight on to the take-off area and, without pausing, increased speed and lifted off in a steep swing away from the ridge of hills. By this time the pom-poms on the plateau were beginning to be difficult so, on the return, they began to fly in very low across the camp to avoid their fire, landed on the taxi strip close to the buildings, swung in at speed through the gate and whipped round the back of the hangars.

Osanna had tried to set up a debriefing system complete with a pile of debriefing forms – time on patrol, time off, that sort of thing, with descriptions of what had been hit – but too much was happening too quickly and in the end he gave it up and left it to the pilots to report any new targets they thought important, with two or three clerks from headquarters to put it down in notebooks resting on the wing of a machine while the engine was still emitting its creaks and clicks as it cooled off.

There was no time for anything else because the casualties were mounting, though it wasn't considered that a small flesh wound or minor damage to an aircraft was sufficient to stop flying. At midday sandwiches appeared from the mess and they ate while the machines were serviced, refuelled and bombed up. The man who brought them had a story of six Irazhi Gladiators appearing from nowhere to attack the station buildings. 'Nearly got AHQ,' he said.

Nobody had noticed them in the excitement but there was considerable joy at his description of senior officers diving under tables and his graphic picture of the row of august backsides sticking out.

'Like a lot of hippopotamuses wallowing in the mud,' he said gleefully.

The Irazhi aircraft had done some damage. Where there had been solid buildings and trim verges was now surrounded by smoke, the crackle of flames, dust-shrouded rubble and an acrid smell of burning. Figures were beginning to appear from the wreckage, but the station warrant officer, his face blackened and his moustache askew, was fully in command, his rasping voice rallying men into coherent groups. Fire hoses were being run out, ambulances were racing through the smoke to where men were digging and pulling rubble aside with their bare hands. Near one of the huts an arm, severed at the elbow, lay on the ground and everybody was carefully taking evading action round it, pretending it wasn't there.

The sound of the fighting, the tremendous roaring of aircraft engines and, above all, the explosions, had terrified Prudence Wood-Withnell. Her helpers had fled at once to the shelters but, feeling somehow that if the water tank were damaged she might have to spend the day filling buckets and baths, she herself had taken refuge under a table in the hospital sluice, where all the containers were emptied. The first bombs to fall near had reduced her to tears but then, realizing that she was doing no good at all in tears, she had pulled herself together and gone to help. The first injured man she saw was

149

an airman who had lost a foot and the sight of the pulpy red mess at the end of his stocking turned her stomach over. Then one of the Indian bearers had been brought in with a splinter in the chest and the whole of his white cotton clothing saturated with shining red and she had realized that it was no time to be squeamish. They were already short-handed and every pair of hands was needed. Gulping down her nausea, she had turned to help.

Despite the formidable shelling from the plateau, which seemed to have blown out every wire mesh window in the place, the explosions had not disturbed the pair of nesting storks with their young on the radio mast above Air Headquarters.

'I bet it gave them a fright though,' Darling had observed.

Shrapnel still clattered on the iron roofs but neither the water tower nor the power station had been hit, though too many aircraft had been destroyed on the ground. The Audaxes and Harts on the polo ground, however, were effectively screened by the trees, while those machines behind the hangars were suffering only superficial damage. There was only one question in everybody's mind as aircraft came in and swung into place behind the hangars to be checked for structural damage: could they be patched up enough to go back into the air?

As they cruised at 1000 feet, which Boumphrey decided would give them maximum accuracy, they could see the Audaxes dive bombing beneath them. The Harts had been designed for just this purpose and the Audaxes, an improvement on the Harts, were also proving quite adept at it. They were falling out of the sky into the ground fire with their bombs and guns, but everybody had his own method, and others were going in low and screaming across the plateau, making use of every available gulley, to arrive almost unseen over their target and drop their bombs from a mere hundred feet.

The air seemed alive with aeroplanes and by this time the Audaxes from the polo field had developed a technique of hammering the gun positions while the Oxfords, Gladiators and Gordons took off from the main airfield. Flight Sergeant Madoc was taking the armoured cars along the perimeter close to the plateau, well within range of the guns, roaring at full speed backwards and forwards between the shells and the aircraft taking off and landing, using his guns to force the Irazhis to keep their heads down.

It was decided they were becoming so successful, in fact, that they might get more of the women and children away. Contacting Wing Commander Atkin, the station admin. officer, normally a desk-bound officer, who'd been given command of the Audaxes and Harts, Fogarty explained what he intended. 'We're sending off the Valentias for the coast,' he said. 'So I want everybody you can put into the air to bomb the gun positions to keep heads down while they take off. Let's make it 1500 hours exactly. Telephone me when you're ready.'

Cars and lorries began to hurry from the camp complex to the area behind the hangars and stopped alongside the Valentias.

'It'll take twenty minutes to get 'em all away,' Fogarty explained. 'Can your people keep up a sustained bombing that long?'

'Yes, they'll do it.'

'The armoured cars will emerge at the same moment and head north along the perimeter to draw fire away from the airstrip. While the guns are occupied in that direction, we'll get the big boys away.'

Promptly at 1450 hours, the Audaxes and Harts lifted off and, climbing to 1000 feet, screamed down to hammer the guns on the plateau. While they were busy replying, the Gladiators took off and joined in, and Madoc's eighteen old armoured cars emerged from the complex of buildings and began to roar along the perimeter, firing at anything that

151

presented itself. The din was tremendous and a lifting cloud of smoke and dust hung over both the camp and the escarpment.

At the height of the fury, the first Valentia appeared from behind the hangars and headed for the field. By this time the fence had been pulled down to widen the gate, and it roared through at a good thirty miles an hour, lurching on the uneven ground, its huge biplane wings swaying. Facing the airfield, the pilot opened his throttles. Almost immediately a second followed, then a third. The Audaxes went in lower, screaming down almost to ground level.

The firing from the plateau, as the gunners were caught between the bombing of the aircraft and the automatic weapons of the armoured cars, began to grow wild, and Boumphrey decided to join the fun. The last of the Valentias was thundering down the airfield now, trailing its cloud of brown dust, and he saw it lift off. A solitary gun, temporarily unoccupied, sent a few shells after it and he saw them explode beyond the ditch at the end of the take-off area.

As he lined up to drop his bombs, Darling was bouncing about in his seat with excitement. 'Left, skipper,' he was yelling. 'Left a bit more. Right. Jesus, there they go – I mean, bombs gone, sir!'

As they lifted away, the Oxford as usual touchy on the controls and awkward to handle, they heard a crash beneath them somewhere and saw holes appear in the cabin walls.

'I suspect we've been hit, Darling,' Boumphrey said calmly.

'You're telling me, sir!' Darling's voice was high-pitched. 'Hole back there big enough to put your head through.'

'The undercarriage light's come on. I think the undercart's come down. We'd better try it.'

They could get no joy from the undercarriage. There was no sound of it moving and Boumphrey began to suspect that only one wheel was down, which was going to make landing a problem. Clearly something had happened beneath the machine because its notorious instability was more marked than ever and Boumphrey realized they were in difficulties.

They were swinging round now over the camp and heading for the landing field and he was hoping to God they could get down safely before the tricky Ox-box dropped a wing and went into a spin. They were turning at the end of the field for their run-in when Darling yelled.

'Sir, sir! We're on fire!'

'Where?' Boumphrey struggled to keep his voice steady.

'Starboard wing, sir. I think it's spreading. It's coming from the starboard engine.'

Boumphrey's eyes flickered to his right where the Armstrong Siddeley engine was pounding away. The machine was not fitted with fire extinguishers and he was aware that it was necessary to get it down as quickly as possible and get out and run, because of the Oxford's tendency to burn fast. It was largely built of plywood and was well known for its ability to become a mass of flames.

His thoughts were racing through his mind like mad mice. How did he get a burning Oxford down safely with a damaged undercarriage? As he glanced about him below, he saw the fire engine racing across the ground towards them. Passing overhead, he saw them turn and one of the crew, riding on the running board, was pointing frantically, gesturing wildly at the aircraft. Boumphrey wasn't certain what they were trying to indicate but he suspected it wasn't that the engine was on fire, because the fact that he must have seen it should have been obvious to anyone. So he could only assume that his guess was right and only part of the undercarriage had come down.

His thoughts were still scurrying through his mind when he spotted the small brick huts of the rifle range. There were two of them, one a store where the targets were kept, the other where the target operators sheltered when they weren't in the orchestra pit indicating hits, and he suddenly realized they might be his salvation. They were about fifteen feet apart – at least he hoped they were fifteen feet apart, though he had never measured them – and he decided to take a chance.

'Come aft, Darling,' he said to the cadet. 'If I put this thing

153

down as she is, you and I are going to be cooked meat because the wheels will collapse and she'll go up in flames. Make sure you're properly strapped in and hold your hat on.'

He turned again, the machine behaving awkwardly as it tilted, dangerously close to a stall and a spin. Righting it, he headed for the rifle range. Darling gave him a nervous look and Boumphrey tried to reassure him.

'See those two buildings, Darling,' he said. 'I'm going straight between them. At full speed.'

Darling's look this time was one of alarm. 'Between them, sir?'

'Yes. You'll see why when we've done it – *if we do it*. Now shut up and let me concentrate. There's going to be only one try and it's got to come off.'

The two huts were approaching now, growing larger and larger. Boumphrey held the machine close to the ground and headed for the gap between them. Suddenly, horrifyingly, he felt it might not be big enough, or even that he might not hit it dead centre so that the machine would slew round and plough into one or the other of the buildings. But it was too late now to do anything about it, and he heard Darling draw in his breath and saw him raise his arms to shield his face.

The buildings were huge now, racing towards them, growing in size until they filled the whole of his vision. He held the nose of the Oxford on the centre of the gap and the crash came in a tearing, rending roar. The machine shuddered, but they were going at such a speed the crash ripped the wings clean off in a shower of flying bricks, and the fuselage, containing Boumphrey and Darling, went racing on.

As the wheels touched, the bounding fuselage tilted to starboard and hit the ground with an almighty rending crash. Splinters of wood flew in all directions, then the fuselage slewed round, and came to an abrupt stop. The nose went down and the tail came up, then it rocked back on to its belly.

'Out!' Boumphrey yelled.

The overhead hatch was jammed so they tossed off their

parachutes and scrambled down the fuselage and over the splintered woodwork round the main spar to the door. The door also seemed to be jammed but by throwing their weight against it, they burst it open and fell out into the sunshine. A machine gun was raising spurts of dust all round the wrecked fuselage and they flung themselves flat. The wings had both fallen off and lay in a splintered wreckage against the huts, the petrol they had contained blazing furiously to send up a coil of black smoke towards the escarpment.

Darling was staring at them with startled eyes as if it had just dawned on him what they had missed.

'If we'd tried to land on one wheel,' he said slowly, 'we'd have gone up like Guy Fawkes night.'

'That we would, Darling,' Boumphrey said cheerfully. 'Are you damaged at all?'

'Not a scratch, sir. How about you?'

'Same here. And it looks as though rescue's on its way.'

Two armoured cars were bounding towards them across the airfield. As they reached them, Flight Sergeant Madoc's head appeared from the nearest. 'Round the back!' he yelled.

The armour-plated door was open and they scrambled aboard. Then, as the car was about to set off from among a forest of small puffs of dust, the driver's voice came.

'Flight! We'll have to hang on! One of the Wimpeys is coming in. It looks as though he's in trouble.'

The big machine was coming down in an uncertain manner, one propeller windmilling, the engine stopped, flying in a nose-up attitude as the pilot sought to bring it in at the minimum safe speed. He left his landing flare just too late, the wheels hit the ground and the undercarriage legs shortened as the rams were compressed. The aeroplane was projected back into the air and the engines roared as the pilot tried to catch the bounce and soften the next impact. But he was too late and the great machine fell back as if exhausted. The wheels struck the earth in another puff of dust, then the pilot slammed down the tail as fast as possible and they heard the brakes squeal. As it slowed, every gun on the escarpment seemed to spot it and, now that the Audaxes and Harts had disappeared, they swung away from the wreckage of the Oxford and began to drop their shells round the better target presented by the Wellington. They saw the crew running through the smoke and dust.

A tractor was heading out of the gate from the hangar towards the Wellington and Madoc yelled to Boumphrey.

'Hang on, sir! That chap's going to need some cover!'

The two armoured cars began to race across the dusty surface of the field to take up positions on either side of the tractor to shield the driver and his mate from the gunfire with their armoured sides. The driver's face was tense and strained.

As they swung round the stern of the Wellington, the driver's mate produced a wire rope and started to secure it to the tail wheel but, as he did so, a shell from the escarpment burst close by and they both went on their faces. The driver lifted his head, his face covered with blood, and crossed to his mate, who managed to raise himself one-handed to his knees.

'Come on, Darling,' Boumphey yelled.

Clambering from Madoc's car, they ran to the men crouched under the tail surface of the Wellington. Shells were still cracking around them as they hoisted them to their feet and stumbled with them to the doors of the armoured cars. Hands reached out and dragged them aboard, then Darling looked at Boumphrey.

'What about the Wimpy, sir?' he asked. 'My old man's a farmer and I've been driving tractors since I was ten.'

Boumphrey managed a grin. 'Get cracking,' he said.

They ran to the Wellington and between them managed to secure the wire from the tail wheel of the big bomber to the heavy hook behind the tractor. After a jerk or two, Darling got the tractor going and swung the Wellington round towards the hangers. Immediately the armoured cars moved alongside them, again trying to provide protection from the gunners on the heights. Slowly they began to head across the field.

The shells were still cracking round them and Darling, glancing backwards over Boumphrey where he clung to the back of the tractor, flinched. 'Sir,' he said. 'I think the bugger's caught alight!'

Because the wind was carrying the flames away from them, they hadn't noticed that the Wellington was on fire but now, as they turned towards the hangars away from the wind they could feel the heat searing their flesh, and Boumphrey could see a pom-pom at the bottom of the escarpment only a few yards from the wire perimeter fence hammering away at them.

'I think it's time we left,' he announced.

As the tractor stopped, he slipped to the ground.

'Back up,' he screamed, shielding his face from the flames. 'The wire's too tight.'

Darling put the tractor into reverse so hard it almost ran over Boumphrey. The wire slackened and Boumphrey struggled to throw it off. But the loop had tightened round the hook and he had to lie on his back to try to kick it off. With the heat scorching his skin, he became aware of another armoured car racing from the hangars towards them. As it reached them, it swung round and slid with locked wheels. A head appeared from the hatch wearing a flying helmet, the jack of the intercom flapping.

'Get away, you bloody idiots!' the owner yelled. 'She's still got bombs on board! She'll go up any minute!'

Boumphrey's eyes met Darling's, then he gave one final frantic kick. As the wire rope came free he ran to the tractor and jumped aboard.

'Go!' he yelled.

As Darling let in the clutch, the tractor hurtled away, the engine roaring, taking them thankfully away from the heat of the flames. They hadn't gone fifty yards when there was a tremendous iron crash behind them as the bombs went off. It was followed by two more and, turning, they saw the Wellington had been torn apart. One of the Hercules engines landed forty feet away, then pieces of metal and burning scraps of fabric glittering like golden bats fluttered down around them. A wheel landed nearby in a puff of dust that blew into their faces as they raced for the gate leading to the hangars, the armoured cars keeping pace with them to shield them. More fragments of steel came down in a shower among the shell bursts and the blowing smoke, then they hurtled through the gate, narrowly missing an Oxford that was moving across their front, and swung round behind the hangars. Darling stopped the tractor so suddenly, Boumphrey fell off.

Someone picked him up and he found himself staring at the helmeted Jenno who had scrambled from the armoured car that had rescued them.

'That was a bloody silly thing to do, Ratter,' he said.

Boumphrey grinned. Then Darling appeared. His face was black and when he laughed his tongue seemed extraordinarily pink.

'You've lost your eyebrows, sir,' he said.

3

With darkness, the shelling stopped and they began to take stock. The Wellingtons, they learned, had dropped sixteen and a half tons of bombs in seventeen sorties, and the flying training school about the same amount in 193 sorties. Some men had taken off nine times and aircraft had been in the air over the escarpment for all of a solid nineteen hours.

The results seemed disappointing under the circumstances. A total of twenty-two aircraft had been destroyed or put out of action, reducing the operational strength from the seventy-three to which it had risen with the new arrivals to fifty-one, and the ground staff looked like working all night to prepare the machines that were left for the following day. In addition to the Wellington and Boumphrey's Oxford, one Oxford had been shot down in flames, killing the crew. One of the Audax pilots had been shot through the shoulder and lung but the pupil who was acting as his gunner had managed to pull him off the controls and, although only half-conscious, guided by the pupil the pilot had managed to right the aircraft with only one hand and had actually landed on the polo ground before fainting. Another pilot had been hit in the jaw but had managed to get down, while Wing Commander Atkin, the desk job who had been given the Audax-Hart command, had been shot through the thigh by a bullet which had broken in two, one piece going into his groin and knee, the other working its way up to his buttock. He also had managed to land. Another aircraft, its pilot injured, had been saved by the cadet acting as bomb-aimer, who had taken over the controls and brought the machine down after half a dozen hairy attempts and a final series of colossal bounces. In addition, one of the parked Gordons had received a direct hit from the escarpment, killing one of the ground personnel and injuring two more, and two stationary Oxfords had also been hit and set on fire. They had simply been pulled out of the way and allowed to burn themselves out.

Altogether there had been thirteen killed and twenty-nine wounded among the airmen and soldiers, and another three killed and twelve wounded among the civilians inside the camp. One shell had landed near the Irazhi mess staff who had dodged behind a wall for safety, only for the wall to be hit by the next shell. Three of them had been killed and two hurt. The remainder hadn't been seen since.

By the end of the day, Prudence Wood-Withnell had found she could look on groaning blood-splashed people without much more than a queasiness in her stomach. Her own clothing was spotted with blood and her skirt was smeared with stains where she had automatically wiped her hands. But she was pleased with herself because she had overcome her nausea and been of some help.

What was most significant was that out of thirty-seven available pilots ten were now either dead or in hospital, and though the Irazhi infantry had shown no inclination to do much in the way of fighting, preferring to remain in their trenches with their heads down, the well-camouflaged batteries were still in position for the next day, while the remaining aircraft looked as if they had measles with the doped patches which had been put over the bullet holes. The record was held by one of the Audaxes which could count thirty-two.

However, the second flight of Wellingtons was reported to have landed at Shaibah from Egypt and, though fighting had now started on the coast, these machines would be available for the defence of Kubaiyah because the situation was not critical in the south and a local army cooperation squadron, aided by Swordfish from the carrier, HMS *Hermes*, lying in the Gulf, had been able to give the ground forces there the air support they needed, while a group of venerable but invaluable Vincents had cut the Shaibah-Mandadad railway.

A few Irazhi aircraft had appeared over the airfield. The newly arrived Gladiators had chased them away but had been able to catch neither the Northrops nor a group of Italian twin-engined Savoias which had come over too high to be reached, but they had swooped on airfields from which the Irazhi aircraft had been joining the fight and had managed to do some damage.

On the credit side, the Irazhis had miraculously still not had the sense to switch off the pumps in the pumping station at Dhubban and the sanitary system still worked, while many more women and children had been flown out, the Europeans to Basra on the coast, the families of the levies to Palestine.

'And,' someone pointed out, 'they didn't hit the water tower.'

'Or the magazine, the petrol dump, the radio mast, the power station or the telephone exchange.'

'They also,' the adjutant said, 'didn't disturb the storks. They're still here. I don't think the Irazhis were trying.'

The air vice-marshal wasn't offering a lot in the way of praise because there was still a long way to go, but it was clear that he was far from dissatisfied.

'Despite our losses,' he said, 'we've more than held our own and the enemy's made no attempt to move forward. However, it's far from over, and the Irazhis are still round the fort at Hatbah, and the Engineers and the cavalry aren't going to be able to move to our help yet.'

'We'll have to reverse the usual procedure, sir,' someone at the back said. 'Instead of the cavalry coming to the aid of the besieged fortress, the besieged fortress will have to go to the aid of the cavalry.'

Someone else laughed. 'It would kill the horse-versus-machine argument stone dead.'

The AVM let them have their say then he held up his hand.

'We know that a relieving force has started assembling in Palestine,' he went on. 'But we can't expect them too soon. They've a long way to come under very bad conditions and we shan't see them for some days yet. So it's up to us. However, I think from today's showing we can not only hold our own here but might even be able to carry the attack to the Irazhi airfields and lines of communications. We're going from the defensive to the offensive.'

There were gasps and exchanged glances. It was a bold decision after one day's fighting but the Irazhis were still preferring to stay inside their fortifications and rely on shelling the camp.

As the AVM sat down, Fogarty rose. He made no bones about what was in front of them. 'Same again tomorrow,' he said. 'From first light until darkness. The only method we have is to swamp them. They've established a few more gun positions. Here – and here – and here.' His hand moved across the screened picture of the map. 'Keep a look-out for them. Wellingtons will be coming from Shaibah again and they and you will keep up constant patrols over the enemy to force the Irazhi gunners to stay under cover. The Wellingtons will also set up raids on Sayid aerodrome near Mandadad to keep the enemy air force down. The idea's to make sure they don't fire more than necessary on the cantonment. We want to keep them quiet.'

As he spoke there was an explosion somewhere on the airfield followed by the rat-tat-tat of a heavy machine gun.

'Or fairly quiet, anyway,' Fogarty said. 'If we get the chance we shall try to get more of the civilians away, using the same method as today – Harts and Audaxes forcing heads down round the guns, the armoured cars patrolling the perimeter.' He paused, glancing at his notes, then lifted his head. 'Now,' he said. 'A few surprises. Workshops have come up with the idea of frightening the Irazhis with noise. After all, Joshua fought the battle of Jericho not far from here and, as all who aren't Philistines among you doubtless know, he blew his

162

trumpets and the walls fell down flat. Well, we can't quite manage that but Workshops have been at it all day making organ flutes to attach to the bombs you're going to drop and sirens to attach to the undercarts of the Audaxes and Harts who're going to do the dive-bombing. I've seen them and they should make a hell of a noise. It's something the Germans did very successfully in France. But that's not all. By the time darkness arrives tomorrow those Irazhis on the escarpment will have been cowering in their trenches for two days running and they'll be glad to climb out of them to stretch their legs. When they do, they're going to get a surprise because Major Verity's levies will be not far away in the shadows.'

The briefing ended with the crews being told to go to the hangars to help with the fitting of sirens. As they rose, Fogarty called to Boumphrey.

'Tomorrow,' he said, 'you won't be flying, Ratter.'

'Sir?'

'I want you and Jenno to get some rest. You've had quite a day. You heard what I said about Verity's levies going for the Irazhis after dark. I want you to take your legion with them. Can they do it?'

'You bet, sir.'

'Talk to Verity. You take one sector and he can take the other. We don't want you cutting each other's throats.'

As the senior officers left, Major Verity approached. He had a map in his hand which he laid on the edge of the stage so they could study it.

'You quite happy with this idea of carrying the battle to the enemy?' he asked.

'Oh, yes,' Boumphrey said. 'We'll have a go. Whose idea was it? Yours?'

Verity smiled. 'My boys are itching to do some damage. They've got no love for the Irazhis and, now that their women and children are being moved to safety, they want to take a few risks. How about your people?'

Boumphrey smiled. 'Suspect they feel much the same,' he said.

Verity's hand moved over the map. 'We know they've got armoured cars here and guns close to the rifle range. Up on the slopes behind them are more guns. Could you follow Jenno's armoured cars on to the slopes? I've had torches coloured red or green. Your people will carry the green ones. We'll carry the red ones. Use them so there'll be no mistake. All right?'

'Got it.'

'Know the road?'

'Like the back of my hand. I've been up on that escarpment many times.'

Verity grinned. 'It ought to stop them laughing in church,' he said. 'Let's go and see Ballantine.'

Outside the cinema, Boumphrey paused for a moment, deep in thought, then he sought out Ghadbhbhan.

'You've heard that we're going into action tomorrow night?' he asked.

'I heard something about it, sir.'

'Told the boys?'

'Yes, sir.'

'Got your map?'

'Yes, sir.'

'If it came to the pinch, could you do it on your own?'

Ghadbhbhan's eyebrows rose. 'Of course, sir.'

'Good.' Boumphrey gave a faint smile. 'Because there's just a faint chance I might not be with you. They say I'm not to fly tomorrow but I think I might.'

Crossing to the hospital, Boumphrey made his way to the room at the back where he found Prudence Wood-Withnell at work. There were patches of damp on the back of her shirt, a strand of hair hung over her face and she looked tired. Like most white women in Irazh, she had always had plenty of servants and had never had to work herself, but she seemed cheerful and even pleased with herself that she had not bolted for the coast.

She didn't tell Boumphrey her part in the bombing, though she secretly longed to – if only to hear his admiration put into words. Chiefly it was because she felt too worn out. Never in her whole life had she worked so hard, so long, and at such speed. The water filling had become only a secondary task, her helpers supervised between all the other jobs which the station medical officer, desperate for extra pairs of hands and recognizing her as an intelligent responsible person, had dumped on her.

'Hello, Ratter,' she said quietly. 'You all right?'

'Bit tired,' he admitted. 'Like you, I expect.'

'Bit,' she agreed. 'But we're managing. There are over thirty casualties in here, some of them pretty bad. There are sixteen dead, they tell me.' She looked at him earnestly. 'Ratter, you *are* all right, aren't you?'

'Yes, I'm all right.'

'Do you want anything?'

'Only to know you're safe and sound.'

She was silent then she looked up. 'I heard you were hurt when an aeroplane blew up.'

'No,' he said. 'I'm all right. In effect, I had *two* blow up. One an Oxford, t'other a Wellington. Fortunately, I'd just got clear of both.'

'One of the sergeants they brought in was talking about you.'

Boumphrey smiled. Boumphrey's smile was rather special. It was gentle and attractive. It didn't often appear because he was rather a solemn individual, but when it did it had a tremendous effect. It did so now.

'It's because everybody thinks I'm a bit dim, I suppose,' he said. 'I'm not really. It's the fault of having a face that looks as if it's been struck by lightning.'

'Oh, Ratter, that's not true! You don't look a bit as if you've been struck by lightning. In fact, when you smile –' Prudence

165

stopped, confused by her thoughts and startled at her temerity. She changed the subject hurriedly. 'Is it going to be the same tomorrow?'

'And the day after. And the day after that, too. Until we've driven the Irazhis away. There'll be Dakotas coming in to take away more women and children tomorrow. You ought to go.'

'Not likely,' she said fiercely. She simply couldn't imagine bolting for the coast and leaving Boumphrey behind. There was no telling what might happen. He might be brought in hurt and need nursing. He might even – she brushed aside the thought that he might be dead because she'd seen one of the bodies as it had been carried to the mortuary to await burial and she couldn't visualize anything as horrible as that happening to him. It had been the body of a sergeant-instructor who had been dragged from a burning Oxford and she tried hard not to think of it.

She once more excused herself with the story that her father had refused to leave – especially after the fighting – and, because of that, neither could she. 'He'll have no one to look after him,' she said.

They talked desultorily, tiredly, until one of the Asian women came with a message for her. Prudence looked apologetically at Boumphrey. 'I've got to go now, Ratter,' she said. 'Thank you for coming to see if I was all right.' She put her hands on his upper arms and kissed him gently. 'It was kind of you. But then, you're a kind man.'

She smiled and, turning, hurried off to where she was needed. Boumphrey stood still for a moment, then quietly he turned and headed from the hospital for his quarters.

4

There was no rest. The key personnel worked throughout the
night to have the aircraft ready for daylight. A second Wellington from Shaibah had been stranded on the airfield just
before dark but it had been dragged safely behind the hangars
past the one that had caught fire, now only a pile of wreckage
in which were embedded such identifiable objects as a Hercules engine with twisted propeller blades, the blackened
framework of a tailplane and a mass of charred geodetic
structure that had been the fuselage. Men were patching the
second machine up in readiness for the morning, working
practically without lights and cursing only because there
weren't enough of them to finish every job that needed doing.
Meanwhile, in darkness, trucks were being filled with earth
and stones from the edge of the airfield which was being
dumped into the shell holes in the take-off area and rolled
flat.

The first shells fell on the camp as soon as the sky began to
pale in the east. The diminishing band of aircrew were taking
their breakfast in the mess when it started.

'Fifty fils they get the water tower today,' someone said.

'Done. And fifty fils that they get the telephone exchange.'

They were watching the shells bursting in the distance when
a shower of bullets coming through the iron roof of the mess
made them dive for cover under the table. Almost immediately there was the shriek of a shell. Heads lifted and hands
holding cups remained still as the shriek increased in volume,
then there was a concerted dive for shelter, so fast it seemed

that the cups hovered unspilled in midair for a second before crashing down.

'Dammit!' The complaint came from under one of the tables. 'That's buggered up my coffee!'

The explosion made them flinch and they heard the crash of falling masonry and a wail. As the station medical officer scrambled to his feet and headed for the hospital, they looked up at the holes in the roof.

'There'll be vigorous complaints in the suggestions book about *that*,' someone said.

'How're the storks, by the way?'

'Still there. Both youngsters doing well.'

The new station admin. officer finished his breakfast hurriedly, picked up his briefcase and headed for the hangars. With the catering officer back, he was due to fly to the coast to deposit currency there and return with a planeload of groceries. The adjutant appeared with a small pile of roneo-ed sheets which he placed just inside the door.

'Stop press,' he said. 'All the news on what's happening.'

'As if we didn't know.'

'The group captain's idea. To let everybody know how the war's progressing. Written up by Signals with the assistance of Osanna. The Germans are in Athens and are expected to go for Crete at any moment.'

'They might even come here.'

There was a little laughter but it died quickly because German intervention at Kubaiyah was a real danger now.

'What about the relief column? Have those clots set off yet?'

'On their way, I think. Suspect it's more bluff than anything, though. Because there's been a bit more trouble down at Basra.'

'Shooting?'

'Striking mostly. The spirit's willing but the flesh's weak. A mob gathered but somebody fired a couple of shots from a 25-pounder over their heads and that was that. The Irazhi police have been disarmed without trouble but the local authorities are being what you might call uncooperative and there's been some looting of shops. Irazhi troops are being bombed along the Euphrates. Quite a lot of party spirit.'

It was all delivered in a light-hearted manner but they all knew the situation was tense. A new campaign had been started and, with things as they were in the Middle East, the Balkans, Crete, even at home where they were still hanging on by their teeth and eyebrows, Britain couldn't afford a new campaign. She still hadn't the trained men, the weapons, the aircraft or the ships to maintain the old campaigns. As the adjutant had suggested, anything they did had to be largely bluff.

The only bright spot on the horizon was the fact that Ghaffer al Jesairi was not popular. The Irazhis set a lot of store by their royal family and Ghaffer had lost a lot of support by forcing the regent to flee. Besides, Ibn Saud, a monarch of some power in the Middle East, had completely rebuffed him, while the King of Transjordan, who was related to the Irazhi royal house, was also unlikely to look favourably on anybody who had kicked out one of his relations, because one kicking-out could lead to another like the fall of a line of dominoes.

The shelling had increased since first light and the shells were dropping in and around the camp now with some regularity.

'Aim's not very good,' Jenno commented.

'Osanna says it's because the Irazhi officers don't like Ghaffer. Ever seen him?'

'Once. Looks like the second murderer in *Macbeth*.'

'Doesn't seem to be a very good judge of timing either. I think he expected the Germans to fly in.'

'They still might. Osanna says they're trying to make the Vichy French release matériel from Syria. He says he's heard they've actually laid on air transport and it only needs the word to start it.'

They stood in the growing daylight, listening to shells bursting near the hangars, their nostrils catching the smell of smoke, dust and high octane petrol.

'Same again, today,' Jenno said. 'How're you feeling?'

'Tired,' Boumphrey said.

'I suppose in view of what's to happen tonight, like me, they've taken you off flying.'

'Yes,' Boumphrey agreed. 'But, as we're short of trained aircrew and we can't let the other chaps do it all, I *shall* be flying.'

Jenno grinned. 'Me, too, Ratter,' he said.

As they spoke, another flurry of shells landed among the buildings and a fire started near the stores complex.

'They'll quieten down once we're in the air,' Jenno said.

As he spoke the first of the aeroplanes started up. They heard the crackles, then the roar of one of the Rolls-Royce Kestrels.

'Audax,' Boumphrey said, and started to run.

Darling was waiting. Like everybody else, he looked tired. Flying put a lot of strain on a man and continuous flying was wearing.

'Ready, old son?' Boumphrey said.

'Yes, sir.'

'Good show. Let's just have your reports properly. But don't let it get you down if you boob. First time I did anything serious, I made every mistake in the book.'

Darling glanced at Boumphrey's kind gentle face and was rewarded with one of the flashing smiles. It made his day because he knew that Boumphrey, trained slowly in the piping days of peace, couldn't have made many mistakes.

'During my initial training I got lost on a cross-country and had to force-land in a Moth before I ran out of petrol. I telephoned the chief flying instructor who told me to stay where I was and after a while he arrived in another Moth and floated above me. I was in rather a small field but he obviously decided if I could get down, so could he. He had three goes then hit a tree stump and turned over. When he'd recovered a little, he said "What I don't understand, Boumphrey, is how

170

you managed to land a Moth in a field this size without damage." "Oh, I didn't," I said. "I landed in the big one next door and bounced over the hedge." '

Darling gave a hoot of laughter. He didn't believe the story for a minute because it didn't sound like Boumphrey's meticulous flying and he guessed it was merely Boumphrey's way of taking his mind off what lay ahead.

They were just about to climb into their aircraft when the station engineering officer appeared, red in the face and in a hurry.

'Cancel all take-offs!' he was yelling. 'There's a flight of Blenheims coming in! AHQ have just telephoned. Estimated time of arrival in five minutes!'

For a moment there was silence, then a yell of delight went up. In France the previous year the obsolescent Blenheims had been found to be very vulnerable but against the Irazhi Northrops they would be a welcome reinforcement.

The chief flying instructor's car roared up, and slithered to a stop outside the hangar.

'Some bloody chairborne pill in Cairo's made a balls-up of it,' Fogarty snapped. 'Those Blenheim chaps are going to know nothing of the conditions here, and they won't know the field's under fire. We've got to get 'em down and behind the hangars as fast as possible.'

He called the technical warrant officer to him and gestured at the Oxfords standing higgledy-piggledy ready to taxi out of the gate and on to the airstrip.

'Get these things out of the way, Mr Farrar,' he said. 'We've got to get the place clear for the Blenheims.'

As he spoke, Flight Sergeant Madoc led two of the armoured cars over the hard standing between the parked aeroplanes, followed closely by two more, and headed for the gate to wait just behind the shelter of the buildings there. As they halted, the Oxfords began to move. Those with crews in them taxied away from the entrance, and those which hadn't yet been started up were seized by ground personnel and any available aircrew or pupils and pushed out of the way.

As they did so, the Gladiators began to take off to keep down the heads of the Irazhi gunners, then the Kestrel engines on the polo field started to roar and one after another the Audaxes and Harts began to take off across the camp. As they passed overhead, the patches over the scars of the previous day's fighting made them look diseased.

They were climbing for height when the first of the Blenheims appeared and, their sirens screaming, the biplanes immediately swung round over the Irazhi positions to plaster them with bombs and bullets to enable the unwary pilots of the Blenheims to put their machines down. But the escarpment sprang to life as the bombs started to fall and all the guns started firing. A haze of dust hung over the slopes and blew gently across the field.

The Blenheims came out of the west low down, wicked-looking monoplanes wearing the sand-coloured paint of the Middle East, their big Mercury radials snarling as they went into the usual formal circuit of the airfield before making their final approach and landing. The bombs dropped by the Audaxes were throwing up great columns of dust and stones and they saw one of the Blenheims actually fly through one of them, waver a little as the blast caught it, then recover.

The first machine's wheels touched in a puff of dust and it began to slow to a stop, waiting to be guided to a dispersal area according to the usual practice. But at Kubaiyah, with the whole airfield overlooked, there was no dispersal area, and no bomb-proof pens of sandbags such as they'd been used to, only the sheltered stretch behind the hangars. As the aeroplane stopped, one of the armoured cars roared up to it. The Blenheim's propellers had slowed and they half-expected to see them stop, but there was a shouted instruction from the armoured car and the propellers began to increase revolutions. The armoured car swung at speed in front of it, heading for the gate, a man standing in the back waving his arms to encourage the pilot to do the job as fast as he could. An airman at the gate waved a green flag and the wildly-zigzagging Blenheim made it through to the shelter of the hangars.

The second machine was down now and, as if the pilot hadn't noticed what had happened to the leader, it was turning idly at the edge of the airfield. An armoured car roared up to it and they could all see its commander shouting to the pilot from the open hatch. Because of the din of the turning engines, the pilot seemed not to hear and appeared uncertain what to do. Then a salvo of Irazhi shells from the escarpment made him realize what was happening and, as the armoured car drove ahead of him, the machine began to scuttle for the safety of the hangars.

One after the other they chased each other for the gap in the fence, the crews trying to understand the frantic signals that were being made to them by ground staff to get them behind the hangars as quickly as possible. The Irazhi guns were making the most of their opportunity and every one of the Blenheims had been slightly damaged. Their crews climbed out wearing dazed expressions. The din from aeroplane engines, guns and sirens was deafening.

'What in Christ's name's going on here?' The first man to appear glared at Boumphrey indignantly as if the uproar were his fault.

Boumphrey gave him his gentle smile. 'You might well ask,' he said.

5

'Get these machines checked, refuelled and rearmed!'

Warrant Officer Farrar's shouts came as the ground crews swarmed over the Blenheims, and the armourers' lorries and fuel bowsers roared up. Men climbed on wings and began to unscrew panels, hoses snaked up and pumps were started.

The Harts and the Audaxes were landing now, whooshing overhead to touch down on the polo ground. Information had arrived that Dakotas were to fly in soon to remove more of the women and children, and there was to be a concerted attack on the Irazhi positions as they appeared and another as they left.

As they waited, the Harts and Audaxes began to take off again, howling overhead to gain altitude as the Dakotas were reported on their way in. As they clawed for height, they were followed by the slower Gordons, then the first of the Oxfords began to move towards the gate, ready for their rush through it on to the airfield. As they did so, there was another flurry of shelling from the escarpment, as if the Irazhis were trying to get in as many shells as they could before the bombing swamped them.

The Oxfords, still bright yellow in their training colours – and with the cupola and the bubble windscreen attracting attention as they caught the sun – stood out stark against the dusty brown landscape. A few shells fell on the airfield, but it didn't deter them and they began to roar down the runway one after the other and lift into the sky. As they climbed, Darling began his running commentary.

'Audaxes going in now, sir,' he said. 'My word, they're low today!'

As they levelled off, he took up his place in the moulded bomb-aimer's Plexiglass window and reported that he was ready. They could see the Dakotas beneath them, coming in to land one after the other and the puffs of dust they trailed behind them as they touched down and headed for the gate and the safety of the hangars. By the time everybody had dropped their bombs, the Irazhi guns were almost silent.

Going down to rearm and refuel, the Oxfords followed one after the other, while the Gordons did their death-defying dive-bombing act to allow them to get in. By the time the Gordons were ready to land the Harts would be available to take their place. It was a technique that had not been thought out but had been developed by individual pilots and followed by others. There were always aircraft in the air, bombing and firing their machine guns to prevent the artillery on the escarpment from shelling the airfield, and as soon as a new batch of machines had lifted off to take their places, their protectors went down for their turn at rearming and refuelling.

As Boumphrey climbed from his machine, the Dakotas were already in place, their engines silent, their doors open and men passing down cartons and crates to ground personnel waiting beneath them. The old Valentias seemed to have been left behind and the work was now being done entirely by the Dakotas which were faster and more manoeuvrable than the huge biplanes. The catering officer was gesturing to the piles of sacks, cartons and boxes he was gathering around him and, as fast as they appeared from the aircraft, they were pushed into lorries and driven away. Armourers were handing down boxes of ammunition and bombs and Sergeant Porlock, the artificer from the Royal Artillery, arrived to take command of several boxes of 4.5 shells for the howitzers from outside AHQ.

As the first aircraft was emptied, lorries and cars began to

arrive, their occupants clutching their few remaining possessions. A child was wailing, its thin cry coming over the sound
of a revving engine and the shouts of men pushing Blenheims
into position so they could get out ahead of the transports.
Among the civilians, Boumphrey spotted Prudence. She was
with her father and two RAF medical orderlies, trying to get a
stretcher containing the wife of one of the Indian bearers
aboard a Dakota.

'Bomb?' Boumphrey asked.

She helped push the stretcher up to the reaching hands and,
as it vanished inside the aeroplane, she turned and gave him a
smile.

'No,' she said. 'Baby. Due any time. She's terrified for it
because of the shelling and we decided she was better off
where it was quieter. She's been sedated. By the time she
comes to life again, she'll be where it's safe.'

She waited with Boumphrey as the Dakotas began to
manoeuvre for their rush at the gate and on to the airfield. She
was stooping with tiredness and there were small dark circles
under her eyes.

'Are we winning, Ratter?' she asked.

Boumphrey wondered. The Irazhis had broken the river
bank beyond Kubaiyah to allow the river to pour out across
the open plain and there was news that Fawzi ali Khayyam had
arrived outside the fort at Hatbah with around 2000 of his
A'Klab tribesmen so that Craddock was now more securely
trapped than ever.

'Well –' he gestured '– so far we're not losing.'

Just how long they could keep it up, however, he didn't
know. What they had achieved so far had been due to unremit-
ting labour and sheer cheek but it still seemed only a matter of
time. Once the water tower was hit that was that.

The Audaxes were in the air now, wheeling beyond the
airfield for their attacks on the escarpment. The Harts followed, and Boumphrey took Prudence's hand and squeezed
it.

'Me, now,' he said.

Darling sat silently as he did his checks. Through the Plexiglass, he could see the explosions in the distance as the Audaxes went into the attack, then ahead of him the Blenheims began to move, one after the other, heading as fast as their pilots dared for the opening in the fence. The Mercury engines snarled as they made a swift turn on to the airstrip, then they were roaring down the field, trailing the usual cloud of brown dust. As the last one vanished, Boumphrey released the brakes and opened the throttle. As he moved foward, the Blenheims howled across the airfield, heading east.

'Somebody's going to get a nasty shock when that lot arrives,' Darling observed.

By the time they had achieved height, the Audaxes and Gordons were already pinpointing targets. One of them screamed past the nose of the Oxford, its siren going so they could hear it even over the roar of the engines, then it went into a near-vertical dive almost to ground level and they saw it scooting along at low level to lay its bomb on one of the gun positions. They saw the flash and the puff of smoke and dust, and running figures, then, howling along the plateau, forcing the Irazhi gunners to keep their heads down, they watched the Dakotas move out from behind the hangars, one after the other, and take off towards the south and safety.

Dropping their bombs, they swung round for their landing, put the wheels down quickly and scuttled along the field towards the hangars as fast as they could while a new flight of Audaxes roared backwards and forwards along the escarpment to give them protection. Jumping down, they were told a lorry was dispensing drinks on the road to the polo ground. As they stood by it, a solitary aeroplane appeared over the airfield.

'What's that?' someone asked. 'One of ours?'

'Must be. There's been no warning.'

Since the air-raid warning system consisted only of the station accounts officer or the education officer on the roof of

AHQ with a pair of field glasses and a large bell, this was no guarantee of safety, and the first speaker stared again at the approaching machine, his eyes narrow with suspicion.

'It looks like a Savoia to me,' Darling said. 'Think it's a bomber?'

'Not for a minute. It'll be a photographic machine.'

For a second there was silence and they were all watching tensely when they heard the scream of the bomb. They all flung themselves down, the lorry with the drinks promptly bolted, scattering mugs and food, and the machine guns round the airfield, which up to then had been silent, began to fill the air with streams of tracer. The bomb struck alongside the road, and a tree was stripped of its leaves as if by a miracle and a huge shower of earth, stones and sand went up. Lifting his head, spitting out grit beneath the shower of descending leaves, Darling glared.

'The bugger must have dropped his camera,' he said.

As the drinks lorry returned and they snatched a hasty meal of sandwiches, they could see the shells falling again and once more the bets started.

'Up fifty fils they get the water tower today.'

'Not they. They couldn't hit a pig in a passage.'

'They hit me!' The voice was indignant. 'Yesterday. As I came in. The bloody aeroplane looked like a sieve!'

The Oxfords took off again an hour later. The sun was high by this time, glinting off the iron roofs of the buildings and picking up glints of metal from the escarpment. Darling's first effort was off-target and Boumphrey suggested they went lower.

Swinging round, he put the nose down and the speed began to build up as the Armstrong Siddeley Cheetahs began to howl. Puffs of smoke appeared on either side of them but Boumphrey held the machine steady. It was shuddering a little now; then, as the speed built up further, there was a tremendous crash and debris flew in all directions through the machine. Boumphrey ducked, thinking for a moment they had received a direct hit, but they were still flying and as he glanced at the air speed indicator he realized he had blown in the bomb-aimer's Plexiglass window.

Part of the nose was hanging loose and flapping noisily so that it sounded as though the aeroplane was falling apart. Darling was looking terrified as he held on by his toenails.

'You all right, Darling?' Boumphrey asked, pulling the stick back gently.

'Yes, sir. What happened?'

'It was me. The Ox-box's top speed's reckoned to be around two hundred miles an hour. I think I overdid it a touch.'

A gale of wind was blowing through the hole in the nose and Boumphrey looked about him to see what other damage had been done. The interior of the machine was full of pieces of wood and Plexiglass but the Armstrong Siddeley engines seemed still to be full of health and vigour. He tried the flaps and undercarriage.

'Everything seems to be working,' he announced. 'How about bombs?'

'I didn't let them go, sir.'

'Well,' Boumphrey said, 'we'd better not waste 'em.'

They landed with the loose Plexiglass swinging wildly. A machine gun was firing across the field and to their surprise they saw holes being punched in the fuselage.

'Here, too?' Boumphrey said irritatedly.

As he approached the gate the man on duty there waved them away.

'We're falling apart,' Boumphrey shouted but he was still waved peremptorily away, so he circled as fast as he dared, expecting all the time the machine guns to open up again. But by this time armoured cars had appeared and were heading across the airfield at full gallop, their guns going. Beyond the perimeter, near the old rifle range, they saw Irazhi soldiers rise from behind a small bank and start to run for the slopes carrying a machine gun. With the machine gun fire stopped, the armoured cars continued to move about, careful not to offer themselves as targets for the heavier guns on the escarpment.

The Gordons were emerging through the gate and, as the last one swung on to the airstrip, a man stepped out and waved a green flag. As they passed through, a machine gun opened up from higher on the slopes and they saw chips flying from the brickwork of the buildings and heard more bullets being punched into the Oxford. As they swung round to a stop behind the hangars, what was left of the Plexiglass fell off.

The station engineering officer's face appeared in the hole. 'What in God's name did that?' he demanded.

'Mice,' Boumphrey said.

'Don't be bloody silly, Ratter!'

'Solid air,' Boumphrey explained. 'We went down a little too fast.'

'Doing what?'

'I would say it was a sort of dive-bombing.'

The engineering officer glared. 'Oxfords weren't designed for dive-bombing,' he snapped. 'They're supposed to be three-seat advanced trainers for aircrew training.' Then his expression softened. 'All the same,' he admitted. 'It was probably a good try.'

'Ten for effort.'

'You hurt?'

'Neither of us.'

'You're bloody lucky. You might have lost the wings.'

As they studied the damage, the chief flying instructor's clerk appeared from the operations room.

'Chief flying instructor wants you, sir,' he said.

To get there Boumphrey had to go through the hangar where an aeroplane was propped up between crutches, the undercarriage legs hanging down. Two cowlings were off and half the starboard wing was missing. Fitters and riggers were doing wonders with spares – begged, borrowed or cannibalized – and were already on the way to fitting a new wing.

As Boumphrey appeared, Fogarty was red in the face with rage. 'What the hell do you mean, going up? You know you were told to stand down because of tonight's operations!'

Boumphrey pulled a face. 'Thought we were a bit short, sir,' he said.

Fogarty sighed. 'Sit down, Ratter,' he said, pushing a cigarette case across. 'How do you feel?'

'Bit tired. But not too much.'

Fogarty looked at Boumphrey. He was a strange young man but the older officer had a great regard for him. Boumphrey, he'd noticed, was always scrupulously polite to everyone from the senior officer to the lowest airman or native bearer. He was shy and, as Fogarty knew, vaguely ashamed of his sense of duty, especially of showing it in front of others. Yet behind his odd self-effacing attitude there was a curious confidence, a strange solid belief in his own ability, an indifference to the opinion of others, as if he didn't find it necessary for anyone else to appreciate what he was doing, so long as he understood it himself.

'You look like death, Ratter,' he said. 'You've been doing too much.'

'Not much choice, sir, is there?'

'There is for the moment. Push off, get a meal and a couple of drinks and arrange to be called for tonight. Then get your head down and go to sleep.'

Even now Boumphrey seemed unwilling and Fogarty pushed his lighter across. 'This is your third narrow escape, Ratter,' he said. 'Nobody can keep that up. Courage's an expendable thing. That's something the RAF discovered while the army was still shooting shell-shocked cases for cowardice.' He paused. 'That was a pretty brave thing you did, you and young Darling, trying to save that Wellington.'

Boumphrey's eyes widened. He hadn't known that the CFI was aware of it.

'And that was an inspired bit of flying when your machine caught fire yesterday.' The CFI smiled. 'I must admit it wouldn't have occurred to me, but it's a pretty obvious solution really. The wings carried the petrol and the wings were on fire. What better than to get rid of the wings.'

'Made manoeuvring a bit difficult,' Boumphrey admitted, a small smile of his own appearing. 'Flew like a brick.'

Fogarty sat back. 'Can you cope with what's planned for tonight?'

Boumphrey considered. As he did so, the CFI studied him. He was by no means the sort of figure that the RAF put into its recruiting adverts, but after his inspired showing in the last two days, Fogarty realized he had been misjudging him badly. Flying often took time to come to some people. While some grasped the essentials at once, with others it was different, though when the knack was acquired these men were often better pilots because they had learned to be cautious, too. There was a saying among aircrew that at 100 hours a pilot thought he knew it all, at 1000 he was sure he did, and at 10,000 hours he was beginning to realize he had a lot to learn. Boumphrey seemed to have acquired both caution and knack simply by having them thrust on him.

6

The mess had been hit again, the bar had holes in the roof and somebody was complaining bitterly about a fusillade of bullets that had slapped into the walls as he was writing his report.

'It was a bit bloody disconcerting, I can tell you,' he said. 'Made my spelling go all to pieces.'

There were glass and wood splinters on the floor and an Indian bearer was sweeping up the debris, one eye on the window, his head cocked for the sound of bombs and shells. A temporary bar had been set up at the end of the anteroom and the native barman handed Boumphrey his drink quickly and dodged back into the cubbyhole where he kept his wares just in case.

Boumphrey swallowed his drink, called for another one, and headed for his room. The shelling was still going on and he could hear the crump of shells all the time around him. Underneath his bed, Archie, the dog, was whimpering a little at the crash of explosions, but when a near miss brought dust down from the roof Boumphrey joined the dog under the bed. The dog moved closer, still whimpering.

'Cissy,' Boumphrey said.

The floor was hard and in the end he climbed back on to the bed and took the dog with him, by this time probably less frightened than Boumphrey.

He was awakened a lot sooner than he had expected and he was surprised to find it was Verity who had disturbed him. He turned over, pushed the dog to the floor and sat up.

'Plans have changed,' Verity said. 'They've planted guns at

the other side of the river and they have to be knocked out.'

'Where?'

'Bisha. Where that clot, Craddock, had his troop of Dragoons to watch the northern perimeter. The idea was that they were to form a strongpoint with their machine guns against any attempt to get round that side. But, of course, the fathead collected them – *and* their guns – and now the whole bloody lot are trapped in the fort at Hatbah.'

'And Bisha?'

'The station education officer saw Irazhis moving into position from the top of AHQ. There are four guns and so far they've only fired ranging shots but from there they could hit AHQ, the hospital and Workshops, and they're a lot nearer the water tower. We expect them to come into action tomorrow.'

Boumphrey blinked away sleep. He had been dreaming that he was at home in England and he was finding it hard to absorb what Verity was saying.

'We've got to take them out,' Verity was continuing. 'From where they are they can send shells straight across the polo ground whenever they like. They could knock off every machine we've got there.'

Showering and having a badly needed shave, Boumphrey stared at his face in the mirror, aware that if the water tower was hit all such ablutions would have to cease abruptly. He had often listened to Wood-Withnell on the sufferings of the men trapped in Kut and he could see similar problems in Kubaiyah. Every drop of water would have to be brought from the river and boiled and, for the number of people still in the encampment, that was a task that was clearly beyond possibility.

The AVM's meeting to deal with the problem was attended by the usual departmental officers, together with the station education officer, who had spotted the movement from his roost on top of AHQ.

'How big are the guns?' Verity asked.

184

'The Royal Artillery artificer says they're 18-pounders,' the education officer said. 'He had a look at them with field glasses. Very common in the last bunfight. Not too big but big enough.'

'Any ideas, anybody?' the AVM asked.

'There are boats,' Boumphrey pointed out. 'One seaplane tender belonging to the station rescue unit, and two belonging to the cruising club.'

'Are they big enough?'

'I doubt if the club's boats are powerful enough with the river in flood after the rains but the seaplane tender's all right. They were built to deal with bad weather and tested on Plymouth Sound. They'll stand up to heavy seas, and ours copes well with the river even in flood.'

'It must be a long time since it was used,' Group Captain Vizard pointed out.

'Nothing wrong with the clockwork, sir. She's got two Perkins diesels.'

'There are four guns,' the education officer said. 'There, there, there and there.' His finger moved over the map. 'They're only about a hundred yards back, set on patches of high ground behind the Dragoons' old camp among the reeds and marsh grass so you can't see them from ground level. So far they've done no more than fire a few shots to get the range but if they start getting ambitious they could fire over open sights.'

'Shouldn't be too difficult to find in the dark,' Boumphrey pointed out. 'Bisha's under the only bunch of palms on that stretch of river until you come to the left-hand turn northwards.'

'Who's going to do the job?' the group captain asked.

Verity was willing to have a go at the guns with his levies but he had only been in Kubaiyah a short time and wasn't sure of the ground, while his men, mostly used on guard duties, weren't much wiser. The Loyals, new to the station, knew nothing at all of the lie of the land.

'Better let me look after the river,' Boumphrey said quietly. 'I know it well. As president of the cruising club and former CO of the rescue unit, I ought to. I've explored the other side too. Bird watching. Pelicans, snake-necked darters, pigmy cormorants, kingfishers, coots. That sort of thing. There should be no trouble getting there. The river runs this way.' His hand moved across the map from left to right to indicate a west-to-east flow. 'If we board the boat from the jetty north of the cantonment, cross immediately then shut down and allow the river to take us down, we could end up just about where we want to be without using the engines again until the last minute. Should inject quite an element of surprise into the proceedings. Of course, I ought to have someone with me who knows something about artillery.'

'How about Sergeant Porlock of the Gunners,' the armament officer suggested. 'He's been complaining that he's sick of cleaning up those two old howitzers when everybody else's doing the fighting. Would he go?'

It didn't take long to discover that Sergeant Porlock not only would go but would be very annoyed if he didn't.

'I can settle their 'ash in no time,' he said. 'I'll need a few chaps with a bit o' savvy who'll do as they're told, o' course. But that's all.'

'Who're you going to use to do the dirty work?' Colonel Ballantine asked Boumphrey. 'I can ask for volunteers from my chaps.'

'Thanks.' Boumphrey gave him his gentle smile. 'I prefer my boys. I know them and they know me.'

It was decided that while Boumphrey and his Belles were attending to the guns across the river, Jenno's cars, plus a group of volunteers from the Loyals, should take advantage of the confusion to do the job originally intended for the Mounted Legion on the southwestern end of the escarpment, while Verity would continue as originally planned to the northeast. Jenno would knock out the Irazhi cars outside the perimeter, and would then lead the Loyals up on to the escarpment. Colonel Ballantine would coordinate the defences and provide men to guard the gates until the raiders could return.

There was only a small gate in the wire to the north of the camp, leading to the river and the little jetty where the rescue tender was moored, among the dhows abandoned since the fighting and the bumboats normally used by the camp labourers to bring earth and stones for repair work in the camp. With its black hull and the red, white and blue RAF roundel, it looked neat and efficient.

'Will it be big enough for all the people you're taking?' Jenno asked.

'I'm going to lash one of the bumboats alongside and tow her across,' Boumphrey said. 'And I'm only taking one troop. Otherwise we'll be getting in each other's way.'

'What about back up?' Colonel Ballantine asked. 'How many of my chaps will you need to support you?'

'None, thank you.'

'None?'

'With all due respect to your chaps, they're a bit noisy when they move about. Those boots they wear. I shall have the rest of my boys lining the opposite bank, with instructions to knock out anything that moves.' Boumphrey smiled. 'If I don't include them all, they'll probably shoot *me*.'

As they got down to details it was decided that six men to each gun would be ample.

'Together with four other men,' Boumphrey suggested. 'Sergeant Porlock and three armourers, to do the dirty work. My chaps will deal with the guns' crews and Porlock and his experts will deal with the guns.' He looked at Porlock. 'How do we go about killing these guns?'

'A shell in the breech, one up the spout, and a length of cord to the trigger.'

'Sounds complicated for amateurs.'

'I'm not an amateur, sah!'

'I am.'

187

'You could always do it with a block of guncotton and a primer detonator.'

'We'd blow ourselves up and *you* can't be in four places at once.'

'OK, sir.' Sergeant Porlock sighed, deciding that the RAF were a right lot of dimwits. 'We take out the breech blocks and chuck 'em in the river.'

As dusk approached the different groups began to muster at their jump-off positions.

The river was still blue and startling as a kingfisher's wing. The yellow grass on the far bank was leaning in the breeze, and through his binoculars Boumphrey could just see the roofs of the village of Bisha, a poor place, its black walls dusty and collapsing. There were a few reed huts on the sandy bank and a ferryboat for donkeys and camels. As the horizon melted to dust in the south, the village seemed to float above a gathering mist.

'That'll help,' Boumphrey said, his eyes on the land where he could see a flock of mixed goats and sheep moving among the shallow undulations.

With darkness, the Loyals, who were to hold the gates through which the raiding groups were to debouch, began to fill sandbags and throw up small fortifications behind which they stationed machine guns. Slit trenches were dug to contain the men who were to hold the gates in the event of a rush.

Verity's levies marched smartly with swinging arms across the airfield to the perimeter fence. They were excited and eager to go and all the doubts that had been entertained about their loyalty had long since been dispersed. Behind them Jenno's armoured cars growled into position, followed by a half-company of the Loyals. Nobody was kidding himself that the noise they made couldn't be heard by the Irazhis on the escarpment. They could only hope that they would put it down as some attempt by the RAF to strengthen their defences and wouldn't expect the gates to be opened and raiders to roar through.

At the other side of the cantonment, beyond the hangars where the work of preparing the aircraft for the next day was in progress, beyond the polo field where the remaining serviceable Audaxes and Harts were being checked and the holes in their fuselages and wings patched, Boumphrey and the Mounted Legion gathered near the cruising club's jetty. With the end of daylight the shelling had dwindled to an occasional bang and it was quiet enough to hear the movement of the river which was still running swiftly after the winter rains. The dark-eyed men in pink keffiyehs, excited and grinning with anticipation, were wearing their black robes to make them difficult to see in the darkness.

Boumphrey wore his ordinary uniform of khaki drill shirt with long trousers, over it his harness, belt and revolver. On his other hip he carried a side pack containing a Very pistol and cartridges, but, because the operation was to be carried out entirely by the Mounted Legion, on his head he wore the yellow keffiyeh which marked him as their leader. His men were quick to notice the headdress and, as he moved among them, white teeth showed and soft voices spoke to him.

'Greetings, Beni Ifry,' they said, addressing him by their version of his name. 'In the name of God, the merciful, the loving kind, tonight we shall do them mischief.'

'The stars are out, Beni Ifry,' another one said. 'Behind the stars we see God and He watches our movements.'

Boumphrey smiled and patted shoulders as he moved to the river bank where the marine fitter who attended to the tender's diesels was bent with the coxswain over the open hatches.

'All well?' Boumphrey asked.

The coxswain looked up. Ever since the beginning of the crisis, he and the other motorboat crew had been digging trenches, humping sandbags and generally working as labourers, and he was glad to get back to doing the job he knew best.

'We had 'em running earlier, sir,' he said. 'They'll not let us down.'

Ghadbhbhan was addressing the Mounted Legion mustered along the river bank roughly opposite where the guns would be. He had them standing in rows and was letting them know in no uncertain terms what was expected of them.

'Listen to me,' he said. 'This night you will behave as soldiers or I shall want to know why. Opposite you, across the river, will be the Irazhi. It will be your duty to kill any you see. But –' he glared at the lines of men '– you will be careful. Beni Ifry will be across there, too, and you will not shoot *him*. Is that understood? If he is hurt, I shall ask questions and I shall find out who was the cause.' He marched up and down the lines. 'Now, let us make sure that we look like soldiers. Most of you would not do credit to a whorehouse. Tighten that belt! Adjust that girdle! Up with that rifle! Beni Ifry will be proud of us when we return or I shall want to know the reason why. You may not realize it but tonight's operations depend on us. No matter how good the men Beni Ifry takes with him, they are nothing without *our* fire power and *our* skill as soldiers.'

It was all good stirring stuff and, even though Ghadbhbhan was educated enough and intelligent enough not to believe it himself, his men did and that was sufficient.

As they marched away to take up their positions, Boumphrey stepped aboard the tender. It was facing upstream and, on the riverside, the coxswain and deck hand had lashed one of the shallow-draft native bumboats with mooring ropes and springs so it could be towed alongside. It was a heavy boat built of strong timbers and big enough to carry a group of heavily armed men.

By this time, night had come with all the grandeur of the marshlands. The chrome yellow sky had turned hotter and hotter, those reeds which stood out against it like black cross-hatching, those to the east still glaring orange. Then gradually the water became purple below a bright half-moon and, as the last of the light went, it was dappled by brilliant silver slots, while the stars burned splendid and still in a sky crossed by two long streamers of black cloud. Boumphrey stared at it thoughtfully, listening to the susurration of the moving reeds.

'Right,' he said. 'Let's have everybody aboard.'

His men climbed nervously from the tender to the boat lashed at its other side. They were landsmen who lived about as far from the sea as you could get, and they didn't look forward to the trip across the river. But Beni Ifry had ordained it so they kept their thoughts to themselves. As they settled down, squatting on the bottom boards and sniffing at the dirty water that soiled their robes as it swilled backwards and forwards in the bilges, they clutched their rifles, uneasy but eager to prove what they could do. They were all men of warrior tribes and so far in the siege of Kubaiyah they had done nothing more than sit humiliatingly in trenches or squat behind barricades of sandbags and count the shells that landed in the cantonment.

As they settled down, Sergeant Porlock and his armourers climbed aboard the tender. They were strapped into harness with revolvers, and for his own entertainment, Porlock had brought along guncotton and detonators. The fact that if he were hit by a bullet he could go up and carry everybody else with him didn't worry him too much. He had served in the artillery in the first war and he was well aware of the chances.

'Right,' Boumphrey said. 'I think we're all aboard. Let go, Corporal, please.'

7

As the deck hand shoved the boat away from the jetty with his foot, the nose swung out and was caught by the current. The coxswain allowed it to turn of its own accord, then, as the boat faced directly across the river, he opened the throttles.

'Not too much, Corporal,' Boumphrey warned. 'Let's keep it as quiet as we can.'

The river was running fast and the man at the wheel had to head slightly upstream to keep them from drifting with the flow. A light breeze was whipping up wavelets and an occasional thin snatch of spray whipped over the bow and sprinkled the men squatting in the boat lashed alongside. Though they said nothing, their eyes moved uneasily and there were low moans as the boat seesawed up and down alongside the tender.

Boumphrey reassured them. 'Not far now,' he said.

'It's as well, Beni Ifry,' a voice came from the shadows. 'My stomach doesn't like it.'

With the engines running sturdily, the tender chugged quietly across the river. Boumphrey's thoughts were busy. Though he had trained his men well, this was the first time he had ever led them into any kind of danger and he wasn't sure how they'd behave. His impression was that they wouldn't let him down but he couldn't take bets on it because they were largely an unknown quantity.

He wondered what Prudence Wood-Withnell was doing and tried to understand his own thoughts about her. He was happy in her company and knew she was happy in his, but he was also aware that she wasn't what he'd dreamed of as an adolescent with ideas of romance. In those days his thoughts had run on the lines of film stars and he had suffered agonies when a pretty girl on whom he had set his sights had jeered at his advances. If nothing else, it had brought him sharply down to earth and he was far from unaware that most of the women he'd met in the Lafwaiyah Club had not regarded him as worth a second glance. They never fell over themselves for his favours as they did for the satanic-looking Jenno, whose dark sardonic good looks seemed to attract them like flies by their very suggestion of evil. Boumphrey couldn't imagine anyone like Christine Craddock wishing to disappear into the darkness with him as she had with Jenno.

A slash of spray wet his face. He wiped it away with his hand, suddenly aware of what he was about to do. But he couldn't imagine merely sitting back and allowing the Irazhi to take over the camp. Quite apart from the fact that Ghaffer al Jesairi was known to be a bit of a dirty dog, an opportunist politician who had repudiated the treaty between his country and Britain and gone for the side of the Nazis. Anybody who supported Hitler, in Boumphrey's eyes, was a dirty dog and, like Hitler, devoid of any of the qualities of a gentleman.

But, above all, what had sustained Boumphrey through all the dangers and excitements of the past two days was the fact that if the camp fell, not only Prudence but all the women and children would be subject to the indignities of being made prisoners. Boumphrey had grown up in an age when the Victorian idea of the British showing the world how to behave was still strong, and many of the books he had read as a boy had featured the rescue of besieged civilians by the manly figures of British soldiers carrying the flag. Always, it seemed, to the top of a hill.

His mind had been filled with stories of Waterloo and Balaclava, when the Light Brigade – quite naturally in the eyes of Boumphrey – had destroyed itself to bring about a victory. Nobody at Boumphrey's school had bothered to tell him that

Balaclava had not been a victory despite the Light Brigade's sacrifice. He had read about the sieges of Lucknow, Chitral, Ladysmith, Kimberley, Bloemfontein and Kut-el-Amara, just down the river.

He had lived on episodes of high adventure and the doings of daring young soldiers and, despite the defeats in Norway and France and the Balkans, he was still full of Britain's good name and military pride, that strange emotion the country had evoked from what were all too often a string of disastrous defeats. Though young soldiers no longer postured proudly before tattered Union Jacks, the emotion that such pictures had roused in Boumphrey still remained strong within him. He would have objected fiercely if he'd been told he was old-fashioned, but his sense of honour was far stronger than his sense of self-preservation and he simply could not imagine allowing the women and children in Kubaiyah to become prisoners while there was still breath in his body and the strength in his limbs to prevent it.

Besides – the thought pleased him in view of what her father had said of her – the siege had proved what he'd always thought; that there was more to old Prue than met the eye. She hadn't said a word to him of what she'd done but the station medical officer had been loud in his praises of his civilian helpers and had even singled her out by name for a special word.

He could see the opposite bank now, a dark line against a paler sky, broken here and there with stunted trees, high tufted reeds and the masts of occasional dhows. There was no sound, no light, no sign of life.

'Let's turn downstream now, Corporal, please,' he said. 'And just enough engine to make her manoeuvrable. Keep well clear of the bank, and call out as the river bends.'

A few minutes later, the corporal turned. 'Right-angled bend, sir. To the south.'

Boumphrey stared at the stars and saw them swinging. 'Five minutes I think, then a ninety-degree turn to port.

That'll carry us east. Another five minutes then a turn forty-five degrees to port. Then the palms and the huts of Bisha should be visible.' He stared at the sky again. The moon was rising and the river was flecked with silver as the sky beyond grew lighter, throwing the land into sharper silhouette.

The murmurings from the boat lashed alongside had died down now that they had turned downstream and the motion of the boat had subsided a little. Boumphrey moved to that side of the tender, checking the lashings and speaking reassuringly to the occupants of the bumboat.

'Ahmed has been sick,' someone said cheerfully. 'He is no sailor. Aziz rather fancies cutting his throat because he was sick on Aziz.'

'Tell Aziz,' Boumphrey said, 'to save his bloodthirstiness for the Irazhis. We shall soon be going ashore.'

The ninety-degree turn came up and, shortly afterwards, the forty-five degree turn.

'There's Bisha,' Boumphrey said.

'I see the palms, sir.'

'There's a wooden jetty running out from the bund. Can you put us alongside without carrying it away?'

'No trouble, sir. I'll come upstream of it and let the current carry us on it.'

The muttering in the boat alongside began again as they turned broadside on to the current and the motion started once more, but this time it was overlaid with the excitement of their arrival. The tender's diesels throbbed as the sharp nose edged in. A slash of spray came over that raised a low wail of protest from the boat alongside and a series of warnings to be quiet. It was possible to see a few faint lights in the mud huts among the reeds beyond the bund, as though crude oil lamps were burning.

'Can I use the searchlight, sir?'

'I've got a torch. Let's use that instead. It'll attract less attention.'

The beam picked out the wooden jetty almost immediately

and the tender edged in. There was a soft thump as the boat lashed alongside touched. It was Bisha all right, a place of crude mud huts festering along the bank, unlovely against the landscape. Among the few date palms and withered trees that struggled upwards, it was basically as medieval as in the days of Genghis Khan, with the same despair, the same ragged people, the same swollen-bellied children. A dead buffalo lay in the water near the bank, the hair all gone from the hide and the white ribs bursting through. Around it the water looked curdled, though the people of Bisha didn't hesitate to use it to drink – or, for that matter, to wash away their defecations. The air was noisy with the croaking of frogs.

The deck hand and the fitter were ashore with ropes, lashing them to the poles that held the jetty, and Boumphrey gestured to the men in the boat alongside.

'Ashore,' he said. 'Quickly. And no noise.'

The boards of the jetty creaked under the feet of the hurrying men. Then Sergeant Porlock and his three assistants, their feet clad in gym shoes, climbed from the tender and followed them. Boumphrey was the last to go. As he reached the jetty he turned to the coxswain.

'If there's trouble,' he said, 'it's up to you to go. But leave it to the last moment in case anybody turns up.'

'Aye aye, sir.'

Boumphrey climbed ashore, reflecting that, despite being in the middle of the desert, the marine craft men still managed to retain their seafaring habits.

His men were standing in a line on the bund. The frogs' chatter had died as they had gone ashore. He waved them over the bank to the lower ground where they weren't silhouetted against the sky, and they organized themselves quickly into four parties, Sergeant Porlock or one of the armourers with each.

'The job's to be done quickly,' Boumphrey pointed out quietly. 'Then away. Don't waste time.'

There was a murmur of assent and he climbed the bank to a

point halfway up and began to lead the way. After a quarter of an hour, he stopped and, as Porlock and the armourers gathered round him, he gestured.

'Four of 'em,' he said. 'There, there, there and there.'

'I can see a wireless aerial, sir,' one of the armourers said.

He pointed and Boumphrey nodded. 'That'll be number one. According to the education officer, the others are stationed at thirty-yard intervals eastwards. Move along the bank, count your steps then halt. I'll give you ten minutes. After that I'll fire the Very pistol. It ought to start a few people moving and there will probably be lights. So go straight in on them. Right?'

There were murmurs of assent and he waved them away, Porlock first, stumping off with his bag of explosives, his small eyes bright with excitement. The armourer stood quietly at Boumphrey's side, behind him half a dozen men of the legion waited patiently.

Boumphrey studied his watch then he lifted his head. 'Ready?'

The armourer nodded and Boumphrey lifted the Very pistol.

'Here goes,' he said.

The gate in the iron fence at the other side of the camp stood open, held by a man of the Loyals. Beyond, outside the camp in what was now enemy territory, Verity's levies had gathered to the left. Jenno's cars had not moved since they had arrived because of the danger of their engines alerting the Irazhis on the slopes. Near them, but on the outside of the wire, stood the half-company of the Loyals, led by a lieutenant and a burly sergeant major who seemed to be the very essence of military hostility.

Jenno stared at the gaunt outline of the hills and then at his watch, his eyes worried. 'What's happened?' he said. 'Boumphrey should be in position by this time.'

He studied the sky to the north, wondering what was

happening, then, as he stared, Flight Sergeant Madoc along-side him flung out an arm.

'There, sir!'

A red Very light was soaring into the sky beyond the camp and they clambered aboard their cars as it burst into a brilliant red glow that shone on the roofs of the buildings and the surface of the distant river. Immediately, Verity's levies set off at a half-run along the edge of the escarpment and turned left on to the road that led upwards to the north and east. Jenno's cars began to growl forward, bumping and swaying outside the wire fence.

Almost at once, they saw two Irazhi armoured cars in front of them, parked among the rocks at the bottom of the escarpment, and as Madoc opened fire they saw his tracer bullets striking the turret of the nearest and leaping into the air. As the Loyals surged forward, the machine gun stopped and the big sergeant major appeared from the shadows, and raised his hand to slip a grenade through the slit of the enemy car's turret. There was a flash and a bang and the turret seemed to bulge. The machine gun, just beginning to move round towards Jenno's cars, came to a halt, and the car seemed to sag back, immobilized. The second car began to move but Jenno's driver jammed his foot hard down and they leaped forward, ramming it with the armour-plated nose. The enemy car rolled on its springs and came to a stop, its front wheels twisted inwards as if it were crippled. Immediately the hatch opened and a man leaped out and thrust his hands in the air.

'They're yours, Sergeant Major,' Jenno said. 'Hang on to them. We'll tow 'em in as we come back. Let's have your men behind us. We're going up the slope.'

Swinging to their left, the four cars began to growl in low gear up the rocky path to the escarpment. At the top they almost ran into two men who were standing on the roadway staring down at the point where the attack had taken place. Jenno's machine gun rattled and they toppled over among the rocks. Almost immediately, they saw more men armed with rifles running towards them. As the gun went again and several of them fell, the rest turned tail, throwing down their rifles as they ran.

'Go ahead, Sergeant Major,' Jenno shouted. 'We'll cover you.'

The Loyals swept past and they saw grenades being flung. A shrub caught fire and in the light of the flames, they caught glimpses of soldiers in the gun positions. There were cries of terror and anguish, a few more explosions, the clatter of rifle fire, then silence. A few minutes more then the Loyals reappeared. They were carrying machine guns that didn't belong to them.

'We smashed what we couldn't carry,' the sergeant major said. 'The bastards were still wondering what hit 'em.'

'Right,' Jenno said. 'Get back down the slope. We'll cover you.'

As the Loyals hurried past, the cars began to turn in the narrow road. It wasn't easy in the dark but they managed it, each taking up a position to cover the others as they manoeuvred. At the bottom of the slope, the Loyals had emptied the two disabled cars of their crews. Two bloodied corpses lay alongside one. Alongside the other four men stood with their hands in the air.

'Like they was trying to claw their way up to heaven,' one of the Loyals said.

The sergeant major gestured at the car that had been rammed. 'Hell of a job to tow that, sir,' he said. 'Wheels all haywire.'

'Right, we'll just take the other then. Put a grenade in the engine as we leave.'

As they struggled back into the camp with the captured car, there was a dull thump and they saw pieces of bonnet panel fly into the air and heard the clang and clatter as they crashed down among the rocks.

'That'll not be used again for a long time,' Jenno said as the Loyals came running past towards the gate. Taking up a position covering the slopes and the route the levies had taken, they waited in the darkness for the returning men.

Moving forward in silence, Verity's levies found the Irazhi gunners outside their trenches, staring towards the southwest where the bang of the first grenade had gone off. They fell on them immediately with rifle, bayonet and grenade. The Irazhis were completely surprised, standing in the open wondering what was happening, and as the levies went in, they yelled and fled among the rocks, heading for the gulleys and safety.

Grenades were dropped, where possible, down the barrels of guns, and abandoned weapons were snatched up. For a quarter of an hour, the levies ranged among the gun positions shooting at anything that moved, then – as the Irazhis began to recover and they began to be fired on – Verity rallied them and they began to hurry backwards down the slope towards the gate.

Reaching the gate, they found the armoured cars waiting. As they hurried through, the cars followed them, swinging round one by one to cover the retreat with their machine guns, then, as the last man passed through, the gate was pulled shut again and rolls of barbed wire were hauled into place by a lorry.

By this time, the Irazhis above them had started firing wildly on the camp. They appeared to be doing little damage and a lot of the shells were going clean over the buildings towards the river where they could hear the sustained rattle of musketry.

'Sounds as though Ratter's enjoying himself,' Jenno observed.

Boumphrey found the first gun without difficulty and his men went in swiftly. Lights appeared and torches glowed but the crew were standing in the open watching the fireworks at the other side of the river and were totally unarmed. They were dispatched quickly and Boumphrey's group had reached the gun when they heard an explosion over on their right.

'Sounds as if Sergeant Porlock's got a few fireworks of his own,' Boumphrey said.

The armourer swung open the breech of the gun and wrestled out the breechblock which was dropped into a sack.

'Right, sir,' he said. 'I'm ready.'

'Back to the bank,' Boumphrey said. 'We'll hold the way until the others pass through us.'

A few moments later, there was another crash from where Porlock was operating and a flare of flame.

'Sounds as if he's found the ammunition, sir,' the armourer said.

As they waited, they saw figures hurrying towards them, then a machine gun opened up from further along the river, followed by musketry. Immediately the whole length of the bank opposite burst into flame as the eager men of the legion, anxious to be part of the fight, started firing with everything they possessed. Tracer bullets arc-ed across the river and the machine gun that had been firing became silent. As more firing started further along, the fire was switched to swamp it.

The party from the next gun were among them now, panting, none of them hurt, the breechblock safely in the armourer's sack.

'See any sign of the others?' Boumphrey asked.

'Not yet, sir.'

A few minutes later, Porlock appeared, flushed with success. 'Blew the bugger up, sir. Guncotton and a detonator just as I said. That one won't fire again. Then I found the ammunition and put a spot more there. We lost one man. That chap who was sick. He was shot by the officer in charge of the gun. I couldn't 'old your boys. They wiped the lot of 'em out after that.'

Boumphrey nodded. 'What about the other party?' he said.

'No sign of 'em.'

The moon was high now and it was possible to see quite

clearly. Then, to Boumphrey's amazement he saw a group of men struggling along the bund with what appeared to be a gun.

'Good Lor',' he said.

The armourer who had been with the third party panted up. 'Holy wars, sir, the buggers decided to bring the gun along. I couldn't stop 'em. I've got the breech and if we do get it here we've got another gun – if we can get the bastard across the river.'

Boumphrey stared about him, then he gestured to Porlock and the armourers. 'Back to the boats,' he said. 'Get planks. We need planks. Tear up the jetty if necessary. We *will* take it with us.'

8

Boumphrey's Belles were tearing round the camp in triumph, singing, cheering and boasting of their achievement. In addition to the 18-pounder, they had brought back a mortar and several Lee Enfield rifles.

Jenno grinned. 'What else did you get, Ratter?'

'One man killed,' Boumphrey said sadly.

At the other side of the cantonment they had added an armoured car, a light gun and numerous other weapons to their armoury, though Sergeant Artificer Porlock didn't think much of their acquisitions. 'They're in an 'orrible state,' he complained. 'Them wogs don't know 'ow to look after a good weapon.'

They had also taken several prisoners who were now busily indicating on the map to Osanna where their gun positions were situated. Though the night's events had amounted to little more than a skirmish, they had clearly made the enemy nervous and as soon as daylight began to appear, shells began to come thick and fast from the escarpment, though the firing died away immediately the aeroplanes lifted off the ground. It was quite obvious that the Irazhis were concerned that their positions were now vulnerable, not only from the air but also from the ground, and their one desire seemed to be to keep them hidden.

There had been no Irazhi aircraft over Kubaiyah for twenty-four hours because the Irazhi airfields had been paralysed by the attacks by the Wellingtons, Gladiators and Blenheims. Leaflets had also been dropped, but the air gunners who had

had to push them out had found that the air that roared *up* the flare chute carried them back in a fiercely whirling mass of paper which stuck to the hydraulic oil that always settled on everything inside an aircraft. 'Just like a bombed lavatory,' Darling informed Boumphrey. After that, the gunners had pushed the packets out unwrapped in the hope that they might hit some aggressive Irazhi politician on the head.

With the station now immune from shelling during daylight hours, things had become a lot easier but the attacks had still not caused the Irazhis to budge an inch from the ridge and, though the water tower remained untouched, the problem of the food supply was still having to be overcome by the shopping runs to the coast by the catering officer.

Apart from those who were working in the hospital and had elected to stay, however, almost all the women and children had been flown out without casualties, though the officer running the Audax-Hart squadron in place of Wing Commander Atkin, had taken a bullet through the backside while escorting the DC2s and was now having to eat his meals off the mantelpiece and sleep on his face. 'Seems to be an unlucky flight,' he said.

To his surprise, Boumphrey was given the flight in his place.

'It doesn't mean that you'll fly nothing but Audaxes or Harts,' Fogarty admitted. 'Like the rest of us, you'll have to fly whatever's available, but it means you'll be running it.' He studied Boumphrey's face. 'Not that *that* means all that much, either,' he said. 'They're crewed by anybody we can get, plus pupils. However –' he sat back in his chair '– you can put up your second ring.'

Boumphrey left Fogarty's office feeling taller even than his six-foot-four.

Though they had achieved all that they had intended, there was still danger. An attempt was now being made to help Craddock at Hatbah and several of the Gladiators and Oxfords had been sent in that direction. They returned to say they had scattered Fawzi's troops, and soon afterwards a radio message was received from Lieutenant Colonel Barber, of the Engineers, indicating that they had taken advantage of the diversion to escape from the fort – though Craddock's horses had had to be left behind – and the whole force had bolted west and were now within reach of the Palestine border.

However, it was now known that German aircraft were known to have arrived from Syria and reconnaissance patrols had been sent northwards to try to find the field from which they were operating. The news worried the AVM a good deal because, despite their daytime failures, the night after Boumphrey's raid across the river, as though in retaliation, the Irazhis on the ridge started firing on the cantonment after dark. It was new and unexpected and meant that after the hard work of the daytime flying there was now to be no rest after dusk.

The AVM climbed to the lookout post above AHQ and stared at the dark shape of the ridge in the distance. As he watched, a gun fired and a shell, screaming across the fence, fell near the polo field.

'They've pinpointed the most important targets in the camp,' Vizard said. 'They must have worked them out and they're firing by map references.'

The AVM frowned. 'I wonder if we could have a go at night bombing to keep up the pressure,' he suggested. 'The Irazhis don't like bombing and I think we ought to try something.'

'There can't be a flare path,' the group captain pointed out. 'Because they'd see everything that was happening from the ridge at a time when we couldn't see them. And that means that those who're going to take part are going to be the chaps with a lot of experience and, for the most part, those at the younger end of the scale. And,' he concluded, '*they*'re the ones who're already the hardest pressed and their number's dwindling.'

The AVM frowned. He was far from unaware of the facts. 'I see no alternative,' he said.

It was decided to make the first attempt that night.

The day went much the same as previous days, with the aeroplanes in the air from the minute it grew light. The Irazhis clearly disliked the dive-bombing of the Audaxes and bolted for cover from their positions as soon as they appeared above them. But a few daring individuals brought a pom-pom close to the wire, at a point near the gate the raiding party had used, and set it up at the edge of the field behind the marker's hut on the rifle range, smack in the path of any large aircraft trying to land.

By great good luck the Dakota at which it fired its first shots was missed by inches and the others were warned off until the gun could be dealt with. Crews were hurriedly scrambled together for the available aircraft and Boumphrey and Darling found themselves flying a Hart in place of a crew who had been wounded by shell splinters. The machine was plastered with patches and the engine was running roughly, but the Hart-Audax series had always been good aeroplanes and, despite their failings, the old machines had responded nobly to the demands being made on them and were well capable of carrying five hundred pounds of bombs beneath the wings and fuselage.

Boumphrey and Darling had the second machine in a flight of three and, as they climbed aboard, Boumphrey warned Darling gently. 'Just don't use that gun of yours when we're doing a bit of intricate manoeuvring,' he said. 'It's been discovered that the gunner has as much control of the machine as the pilot. In return, I'll try not to stand you on your head.'

Darling wasn't sure what the last cryptic remark meant.

They took off from the polo ground and lifted over the trees, Darling crouching in his seat behind the armadillo plates of the heavy revolving turret. The Harts had originally been built as light day bombers and later converted to two-seater fighters but, with the arrival of fast monoplanes, had become obsolete overnight and were now reduced to the status of trainers or the drudgery of target towing. Only the crisis at Kubaiyah had restored to them some of their former dignity and the machine still looked a thoroughbred despite the patches and the oil smears on the cowling.

Fogarty was flying the leading aircraft, with Jenno – like Boumphrey, again brought back to flying duties because of the dire need for aircrew – flying the third machine, and as they roared over the trees that lined the polo ground, they could see faces lifting up to them. It was Darling's first trip in the open rear cockpit of a Hart and the whip of air from the propeller as the speed built up began to lift his helmet. He hadn't strapped it on as tight as he might have and, as it began to balloon above his head, he had to open his mouth and hold it in place with his jaw.

As Fogarty led them over the guns to take a look at the situation, he saw bullet holes being punched through the wings. As they turned for their run in, one of the anti-aircraft guns opened up on them and Boumphrey banked steeply to the left. Darling, who had just swung the turret to the left in the hope of getting in a pot shot, suddenly realized what Boumphrey's warning meant. The turret seemed to run away with him under its own weight and swung down sharply so that the bank became steeper and he found himself hanging head-down in his straps over nothing at all.

The CFI's machine banked sharply. The starboard wing came up, the nose went down and the machine dropped almost vertically, flattened out and streaked across the ground at not much more than six feet, hidden by the buildings. As it lifted and pulled away, Darling saw puffs of smoke and the flashes as the bombs landed twenty yards beyond the gun.

As Boumphrey followed Fogarty down, Darling was fully expecting the Hart's wings to fall off. His face was drawn down, his eyes seemed to be bulging from his head and for a moment he thought he was going to black out. Then they were racing across the airfield close to the ground. He stared in alarm at the tracers whipping past and the holes being punched in the wings, then he heard a tremendous bang and the whine of a bullet whirring off whatever it was it had hit. As Boumphrey dropped his bomb, he saw the look of horror on the faces of the gunners.

Everybody was a little subdued as the end of the day came. Jenno's bombs had destroyed the gun but, in the afternoon, during the attacks on the airfields round Mandadad, one of the Oxfords had been hit by a shell as it was taking off, while one of the Audaxes had failed to return. They were silent as they walked away from the machines because, in the past, men landing in the desert had been subjected to ghastly mutilations by the Irazhi tribesmen.

By this time only six of the original twenty-seven Oxfords were still serviceable and these had had to be given to the more advanced pupils who were ordered to fly a straight course, drop their bombs and land again as quickly as possible. The crews had been made up by ground staff, one of them even a sergeant of the Loyals who claimed to be a dead shot with a machine gun.

All the machines were looking battered now and the technical warrant officer's face was growing longer. There were problems with temperature, mag drops, hydraulics and a variety of other things, and a tremendous reality in the minds of the men who were doing the flying. They had always known there was an element of doubt about their future but it seemed to be increasing with every day. There had been no rest, no time off, and the diminishing band of pilots was weary to the point when they could hardly bully the remains of their machines into the air. The early enthusiasm and defiance was wearing thin and they were beginning to look strained and jaded under a feeling of blank resignation.

And with darkness the guns, which had been silent during the day, started again – and with growing accuracy.

Boumphrey had managed to get Prudence Wood–Withnell to himself for a moment and as darkness came they were among the trees near the hospital. She was glad to be out of the building. Twice that day, with bullets ripping through the roof and walls, she had had to lie flat on the floor with the nurses and patients. She was tired enough simply to be happy to be doing nothing and to be with Boumphrey was a bonus. It was some time before she noticed the extra stripe on his shoulder.

'Ratter,' she said. 'They've promoted you!'

'They gave me the Audax-Hart flight.'

Her pride was unbelievable. 'Oh, Ratter,' she said. 'How wonderful!'

'Nobody else,' Boumphrey said deprecatingly. 'Had to be me.'

'I don't believe it,' she insisted. 'It's because of what you've done. I've heard about it. People in the hospital have told me.'

'Nothing, really,' Boumphrey said modestly. 'All I did was say "Go". It was the boys who did the work.'

'What about the others?'

'Others?'

'Your friends.'

Boumphrey was silent for a moment. 'A few have bought it,' he admitted.

She felt her eyes prickle. Her father was a soldier, so she knew what Boumphrey meant, and she thought of the few she knew personally, who were suddenly symbolic of all the dead pilots all over the world, all the young men who were dying to destroy Nazism.

They were still silent when they heard the first bang. As they heard the shell whistle overhead and drop just beyond the perimeter near the river, Boumphrey pulled her into one of the drainage ditches that bordered the road, empty and dusty in the dry season.

'Better keep our heads down, old thing,' he suggested. 'Splinters and so on.'

She sat alongside him in the ditch, making no fuss. She was quite calm and unafraid and he gave her a glance of admiration. Unfortunately, the next shell was nearer and dropped close by, then there was a whole flurry of shelling and they could hear the splinters whirring overhead. Instinctively they clung together, Boumphrey's arms round her, her cheek against his, her eyes blinking at the bangs, flinching at the earth and stones that were flung over them.

'It'll stop soon,' Boumphrey said.

'I'm not afraid,' she replied. 'Not with you here, Ratter.'

'Wouldn't have thought it made that much difference.'

'You'd be surprised.'

They were silent for a moment then between the explosions she asked, 'What'll happen here when it's all over, Ratter?'

'Go back to the usual somnolence, I expect.'

'I meant, what about you?'

'Same as before, I suppose. Bit of instructin'. Bit of work with the armoured cars under Jenno. Bit of work with the Mounted Legion. Nothin' very excitin'.'

'They might promote you again and send you somewhere else.'

'Not me.'

The shelling intensified and this time it was a little more erratic so that the shells seemed to be landing everywhere. As they ducked, they heard the scream of another missile approaching. It grew louder and louder until it filled the ears and they were convinced that someone was aiming at them personally. Boumphrey grabbed Prudence and pulled her to the bottom of the ditch. As the shell burst with an ear-shattering crash at the other side of the road, they were covered with dust and fragments of palm fronds torn off by blast. Then suddenly the shelling died as suddenly as it started.

They lifted their heads cautiously, kneeling together in the bottom of the ditch, face to face as if they were praying together. Without even thinking, Boumphrey kissed her.

There were flames nearby that lit up the angles and planes of their faces and he saw she was staring at him wide-eyed. Faintly embarrassed by her expression, he started to brush the dust and fragments of palm fronds from her. But she caught at his hands, though not to put them away from her, and instead pulled him to her, making joyous little sounds in his ear so that the noise of the camp was shut out as their mouths began to search eagerly for each other. Boumphrey held her tight, suddenly a little afraid, of dying, that he might lose her, and he could feel her trembling, almost as though shock waves were passing through her body to his.

After a while they came to their senses and sat back on their heels.

'Funny sort of place to start kissin' a girl,' Boumphrey said. 'In a drainage ditch in the middle of an air raid.'

'Best place in the world,' she replied cheerfully. 'Has to be genuine in a place like this.'

He stared at her. 'Marry me, Prue,' he said, almost without thinking.

'Of course, Ratter. I wondered when you were going to get round to it.'

'Won't be just yet, of course,' he admitted. 'Because we don't know what's going to happen.'

'It'll work out all right,' she said. 'Now. It's bound to.'

He smiled. 'Well, you know the old saying. "Captains might marry. Majors should. Colonels must." They upped me to flight lieutenant, which is equivalent to a captain. It'll be all right.'

They stared at each other, half smiling, indifferent to what was going on around them. The guns had stopped completely now but they could hear voices and the growling of engines as vehicles moved about. Gradually the sounds forced themselves into their consciousness, and Boumphrey looked up.

'Think we'd better move,' he observed. 'People will be asking questions.'

'I expect there'll be work for me at the hospital, too,' Prudence said.

'Just as well nobody saw us here. People would talk.'

'I don't mind. I don't mind a bit. Can we tell people, Ratter? Father, for instance?'

'I suppose he's entitled to know. Why not?'

They climbed out of the ditch and began to hurry towards the hospital, their hands clutching each other. At the door, they stopped and Boumphrey gave her another quick peck.

'Oh, Ratter,' she said. 'I'm so pleased! And so proud!'

As he turned away, she called after him. 'Ratter,' she said. 'Do be careful. Especially now.'

The damage from the shelling turned out to be not too bad. A corner of the hospital had been hit but nobody had been seriously hurt, though the station education officer had been slightly wounded when a shell had burst on the roof of AHQ. It had brought down slates and iron sheeting, together with the education officer, who now had a sprained wrist, a knee cut on corrugated iron, and a small wound from a shell splinter in his thigh.

'The storks are still there, though,' he said with a weary attempt at cheerfulness. 'The youngsters are growing like billyo, too. Any day now they'll be off on their first solo.'

There was a little moon and it was decided that the Audaxes should try to get off from the polo field by its light. But first of all an attempt was to be made by the CFI himself with Flight Sergeant Waldo to take off from the main airfield under instruments in one of the few remaining Oxfords. Everybody who wasn't asleep turned out to see what happened.

Fogarty's face was grim and they noticed that both he and Waldo had stop watches. They had worked out that by setting the throttles for a fast tick-over to give a taxiing speed of between eight and ten miles an hour they could be led through the gate by torches then turn on to a course of 135 degrees for four and a half minutes, which would take them to the edge of the airfield where they were to turn 300 degrees to leave the hangars on their right, open the throttles to full and do an instrument take-off. It was something that needed skill and Fogarty had decided that, under the circumstances, he was the one who ought to have first try. If all went as it should, the aircraft should clear the ten-foot dyke that lay at the end of the airfield. Once airborne, they would turn on the cockpit lights to give their eyes a chance to recover.

The return would be somewhat more alarming because their lives would depend on instrument flying at a time when they were tired and under stress. They were to follow the line of the river which would be visible in the starlight, flying at 1000 feet with the camp on their right, and turn off the cockpit lights in time for their night vision to return. At the far end of the field the river made two right-angle bends and when Waldo informed Fogarty that the machine was directly above them, Fogarty was to throttle back and begin a careful rate one turn to the right, descending by instruments to two hundred feet, which would leave them fifty feet above the highest part of the escarpment. When they reached the reciprocal of their original heading, they expected to be just over the lip of the plateau and facing the airfield, and they could then descend to fifty feet by instruments. At that height they would be in a position to turn on their landing light and descend to just above ground level. They would see the road and the ditch at the end of the airfield, so they could land straight ahead, snap off the landing light and keep the aeroplane straight by compass. By the hangars someone would be waiting at the gate to guide them quickly through to safety. It all sounded very tricky.

As they climbed into the Oxford and the engines were started nobody spoke. A jackal somewhere out on the plain was skirling to the moon. It sounded eerie as it always did and Boumphrey shivered.

'I'm glad I'm not having first go,' he murmured.

Because of the darkness, it was safe to wait on the airfield to watch what was to happen. If the experiment worked, everybody using the airfield was to use the same method for night flying, while, as the moon rose, the Audaxes would take off from the polo field to give support. It was a bold piece of improvisation but, because of the wastage among the aircraft, only a limited number could be used and the number of pilots with sufficient experience was small. While the aircraft were on the move, however, night patrols by the levies, the Loyals and Boumphrey's men under Ghadbhbhan were to stir up alarm and despondency among the besiegers.

The fire engine edged out on to the field, followed by the ambulance and the crash truck, then they heard the roar as Fogarty revved the Oxford's engines. Boumphrey found he was holding his breath.

'Here he comes!'

The dim shape of the Oxford appeared through the darkness, following a man with a torch. At the gate, more torches flashed to indicate the opening and the Oxford rolled through. Immediately, it turned on to its course and vanished quickly into the darkness, though they could hear the engines echoing and re-echoing from the flat sides of the hangars. By this time it was totally invisible.

There was a moment as the engines' pounding dwindled, then they heard the throttles opened wide and the howl as the engines gave full power. Very faintly they saw the machine roll past them, its tail already in the air, then it vanished again into the darkness. The blood waggons followed cautiously.

'He's up!'

It was possible to see a faint light at the end of the airfield that indicated the cockpit lights had been switched on, then someone spotted a tiny moving shape against the paler sky.

'All he's got to do now,' Jenno observed, 'is get down. And, as everybody knows, it's getting down that's important.'

It was impossible to see the machine now but they heard it to the north, apparently following the river, and shortly afterwards they saw a line of flashes along the plateau and heard the crack of the bombs.

'So far, so good,' Jenno said.

The aircraft passed overhead as it turned away from its bomb run, and they heard it cross the airfield and finally turn north. Heads turned with it, listening as the sound of the engine passed from west to east, following the river, then they heard it approaching the plateau, the sound taking on a strange note as the engine's roar raised an echo from the plateau.

'He's coming on to final approach.'

Boumphrey found his hands were clenched as he waited, then suddenly, abruptly, unexpectedly, the aircraft's landing light appeared, shining its beam along the airfield. The machine was at the decided fifty feet.

'My God,' Jenno breathed, 'it's going to work!'

They saw the Oxford pass in front of them, landing away from the plateau. A machine gun opened up against it and they saw tracer bullets streaking like white slots through the darkness and leaping into the air as they struck the ground. But the landing light snapped off immediately and the roar of the engines died; the machine gun stopped firing at its target became hidden once more in the darkness.

Eventually they saw the machine appear through the shadows. Torches flashed as it rolled through the gates, turned and vanished behind the hangars. As the propellers stopped everybody crowded round to watch Fogarty and Waldo climb out.

'No trouble at all if you do exactly as you're instructed,' Fogarty said. 'You can see their camp fires and lights all over the place once you're up. We'll have the instructions typed out and roneo-ed. Any moment now we can start chivvying our friends up there with a supply of high explosive throughout the whole twenty-four hours.'

9

There was growing feeling that they were winning. Bombs had been dropped in darkness by Oxfords taking off from the main airfield and by Audaxes taking off by moonlight from the polo ground. None of the machines had been lost despite one or two heavy landings, and patrols probing the slopes had discovered that the Irazhis had even withdrawn their outposts rather than have a repetition of the disasters on the night of Verity's raid.

They were certain now that the Irazhis had lost the initiative and, if they could keep up the air activity, were unlikely to regain it. Not a single patrol had penetrated the British lines. Not a single Irazhi who was not a prisoner had set foot inside the cantonment and, for the coming night, in addition to what bombing could be undertaken, it had been decided between the AVM, Group Captain Vizard, Fogarty and Colonel Ballantine, in command of the ground defences, to hit out hard.

Jenno and Boumphrey were ordered to report to AHQ, where they learned that during the coming hours of darkness a major sortie was to be launched. This time it was to be the Loyals who were to do the attacking, with the armoured cars, the levies and Boumphrey's Belles assisting on the flanks, the aircraft giving what aid they could. The attack was to be directed at Sin-ad-Dhubban, the village on the bend of the road just to the east of the cantonment from where much of the artillery spotting was done. Dhubban was the key to the escarpment. It commanded the northern end, the lower slopes and the safe route to the heights. With Dhubban in the hands of the British, the Irazhis would be cut off from their supplies.

'It's got to succeed,' Ballantine explained. 'There can be no mistake because failure would set us right back where we started. This time we must hit them so hard they'll be glad to call everything off.'

The day had started as usual with aircraft patrols along the escarpment to keep down the shelling, and strikes against airfields to keep the enemy aircraft away. As soon as it was daylight the aircraft had gone into action and, with the guns silenced, Dakotas and Valentias arrived from Shaibah and the coast with more men of the Loyals. Ammunition, machine guns, bombs, food, medical supplies and spare parts were also unloaded and lorries and cars arrived with the remaining women. Away went the Audaxes from the shelter of the trees round the polo ground and, as they started their systematic bombing of the gun positions, the last of the Oxfords roared off to join them. While they kept their heads down, the Dakotas took off. They were becoming remarkably expert at coordinating their attacks.

During the day, airfields were again attacked, together with convoys on the road from Mandadad attempting to bring up supplies to the heights. Spirits lifted as they realized that more and more the besiegers were becoming the besieged.

'I've questioned the few prisoners we've taken,' Osanna said at the afternoon briefing, 'and the endless bombing's beginning to wear down morale.'

'Mine as well as theirs,' Boumphrey remarked wearily to Jenno.

'We think a good hard blow will force them to throw in the sponge. Ghaffer's failed to defeat us and at the coast our people are now taking over more and more of Basra. There's been some sniping there.'

'There's been some here,' the AVM remarked dryly.

Osanna acknowledged the fact. 'However –' he paused '– there are more and more signs of German intervention. Aircraft are arriving in Syria, clearly on their way here, and

Vichy officials are being forced to give every assistance. Lorries are being loaded with supplies to support them and trains full of arms, ammunition, aviation spirit and artillery are ready to leave. We have to take away the reason for their coming. If Ghaffer's no longer here there'll be no point in their setting off.' Osanna paused again. 'It's hoped in Cairo that there'll be a diplomatic solution,' he ended.

'With all our aircraft destroyed and our men killed?' Fogarty sounded astonished by the workings of the diplomatic minds.

'It's not all-out war yet, sir,' Osanna pointed out.

Fogarty's eyebrows came down quickly. 'I'd have said it was,' he snapped.

Gladiators, their lower wings painted in the old colours of white on one side and black on the other – 'To give the impression that there's only half a plane,' most people argued – were escorting the bombers back from their raids on the Irazhi airfields when several Irazhi machines appeared unexpectedly from nowhere in the air over Kubaiyah. It was the first daylight raid for some time and it caught everyone by surprise.

Several airmen and civilians were killed or injured and a bomb hit one of the huts near the hospital so that the end collapsed, burying one of Prudence's Asian helpers. She was not dead but, as they dragged the rubble aside, they could hear her moans and her pleas for help.

Eventually a medical sergeant appeared with an AC2 orderly, a syringe and an ampoule of morphine, and as they pulled the rubble away, attempted to get in to the woman. But the rubble clearing had been done with more haste than skill and, as the sergeant wormed his way beneath it and reached back for the syringe, the wreckage settled so that he was dragged clear unconscious with broken ribs and a badly cut head. As they carried him away, Prudence stared at the orderly, waiting for instructions what to do. The woman's cries were becoming heart-rending.

'Somebody's got to go in there and give her this,' the airman said.

'Well, go on!' Prudence was beginning to grow impatient at the delay.

'It's going to collapse.' The orderly was young, spectacled and nervous. 'I can't go under that lot!'

She stared at him angrily then snatched the morphine and the syringe from him. She knew what to do because she'd seen it done many times in the last few days and was well aware that she could do it herself, even if only clumsily. 'Then get out of the way,' she snapped, 'and let me go!'

She not only administered the morphine but, finding the woman terrified, stayed with her and even helped to push her clear. When she crawled out, her hands were red to the wrist and she was covered – her clothes, her skin, her hair – in red sand and grey plaster dust. She was surprised how much of an effort it had been to jab a needle containing a quarter of a grain of morphine into a lump of pinched-up flesh, and was more nauseated by it than she had been by attending the wounded of the earlier raids.

The attackers had not had it all their own way. A Pegasus-engined Irazhi Audax was chased by a British Kestrel-engined Audax and, as the British pilot fired, the Irazhi machine lost height, began a graceful turn to the left, straightened out, then slid along the ground in a cloud of dust and smoke. As it came to a stop the fuel tank erupted with a sickening 'crump' and the lorry-load of Loyals rushing up to capture the pilot found that, with the wind carrying the smoke and flames away from them, they had a front-seat view of a man burning to death. They had watched with horrified fascination as the pilot's flying clothing disintegrated and his body slowly bowed forward, shrinking until it was no more than a charred shape.

'Jesus,' one of the soldiers said as he turned away to vomit.

A second Irazhi Audax flew into the face of the escarpment and exploded in a spectacular ball of flame, and a Fiat CR42, with the black, red, green and yellow Irazhi markings on its tail, crash-landed on the marshy ground near the river. The pilot was seen swimming to safety so the seaplane tender, crammed with as many of Boumphrey's Belles as could pack into it, set off to pick him up, while the rest of them kept up a withering fire on an Irazhi lorry that tried to push out of Sin-ad-Dhubban to stop them. In addition to Boumphrey, Darling had somehow managed to scramble aboard the tender. He was clutching a rifle and, Boumphrey noticed, was wearing one of the Belles' pink keffiyehs.

The Fiat had lost its wings and its fuselage was still burning with intermittent popping as the ammunition exploded. The pilot turned out to be an Italian who was found in the village of Bisha. He was a tall handsome man in a splendid but soaked uniform, wearing a spectacular wristwatch which seemed to have as many dials on it as the machine he'd flown; it was promptly claimed by Ghadbhbhan. The Italian gave them a fascist salute and explained in broken English that he was exhausted.

He had left the island of Rhodes the day before, he said, refuelled in Syria, alighted in Musol, got up at dawn, flown two hundred and fifty miles to Mandadad, become involved in the dogfight, been hit in the engine, taken to his parachute and landed on the British side of the river so that he had to swim all the way back to the Irazhi side.

'No wonder the bugger's tired,' Darling said.

During the raid, an RAF Audax and a Gladiator had been lost, reducing the numbers to a dangerously low ebb and making the attack on Dhubban more urgent than ever.

There were, in fact, very few of the original aircraft still serviceable now and the number of dead and wounded had increased, so that those who were left found their minds wandered back to seek faces they realized they'd already almost forgotten. But a few more Gladiators and Blenheims had been ferried in, together with three Battles which were to have gone to South Africa for training purposes and had been

220

diverted. They were all old machines, badly worn, heavily scarred and far from being the answer to a pilot's prayer, but they were added gratefully to the strength, serviced, admired, patted affectionately and regarded with as much pleasure as if they were brand-new Spitfires. Especially since Osanna had come up with a report of reinforcements gathering in Mandadad. If the Irazhis were about to force the issue with a major sortie from the capital, the need for the attack on Dhubban had suddenly acquired an increased urgency. Boumphrey's Belles were delighted that, for the first time, they were to go into action as mounted troops.

Part of the fence was opened to allow the attackers to move out with their lorries, horses, men and guns. The two howitzers from outside AHQ and Boumphrey's captured 18-pounder were attached to the backs of lorries and moved off on their iron-shod wheels like some relic from another age.

The levies and the Loyals took the Irazhis completely by surprise, but they recovered quickly and, watching with his men from the north side of the village, Boumphrey could see the flashes and the flying slots of coloured tracer and could hear the crash of Porlock's 4.5s. Stopped in their first surge forward by machine guns, the Loyals and the levies had had to go to ground and, as he became aware of movement towards him, Boumphrey realized that the Irazhis were mounting a counter-attack on his right to encircle the attackers.

The moon had risen and it was possible to see men and guns beginning to move across his front, heading for the road across the uneven ground. Once they reached the road, they would be able to move more swiftly and cut off the Loyals and the levies from their base, but they seemed to be totally unaware of Boumphrey and his men on their flank.

He glanced at his soldiers as they waited by their mounts, hands to the horses' noses to stop them whinnying, their dark faces under their pink headdresses tense and alert. Quietly he gave his instructions and the horses were led to the rear by horse-holders. The Irazhis' lorries were making sufficient noise to drown the sounds they made. Drawn up parallel with the Irazhis' line of movement, they set up their machine guns quickly.

Ghadbhbhan stood near Boumphrey with his hand raised, and heads turned in his direction, waiting for the signal to fire. As Boumphrey nodded, Ghadbhbhan's arm came down and his high scream of command set the whole line ablaze. As the rifles burst into flame, the machine guns alongside began to hammer.

They had caught the Irazhis in a classic ambush. A lorry managed to turn and head back the way it had come but two others collided with it and brought the rest to a confused stop. Very lights went up all round the village, illuminating everything.

The yells from the Irazhis changed to panic-stricken cries and Boumphrey could see them beginning to bolt at full speed back to the village. Then Porlock's 4.5s opened up again and they saw the shells exploding among the mud huts. Fires started and by the light of the flames the Loyals and the levies began moving forward again.

Boumphrey ordered the horses forward. They came up at the run, the men yelling with impatience.

'Mount!'

The order to advance came as they were still settling themselves in their saddles, and they swept forward in a wave. The shadows were filled with shouts and screams. A machine gun opened up and several horses fell, then the gun stopped as abruptly as it had started, and the mounted men rode up and down among the fleeing Irazhis, shooting and swinging their rifles at any who were near enough. Within minutes they were entering Dhubban, driving the Irazhis like partridges before them.

Almost the first recognizable face Boumphrey saw was that of Jenno. An armoured car, its headlights blazing, appeared from the west, roaring into the village and narrowly missing a group of Belles chasing a horde of fleeing Irazhis. Another attempt at a counterattack against the Loyals was started but a lorry manned by levies drove up at speed to stop it with Vickers guns and the Loyals were given breathing space once more. More shells from Porlock's 4.5s crashed down and the resistance began to crumble.

The Loyals had swept clean through the village now and had reached the slopes leading to the escarpment which had been liberated by Jenno's cars, and as the fighting died down they realized they had gained not only the key to the plateau but the lower slopes as well, so that the vehicles and guns up there were trapped. By daylight the extent of the victory was clear. Dhubban had fallen and they were rounding up dozens of prisoners.

It had been intended originally to halt in Dhubban but the momentum was such it seemed pointless and, with the aircraft already beginning to appear in the air, they swept up on to the plateau. The pupils had long since decided they could win the war in their patched-up aeroplanes and Boumphrey's Belles were convinced they could beat anyone with their bare hands.

The sweep up the slopes of the escarpment continued until they found themselves, to their surprise, in command of the place, with the Irazhis scrambling to safety down the other end into the desert. They began to count noses. The British casualties amounted to no more than seven men dead and fifteen wounded, while the Irazhis had lost over four hundred. The rest of the besieging force had taken to their lorries and cars and scuttled to safety and were now heading in a dis-organized mass towards Mandadad, peering anxiously over their shoulders for the expected pursuit.

The startled victors found themselves staring at abandoned lorries and guns, at tumbled sandbags, discarded clothing and equipment, the remains of half-cooked meals. There were sprawled dead among the debris, a few wretched prisoners and a few badly wounded men who had been left to the tender mercies of the victors, but no sign of any stand, no attempt to

223

resist, and it slowly dawned on the attackers that the Irazhis had fled. The siege was over.

The prisoners claimed that they hadn't been able to fight because they had always been short of water and that they hadn't eaten since the beginning of the bombing because supplies couldn't get through.

'Nine 3.7 howitzers,' Osanna announced when they had collected the spoils and lined them up at the edge of the airfield. 'Two anti-tank guns, forty-five Brens, sixteen other machine guns, ten armoured cars, one light tank, three gun-towing tractors, and a lot of rifles and ammunition. We seem to have picked up some very useful equipment. In addition, the pumping station's back in our hands.'

The celebrations started slowly. It still hadn't got through to most of them that there was no longer a danger from Irazhi shells and that it was possible to walk upright without having your head blown off. A couple of tired nurses were invited to a drink in the officers' mess and gradually more joined them and a party started. Nothing very exciting because they were all too tired and they knew the situation wasn't yet resolved. The next thing was to reach the embassy and remove all the women and children who had been held prisoner there.

Somebody discovered that Boumphrey and Prudence Wood-Withnell had somehow managed during all the uproar to get engaged and there were a few cheers and congratulations and toasts. Once upon a time the cheers might have been derisive but no one was inclined these days to jeer at Boumphrey. He hadn't altered much. He was still shy, still polite, still a long streak of nothing, but they'd all seen him in action and they knew what he was capable of, and, after all, soldiers, sailors and airmen came in a variety of shapes and sizes. Boumphrey had proved himself beyond all doubt.

They were just beginning to enjoy the situation, sit back and stretch their limbs when there was a panic call for all aircrew – repeat all – to report to the camp cinema for briefing and the party broke up abruptly. The drama, it seemed, was not yet over.

The air vice-marshal was waiting for them with the group captain and the chief flying instructor.

'The ambassador's reported that Ghaffer's declared a jihad,' the AVM announced at once. 'And you all know what that means. An all-out war.'

'Wasn't it before?' Boumphrey whispered.

'The Mufti's also put his spoke in and declared that all Muslims – and that means the whole of Irazh – are involved, not just the army. The Christians, the British, everyone, is to be kicked out of the country and, to restore the situation, Ghaffer's organized a column of motorized infantry and artillery which is due to head at once for Kubaiyah.'

The news flew round the camp as the briefing ended.

'What does it mean, Ratter?' Prudence asked as she met him leaving the cinema.

'It means we've got to do better, old thing,' he said. 'Push the old boat out one more time. They get all their muezzins and mullahs or whatever they're called – sportin' parson types, I suppose you'd call 'em in England – and they stir everybody up to knock on the head everybody who doesn't think like they do. It could be nasty.' He gave her a quick peck on the cheek. 'Got to go now. Bit of a hurry.'

She stared after him, her eyes anxious. Somehow the movement of men towards the hangars reminded her of what she'd read of the British soldiers leaving the Duchess of Richmond's ball in Brussels to head for the field of Waterloo, many of them to meet their death there. She watched the long figure of Boumphrey disappearing and found tears pricking at her eyes.

There was more news as the crews gathered in the crew room, and the air vice-marshal didn't pull any punches.

'Ghaffer's got the promise of more aircraft from the Germans,' he announced. 'The ambassador's just informed us. And two of Ghaffer's Golden Triangle are trying to recruit the tribesmen. If they're involved there'll be no end to the fighting.

The ambassador's also been told by Ghaffer's representative that there'll be no mercy unless we all pack up and leave at once. We don't intend anything of the sort, of course, but it does mean that we've got to break up his attempt to restore the situation here or it'll be too late. Messerschmitt 109s and 110s are assembling to fly to Syria. From Syria they'll fly here and you all know what a couple of squadrons of Messerschmitts could do to what we've got.'

They did indeed. A few 109s could wipe the floor with the remains of their pathetic force without losing their breath.

'The Gladiators have spotted Ghaffer's column,' the AVM continued. 'It's left Mandadad and is near Fullajah. We have to stop it before it gets any further. Every man and every machine which can get into the air will take part. Shaibah is sending machines to attack the airfields to keep the Irazhi air force down.'

The chief flying instructor was to lead the attack and, to make sure nothing went wrong, he once more had as his observer Flight Sergeant Waldo, the man with eyes like a hawk and a reputation as an expert. The newly arrived Gladiators, Blenheims and Battles were put into the battle order but because their pilots were ferry crews and not operational – four of them were even civilians – the old hands who knew the conditions were given their machines, to give the striking force some punch for its first blows against Ghaffer's column. Those ferry pilots who were in the RAF were given places in the follow-up machines and three of the civilians who volunteered were crewed with hurriedly briefed pupils who were to drop the bombs, and told to go in after the first strike and release their loads from a safe height.

As one of the few remaining regulars who had been trained under the exacting stands of the pre-war RAF, Boumphrey found he had been allotted one of the Battles and was given half an hour to familiarize himself with its controls and habits. It was a big machine, all metal and very different from the Harts, Audaxes and Oxfords he'd been flying and was able to absorb an enormous amount of punishment. Turning it was like trying to get a heavy lorry round a corner but it carried twice the bomb load of an Audax or a Hart. Though they had been lost in dozens to German 109s in France, here it was a different matter.

The machines began to head for the gate as soon as they had been briefed, first the Battles, then the Audaxes, then the Harts, finally the Gordons, the remaining Oxfords, the Blenheims, and the Gladiators. They were still inching forward, when one of the ground crew began pointing frantically and, though Boumphrey couldn't hear him over the sound of the engine, it appeared that the air-raid warning had gone. The education officer on the roof of AHQ had seen approaching aircraft and rung his bell. The telephone had gone in the Operations Room and suddenly everyone was in a panic to get the aircraft off the ground before the enemy arrived.

The enemy machines were identified at once as Blenheims. For a moment it was thought they were reinforcements then they saw the Irazhi colours on the wings and tails. Trying to swing the heavy Battle away from the line of moving aircraft, Boumphrey saw the bombs fall away as they screamed overhead and, horrified, he saw Fogarty's Battle lift from the ground and flop sideways, its starboard wing wrecked and on fire. Men ran forward and he saw Fogarty struggle from his cockpit. The air gunner dropped on to the port wing and began to run, then the fire engine arrived and began to smother the flames with foam. As the ambulance appeared with the medical officer, the technical warrant officer ran forward and jumped on the wing to warn Boumphrey that the proposed attack on the Irazhi convoy had been temporarily halted.

'Chief flying instructor's orders, sir,' he yelled.

With the wrecked Battle jamming the exit, the attack had thrown the British sortie into confusion and had cost a Battle, an Oxford, a Gladiator and an Audax, together with seven men killed and eight wounded.

As the ambulances roared up, men were running forward with foam appliances to burning aircraft and the whole assembly area was covered with a black pall of oil smoke. Eventually, Fogarty appeared. He was limping, his face pale, blood still running down his cheek from a head wound. He scrambled awkwardly on to the wing root of Boumphrey's Battle and yelled at him.

'Who've you got as bomb-aimer, Ratter?' he yelled.

'Darling, sir. AC2 observer under training.'

'What's he like?'

'First-rate, sir.'

'Right, then, get cracking. Take over as leader. For today, Darling's a sergeant and a fully qualified observer. They killed Waldo so he's got to do the job for him.'

As Fogarty dropped from the wing, a tractor appeared, trailing heavy chains which were attached to the smoking Battle and, as it was dragged out of the way, the Gladiators and Blenheims got away in a rush to join aircraft already on their way from Shaibah to attack the Irazhi airfields. Because of the Irazhis' attack, the Shaibah machines would have been and gone by the time the Kubaiyah contingent arrived, but there wasn't time to change plans.

As the remaining aircraft moved into position, no longer worried by the guns on the plateau, Boumphrey spoke into the intercom.

'Darling,' he said, 'this is your chance. It's a long straight road to Mandadad and I'm going to fly low along it. As soon as you see the first vehicles in your sight, let half your bombs go. I'll give you a yell when the other end of the column's coming up. Your remaining bombs should take care of that. OK?'

Darling's voice was brisk and confident. 'Bang on, sir.'

They discovered the relieving column halted near Fullajah where it had run into the column of men bolting from the plateau after their defeat. In their panic, the vehicles of the retreating column were all over the road, so that the column advancing from Mandadad had been brought to a complete halt just beyond the river, unable to disperse because of the flooded ground on either side of the road. The aircraft fell on them like avenging eagles.

A storm of anti-aircraft fire rose but the Irazhi conscripts were only half-trained and a lot of it came nowhere near them. Boumphrey made no attempt to climb away from it.

'Column coming up – *now*!' he yelled and Darling pressed the tit and saw the bombs fall away. They couldn't fail to hit the vehicles at the front of the column.

'End of column coming up,' Boumphrey yelled. 'Stand by to let go . . . now!'

Darling pressed the tit again without thinking, relying entirely on Boumphrey's judgement. The big machine lifted, trudging upwards like a bus with wings and, as they clawed for height, Boumphrey levelled off into a slow right-hand turn. Lorries at the head of the column had been hit and, as the smoke drifted away on the breeze, he could see two of them blazing furiously. There was another column of smoke at the rear of the advancing column and as it cleared he saw a burning lorry on its side, cutting off the retreat.

'Darling,' he announced. 'That deserves a gong.'

With the road blocked at either end, there was no chance for the Irazhis to save much. As the following aircraft came down and more and more vehicles went up in flames, the anti-aircraft gunners fled and the last machines swept over the destruction almost unharassed by ground fire.

Returning to Kubaiyah, Boumphrey put the machine down heavily. It bounced badly and he grinned sheepishly as he scrambled out. 'An arrival not a landing,' he said.

Together, he and Darling went round the machine with the technical warrant officer checking for damage. There were a few holes but nothing serious.

'Ought to have those patched, sir,' the warrant officer said.

'Not at the moment, Mr Farrar,' Boumphrey said. 'This is the end of the siege and it's got to stay that way. Like the beginning, it's a flat-out effort. Fill her up and we'll be off again.'

The aircraft swept down on the halted columns again and again. Returning to rearm and refuel, they kept it up for two solid hours, not a man nor an aircraft wasting a moment. Audaxes, Harts, Gordons, Gladiators and Battles fell out of the sky, with the Oxfords and even the Rapide, dragged out of the shelter of the hangar and pushed into the air, sailing sedately overhead to drop bombs from a mere five hundred feet and leave the road a strip of flame two hundred and fifty yards long.

A few brave men attempted to fire back but it was ineffective and they could see them abandoning their lorries and splashing into the water to escape the horror. Ammunition waggons, cars, lorries, light tanks, guns, lay everywhere across the road, burning and exploding and filling the air with black smoke.

When they finally landed they were well aware that the Irazhi attempt to restore the situation had ended in a disaster. As they climbed from their machines, their hands unsteady, their brains numb with the roar of engines, Boumphrey laid a hand on Darling's shoulder and beamed at him in that gentle but devastating way that made him feel he would willingly lay down and let him walk up his chest.

'Darling, old son,' he said, 'that was absolutely splendid. If I have my way – and I suspect it won't need much pressure – the chief flying instructor's going to waive the rest of your training.'

They were still celebrating when the AVM called Group Captain Vizard to his office. His face was grim as he skated a message form across the desk.

'The relief force from Palestine's made contact,' he said.

'When do they arrive?'

'They don't. They made good progress at first but now they're stuck and screaming for help.'

'What sort of help?' Vizard asked. 'Aeroplanes?'

'Aircraft can't help much this time. They're stuck in the sand and running out of food and water. And we need them here. Ghaffer isn't finished yet and if he learns they're held up he'll probably have another go. We've got to put paid to him for good and all and the only way is to go for Mandadad. For that we need Lindley's column. Can we bring them in? They need a guide.'

Vizard frowned. 'There's only one man who could do it,' he said. 'Young Boumphrey.'

The AVM looked up. 'Seems a bright boy. Lot of initiative.'

Vizard protested. 'I think we're asking too much of him,' he said. 'He's been flying non-stop since it started. He liquidated the battery at Bisha and led the attack against Ghaffer's column. He's had too many narrow escapes.'

'Is there anyone else?'

'No.'

'Bit of an explorer, isn't he?'

'He's a lot of things,' Vizard said. 'I don't think we really appreciated until now just *what* he was.'

'Knows the country round here like the back of his hand, doesn't he?'

'I believe so.'

'Would he do it?'

'Of course he would.'

The AVM knew what Vizard was thinking because he himself had been flying out-of-date machines on the Western Front in 1917 when a pilot's life span was reckoned in days rather than weeks, and he was well aware that it was always the brave and the willing who were pushed too far. But now he had bigger issues to deal with and they had taught him what responsibilities his superior officers must have carried when he was still a fledgling fighter pilot bitter at the death of his friends. A single life couldn't be weighed against a whole campaign, the outcome of a war. He sighed and gestured.

'It'll have to be Boumphrey then, won't it?' he said.

The aircrews were still talking excitedly and describing aeroplane movements with their hands when a message came through that Jenno and Boumphrey were wanted at AHQ. Vizard was still there, with Osanna and the AVM.

'You chaps feeling all right?' Vizard asked.

'Yes, sir.' Jenno answered for both of them.

'Tired?'

'Of course, sir. A little. But that doesn't mean that if something needs doing we couldn't go up again.'

The AVM interrupted. 'Something does need doing,' he said. 'But not in the air. Not this time. Brigadier Lindley's relieving column from Transjordan's stuck.'

'You know that part of the desert, don't you, Boumphrey?' Vizard asked.

'Yes, sir.'

'Explored it?'

'Often, sir.'

'How? Lorry or horseback?'

'Both, sir.'

'This time it's got to be in lorries,' the AVM said. 'Because it's got to be done quickly. German and Italian aircraft have found them and they're being bombed. They're also short of water and growing short of rations, and they're losing lorries not only to the bombing but to the sand. They have to get here because we've got to consolidate our success by moving on as fast as possible. The Germans are expected to attack Crete at any moment and there's to be an attack in North Africa to try to force the Germans back. The C-in-C's demanding a final clearing up here and we need Lindley's column. Can your people bring them in, with Jenno to look after your flanks?'

Things seemed to be growing complicated, despite the successes.

The relief column appeared to have come to a full stop about forty miles west of the camp. From what they could make out, they had followed the trans-desert road that ran from Palestine to Mandadad past the fort at Hatbah where the Engineers had been shot up. To avoid Howeidi, where there was still an intact Irazhi brigade, they had turned south but, because of the floods caused by the Irazhis breaking the bund of the river, they had not been able to follow a route close to the road and had moved into the Karymat Heights, a line of low sandy hills that ran north and south for a matter of twenty miles. There they had stuck and had even been forced to turn back on their tracks. They were now seeking a way round.

Jenno's column headed out of the camp for the south end of Lake Kubaiyah. The armoured cars led the way, followed by Boumphrey, with his dog beside him, his solitary armoured car leading the lorries containing the Mounted Legion. The Belles were excited, their eyes shining with eagerness.

By the lake they passed the headquarters of the RAF Sailing Club. The jetty was still there but the boats had all been sunk at their moorings, only their masts visible. There was an Imperial Airways resthouse nearby where before the war passengers from flying boats on their way to India had been brought ashore to stay the night. Now there were no flying boats and the marine section huts had been set on fire. A refueller, a seaplane tender and two dinghies had been run ashore and lay on their sides, the refueller's pumps wrecked. The ground about was strewn with paper and on the steps of the resthouse was a woman's green silk shoe. A Bedou woman with a child watched them pass with smouldering eyes, stately and beautiful and silent.

As the column circled the southernmost extremity of the lake, a Gladiator appeared overhead, turned and came back low. A small object that was seen to fall from it struck the ground just ahead with a puff of dust. It was one of the metal tubes with streamers attached by which messages were dropped.

As the men ran towards it, Jenno's car drew up alongside Boumphrey's. 'Trust us to do it the hard way,' he observed. 'There's something about all this that reminds me of the *Boys' Own Paper*. British outpost, women and children defended by a gallant handful of British troops and their native allies.'

Boumphrey smiled. 'And, in the best tradition, a column's on its way to rescue 'em.'

'While *we*'re on the way to rescue the rescue column.'

Boumphrey laughed. 'It'll come out all right in the end. They'll arrive in the nick of time, save the beleaguered British ambassador and all the women and children, overthrow the rebels and restore the rightful ruler.'

'Pro-British, of course.'

'But of course. Straight out of a Victorian picture book.'

When the message tube was brought to them, Jenno opened it. 'Fawzi waiting you in sandhills. Two armoured cars and several lorries. Machine guns seen.'

He showed it to Boumphrey. 'Complicates things a bit,' he said.

Boumphrey frowned. 'I thought we were supposed to be fighting the Irazhi,' he said. 'Not some tinpot sheikh who likes to stir up trouble.'

'Fawzi's not so tinpot,' Jenno pointed out crisply. 'He's a superlative ruffian and has boundless support among the

A'Klab tribe. He's sold himself to the Turks, the British, the Arabs and the French in turn.'

Boumphrey smiled. 'Not at bargain prices either.'

'Gone up a bit, in fact, I'd say,' Jenno commented. 'I bet the Germans are paying him top rates. All the same, what's he doing *here*? I thought he'd be in the fort at Hatbah with the Irazhis by this time. I think we'd better see what he's up to.'

Leaving Flight Sergeant Madoc in charge of the cars and Ghadbhbhan in command of the Belles, Boumphrey and Jenno moved forward. They took two cars in case of accident or ambush so that if one had to be abandoned the crew could escape by clinging to the other. It was a still hot morning but eventually the wind got up, filling the air with flying dust that peppered their faces like buckshot. It lay in the folds of clothing, clung to sweating skins and caked lips and nostrils to give them paste-like masks that cracked in wrinkles round their mouths as they spoke.

They drove in silence, exhausted by the wind and the flying grit. They were growing tired now. The cars were over-crowded and full of the smell of sweaty bodies. As they gasped for air in the stifling atmosphere, the sight of gazelles leaping across the horizon woke them up.

'Something there,' Boumphrey said. 'They've been scared.'

The Rolls-Royce engines were silent as they murmured their way to the edge of the sandhills, then Boumphrey and Jenno moved forward on foot with the dog. The wind was still picking the sand off the ridges and tossing it in malicious bursts at their eyes, throats and noses. Climbing one of the hills, they lay flat on top, careful not to raise any dust. The dog crouched between them, its nose twitching.

Below them in the valley they saw Fawzi's group. They had fires going, burning in tins filled with sand on which petrol had been poured, a trick they'd picked up from the British army. Their tins were even the old square British petrol tins cut in half, and they could see the pale flames. The A'Klabs were grouped round them, eating, the metal of their accoutrements picking up the sunshine so that there seemed to be constant movement in the group. They were a few hundred yards away, some of the men in Arab robes, others in khaki trousers and shirts, but all wearing the Arab keffiyehs – and all armed and slung about with bandoleers of cartridges. Jenno indicated a tall man standing near one of the trucks.

'That's Fawzi himself,' he said.

'Two armoured cars,' Boumphrey counted. 'Nine lorries. I can also see machine guns.'

'How many men, do you reckon?'

'Hundred and fifty?'

'About that. They won't be moving before daylight. Some of them are getting blankets out. I'm surprised they hadn't a lookout up here.'

'Overconfidence,' Boumphrey suggested. 'I expect they thought we were still tied down at Kubaiyah.'

'I wonder,' Jenno said slowly. 'Perhaps they've guessed we'd make some attempt to reach Lindley's column and they're waiting for *us*. They can't be waiting for a column as strong as Lindley's. Fawzi's clever enough not to go for someone he can't wipe up properly.'

Boumphrey studied the men in the valley. 'Think a chap's entitled to dot another chap who's waiting round the corner with a club to dot *him*.'

'Best way to deal with that is to have a bigger club,' Jenno said. 'Which we haven't got, so I'd say the AVM's idea was best. Get our blow in fust. Fawzi wouldn't feel it wrong. He's killed plenty of our chaps.'

'How're we going to go about it?'

'Any ideas, Ratter? You know these hills.'

Boumphrey studied the land below him. 'They run in two ridges that are joined at both ends,' he said, 'with this bowl in the middle. But there are openings in them where the road runs through. If we appeared up here, they'd head for the gaps like the field going for the first fence at a point-to-point as soon as we started firing. But they wouldn't go west because the relief column's on that side. They'd go north or east. It'd be awkward for them if we had armoured cars waiting for them.'

Jenno nodded. 'We can handle 'em if we take 'em by surprise. Who's going to fetch the rest of the chaps up?'

'You,' Boumphrey said. 'I'll stay here and watch. If they start moving, I'll come back and let you know.'

Jenno slapped Boumphrey on the shoulder and began to move down the hill, his feet sliding in the soft sand. Boumphrey's car remained tucked out of sight in a wadi with its crew in case one of Fawzi's men climbed the hill to where he waited.

Fawzi had posted sentries but their discipline was slack and they had moved close to the fires for fear of missing their meal. There were men sitting by machine guns mounted on circular bars above the cabs of the trucks, however, though the rest seemed to feel they were safe and had dug no cover.

Little gusts of steam lifted from the pans on the fires and once Boumphrey even thought he could smell boiling mutton and rice. Occasionally the wind that blew the sand in his face brought the faint sound of laughter. Some of the men were smoking cigarettes and they seemed relaxed and sure of themselves, moving about in a deliberate, easy way.

The sun was just beginning to disappear and the brassy sky had turned lemon yellow when Boumphrey's dog swung round with a tiny whimper of anticipation. Boumphrey turned quickly. It was Jenno. Behind him men were climbing the hill.

'All yours, Ratter,' he advised. 'I'll leave it to you to start the ball rolling. In the morning, do you think?'

'First light.'

'Fine. I'll have my cars covering the exits, with two spare ones ready to nip in and clean up and stop them bolting north or east. OK?'

'OK. The signal for the off will be when I start shooting.'

As Jenno vanished down the hill in the growing darkness,

Boumphrey positioned his men along the top of the hill. They nodded and grinned at him.

'And make sure they keep their hands off their weapons, Ghadbhbhan,' Boumphrey warned. 'We want nothing going off by mistake. If the wind bothers them, they can back off the top for shelter. We'll rouse them at first light.'

The night was cold, despite the heat of the sun during the day, and Boumphrey sat with the dog huddled in a blanket, his eyes on the little fires in the valley. The sound of chattering died as Fawzi's men slept but, though his own men dozed just off the crest of the hill, Boumphrey didn't.

He suddenly realized how tired he was. He and Jenno and one or two others hadn't had a single break since the start of the siege. They had flown constantly and in the intervals between had been involved in the counterattacks against Ghaffer's forces. But he kept his eyes on the camp below and to help him stay awake began to think of Prudence Wood-Withnell. He needed to be married, he felt. He was twenty-nine now and needed to put down roots. It was a feeling that had come on him a lot recently. His parents were growing old and there was a house and land in England that would be his in time – providing, of course, that he survived the war – and he needed someone to share it with.

There was the faintest light in the east when Ghadbhbhan appeared.

'Now, sir?'

'Yes. Wake 'em up. Get 'em in position. When they're ready, let me know.'

The fires down below had died during the hours of darkness, but now he heard the clink of metal and saw the flare of a match. There was a small flower of blue flame as the first of the stoves was lit. As the daylight increased, he saw the A'Klabs begin to move, first one, then another, then two or three. He began to count them.

Ghadbhbhan appeared. 'Everybody's ready,' he said.

'Guns in position?'

'In position, sir.'

They were only Lewis guns. Far from the best and susceptible to jamming but, with Ghadbhbhan's help, Boumphrey had shown his men how to care for them, how to keep them covered up, so that no flying particles of sand clung to the thin film of oil they wore. They had become so particular, in fact, there were occasional fights when one man accused another of carelessness.

'Right,' Boumphrey smiled at Ghadbhbhan. 'Give 'em the word.'

The crash of the first shots turned every face in the valley upwards. As the machine guns were pushed over the ridge, raking the vehicles, the A'Klabs began to run, one of them straight for the hill where Boumphrey waited, as if he had no idea where the firing was coming from. Then suddenly he realized what he was doing, stopped and tried to turn, but someone shot him and he rolled down the slope.

One of the trucks began to head for the gap in the hills nearby but it blew up unexpectedly in a wide pall of smoke. Pieces of steel whistled over their heads and they had to duck as they landed in puffs of dust. When they lifted their heads again one of the men below was leading a charge up the slope, firing a Tommy gun from the hip. He was hit in the chest and sat down abruptly. He was still firing but he was shot again and, as he fell back, the charge he had started crumbled and the men who had followed him began to run back the way they had come.

By this time the A'Klabs were climbing into the lorries and beginning to scatter, heading for any shelter they could see. As they vanished among the folds of ground, Boumphrey heard the roar of more machine guns and knew that Jenno's men had found them. For a while the firing continued then suddenly, abruptly, there was silence.

Walking down the slope towards the remains of the camp where a lorry burned and an armoured car leaned sideways over a punctured front tyre, Boumphrey was wary. Abruptly, a man stepped out from behind the armoured car, his rifle raised, but Ghadbhbhan shot him before Boumphrey had even reached for his weapon. The man fell backwards out of sight.

There were several weapons lying on the ground, and a lot of dead. There were also a few wounded and Ghadbhbhan, restraining his men from throat-cutting, gave orders for them to be gathered together. As they worked, Jenno's car came roaring into the valley from the north. He was gasping for air and rubbing his neck where hot empty cartridge cases, falling from the gun on to him, had burned his skin. His head through the hatch cover, he waved and shouted.

'Four lorries back there,' he said. 'All disabled. I think we can make two of 'em go and give 'em to Fawzi's boys to shift their wounded.'

'Two here,' Boumphrey said. 'That means only three got away, plus one armoured car.'

'*No* armoured cars,' Jenno corrected. 'One of my chaps shot the driver and it stopped. We've got it.'

'There's one here with a punctured front tyre but we can change the wheel and that'll give us another. I think we've blunted Fawzi's weapon a bit. How many do you think got away?'

'Hundred or so, including Fawzi,' Jenno said. 'But he's lost a lot of weapons and almost all his transport. That should keep him quiet for a while. I think we can now push on to the relief force.'

They found Lindley's column a few miles to the west of the hills. They were strung out and very vulnerable, a long line of black dots across the desert like the beads of a broken necklace, sometimes hardly visible in the distance through the shimmering heat.

As they approached, an Irazhi Blenheim screamed overhead and they saw two black tulips of smoke blossom ahead and the white-hot flash of anti-aircraft fire streaming up. A truck was hit and a long black column began to lift into the brassy sky.

There were cheers as they were spotted, then, as they swept forward, they found themselves surrounded by men who looked exhausted and shrivelled by the tremendous heat, worn out by the struggle they'd been having. The first man they spoke to was a captain in the Life Guards from Lindley's staff. He was struggling to free an armoured car and was lightening it by unscrewing every scrap of armour it carried.

'It's like Flodden Field back there,' he said.

The lorries seemed to have straggled all over the desert, as one group after another had tried to find the way through.

'Which way did you come?'

'By the sandhills,' Jenno said.

The cavalryman looked as if he didn't believe them. 'Anyway,' he admitted, 'we're damn glad to see you. At the moment everybody's trying to find somewhere firm to park without sinking up to their hubcaps. It's a bit like a small boy trying to shepherd a herd of angry elephants into a kraal.'

They had set off enthusiastically from Palestine, making excellent progress at first. At Hatbah, they found the Irazhi police who had first surrounded it had been replaced by Fawzi ali Khayyam who had occupied the place as Craddock and the Engineers had escaped. The first attempt at recapturing the place had been driven off with casualties and the loss of several vehicles but, with the threat of bombing, Fawzi had apparently decided that the interior of a fort was no place for a guerrilla leader. He and his men had slipped away during the night and the following morning the column had found the place deserted.

'Looked like something out of *Beau Geste*,' the cavalryman said. 'Except that there was a dead horse in there that stank to high heaven.'

Despite the delay at Hatbah, they had still hoped to reach Kubaiyah in record time, but then the crusty surface of the desert had started to give way under the wheels of the heavy

241

vehicles. Digging had not helped and the sand channels, objects like ten-foot-long cheese graters, had been ground down by the wheels until they were out of sight. Half the lorries in the column were stuck, and the others daren't go near them to haul them free in case they got stuck too.

Brigadier Lindley was a brusque red-faced man wearing no badges of rank and he was in a bad temper.

'It took you a bloody long time to get here!' he snapped.

When they explained what had happened, he calmed down to a normality of simmering sourness. 'Craddock's bloody cavalry led us into this,' he said. 'Who're you?'

They introduced themselves and the brigadier stared at Jenno's armoured cars and Boumphrey's lorryloads of dark-faced men. 'Boumphrey's Belles, eh?' he said. 'Well, Boumphrey, I shall need your dark-eyed beauties to help me find an alternative route. Can you do it?'

'Without doubt, sir,' Boumphrey said.

'You sound bloody confident.'

'Absolutely sure, sir.'

'Know this area, do you? Right –' the brigadier dismissed them, looking a lot happier '– we set off at first light tomorrow morning.'

Jenno and Boumphrey squatted Arab-fashion round a candle stuck in a bottle to discuss the next day's plans. The air was hot and stuffy but tea and sardine sandwiches had appeared and they drank out of china mugs which appeared to have been stolen from a NAAFI.

The disaster to the column had been laid firmly at the door of Colonel Craddock and the whole group had spent an exhausting day trying to dig themselves out in a temperature that had risen to 120 degrees in the shade. Rations were running short and there was a lot of worry about water. Boumphrey seemed to be bored by the worrying and Jenno grinned. Boumphrey's men never carried much water and still managed to travel great distances.

There was a lot of concern in the column about the Germans

because they'd heard that the RAF men at Kubaiyah had been fired on by a Messerschmitt.

'Rather more than a Messerschmitt,' Jenno said.

They had seen nothing of Craddock who seemed to be lying low. They'd heard rumours that he wasn't in Lindley's best books. Not only had he brought on the crisis in Mandadad – and it seemed everybody with the column had heard about it – but he had over-ruled Barber of the Engineers, and got them both holed up in the fort at Hatbah, from which they had managed to escape only in a hurry and minus their horses and a great deal of valuable engineering equipment. Finally, he had compounded his earlier errors on their return by trying to lead a headlong charge against the fort which had resulted in casualties and the loss of several vehicles.

'Living in the past.' Their Life Guardsman informant tossed the remains of his tea on the floor and mopped up the residue with a handful of twigs. 'You don't make headlong charges these days.'

'Bit out of date,' Boumphrey agreed.

'Your chaps ever charge?'

'Not if we can help it.'

'Expect he can't forget that bloody charge he made for Allenby at Assoum that finished the Middle East campaign in 1918 and won him a medal. He's been behaving like a hero ever since and wondering when he can do it again.'

When Craddock finally appeared, he seemed to have lost none of his confidence and immediately glared at Boumphrey.

'Young Boumphrey,' he said. 'What the devil are you doing here?'

Boumphrey was conciliatory. 'Came to meet you, sir. Thought a little help might be useful.'

Craddock stared at him arrogantly. It had clearly never occurred to him that his precipitate action near the Habib abi Chahla had brought on the crisis that had involved the whole Middle East.

'We're doing very well without native troops,' he growled.

'And I see you've had to leave your donkeys behind.'

Since Craddock had had to abandon his vast hunters too, any retort along those lines might have produced an arid sort of argument and Boumphrey avoided it by merely smiling.

'Jenno, too, I see,' Craddock went on. 'With his armoured cars. Pity you chaps couldn't have been doing your stuff in the air at Kubaiyah. From what I hear, they could have done with you there, instead of swanning around the desert.'

Jenno followed Boumphrey's example and smiled. It didn't seem to be worth arguing about.

They set off the following morning as soon as it was light, Boumphrey's lorries in the lead, with Jenno's armoured cars watching the flanks. Behind them the salvaged lorries growled forward, filling the silent desert with their rumblings. As they approached the sandhills, Boumphrey began to head for the valleys between them and almost immediately a staff car containing the brigadier came roaring up.

'Where the devil are you taking us?' he demanded.

'Safely to the other side, sir,' Boumphrey said mildly.

'We've already got stuck once on those hills,' the brigadier snapped. 'We'll get stuck twice as quickly in the valleys.'

'I rather doubt it, sir,' Boumphrey said, again mildly. 'Doubtless you were following the line of hillocks because at home high ground's usually harder than the valleys which tend to be soft and waterlogged. In the desert it's a bit different. The high ground's covered by light friable soil and gives way. The floor of the valleys becomes compacted by water in winter and that supplies a solid surface in summer.'

'Is that correct?'

'It is indeed, sir.'

Lindley frowned. 'The advice I was given by –' He stopped dead and gestured. 'Are you sure of your facts?'

'I've driven through these hills many times, sir.'

Lindley stared at him questioningly for a moment then he waved his hand. 'Well, I've got to trust someone. Go ahead.'

Moving cautiously, they picked their way forward, winding from valley bed to valley bed in a long snake of slow-moving vehicles. On their right was a vast lake of dried asphalt like a dead crater of the moon, stretches of greenish water lying like a film over the black pitch. The heat between the hills was fiery and the asphalt bubbled; from time to time they saw black- and white-robed Bedouin watching them in amazement.

At lunchtime a large black Heinkel appeared. As it circled, two Gladiators flew past it, apparently without even noticing it, and it dropped its bombs in leisurely fashion but with little more damage than swamping the nearest vehicles with showers of earth, sand and small stones. Later on, an aeroplane flashed past wearing French colours on its tail, then four black fighters roared out of nowhere, their guns going in an insane chorus.

Every weapon in the column burst into flame and the leading lorry came back towards Boumphrey, full of men shouting, chattering and gesticulating. There was a tear in the metal of the cabin roof and a wounded man inside who was rushed back along the column to where the doctors rode in the ambulances.

During the afternoon they broke free of the sandhills and reached firmer ground to the south of Lake Kubaiyah, then late in the day they caught sight of khaki figures in a sand-bagged trench near a bridge that was a picket of the Loyals. As they thundered into the camp, they were greeted with yells of delight. As they halted, Lindley's car stopped alongside Boumphrey's and he climbed out.

'Thanks, Boumphrey,' he said crisply. 'Until you arrived we were buzzing about like blue-arsed flies in a tripe shop. I'll be letting your senior officer know what happened.'

11

The relief of the relief column had taken place only just in time. Lindley could hardly claim to have relieved Kubaiyah because Kubaiyah had relieved itself. The cantonment looked a wreck, however. There were black scorch marks everywhere where shells had landed, and scattered rubble where buildings had been destroyed. There were also piles of charred metal where aircraft had gone up in flames, and those machines that were left were battered wrecks that no longer looked airworthy.

And the danger was not yet over, because Heinkel 111s had appeared over the place just after Jenno and Boumphrey had left and done more damage in one raid than the whole Irazhi air force and army had managed to do in a week of sustained effort. From then on there had been daily attacks, but a few more Blenheims and Gladiators had arrived from Egypt and finally two Hurricanes – and a great many German aircraft had been destroyed on the ground. Since then more machines, released by Middle East Command in an attempt to clear up the situation quickly so that everything could be concentrated on the Germans in North Africa, had begun to arrive in trickles, which was just as well because Messerschmitt 109s and 110s were now being reported on Irazhi airfields.

Imagining that the relief was likely to arrive too late to be of much help, the AVM and Colonel Ballantine had started to plan their next move and were intending to advance on Mandadad. The attack had been proposed for the next morning and, with the arrival of the relief column and a Gurkha battalion by air from Basra, they could see no reason to put it off.

Lindley hummed and hahed but he could see the advantage of keeping up the momentum. To advance on the capital at once and topple Ghaffer was the obvious strategy and he agreed to the plan and, as senior officer, took over its implementation from Ballantine.

'You'd think they'd give us time to have a fag and a bottle of beer,' Boumphrey said.

Jenno smiled. 'You ought to know, Ratter, old son,' he said, 'that once the British have set an operation in motion, they're never disposed to abandon it, even if the reason for it has long since disappeared. Though there are no longer any heroes to be rescued, there are still villains to be chastised.'

Boumphrey made a point of going to the hospital with the men who had been injured by the aircraft. Prudence greeted him delightedly.

'Ratter,' she said softly. 'Dear Ratter. How lovely to have you back.'

'Not *quite* back,' Boumphrey pointed out, briskly because he'd much have preferred simply to clutch her and go on clutching her, drowning his tiredness in the warmth of her flesh and the smell of the perfume she still managed to use. 'Tomorrow morning we're going for the capital.'

Her face fell. Boumphrey seemed thinner than ever, his face was deathly pale, and there were deep purple hollows under his eyes. 'But you've only just arrived,' she said. 'Surely they can give you a rest.'

'Not just yet,' Boumphrey said. 'Perpetual motion, me and Jenno. But, given a bit of luck, the whole thing will be over in a day or two. Must be off now, old thing. Conference for all concerned officers. I'm one.' Without thinking, he leaned forward and kissed her on the lips. It was unexpected and she looked startled, then she hurriedly kissed him back. He seemed to come to life and grinned at her delightedly while she looked at him with shining eyes.

The AVM, with Lindley and Colonel Ballantine alongside him, made things clear as they gathered in the cinema. 'There can be no delay,' he said. 'The Germans are expected to attempt a landing in Crete in the next forty-eight hours. And while there's every hope of holding on to the place, we're all aware that there's a desperate shortage of matériel. At the slightest sign of success there, inevitably the Germans will attack again in the Western Desert, which has already been weakened by the withdrawal of troops for Greece and Crete and now here. It's up to us to clear up the situation in Irazh as quickly as possible to make the troops here available elsewhere. The C-in-C's demanded an immediate advance.'

So that was that. They were in a mess again and everybody had to work like the clappers of hell, get their backs to the wall and do the old greater-love-hath-no-man thing. Considering that the Irazhis were known to have two divisions they could use for the defence of Mandadad, that the Luftwaffe might well intervene in force, and that there was still an undamaged Irazhi brigade at Howeidi to the west which might well attack Kubaiyah while they were away, they were taking a hell of a chance. Especially as Mandadad might well be defended by as many as 20,000 men and they were proposing to attack it with a force of less than 1200, plus a couple of hundred of the Bedou Legion and a few armoured cars and guns, a force in fact about the size of a battalion and a half.

'You know what Foch said in the last show,' Jenno murmured. ' "My centre is giving way. My right is in retreat. Situation excellent. I shall attack." It's one of those.'

That night, as they tried to snatch some sleep they could hear aircraft taking off to bomb aerodromes known to be used by Germans – some even in Syria. It was no encouragement to know that the Vichy French were allowing their airfields to be used as a staging post, but there was one cheerful piece of news. A German Luftwaffe colonel, the son of one of Hitler's field marshals, who had arrived to direct the air operations against them, had had the misfortune as his machine flew low in its approach to Mandadad, to be fired on by irresponsible tribesmen loosing off a few pot shots for the fun of it, so that when the machine had landed the coordinator of Axis operations was found to be dead in his seat with a bullet in his head.

Because of the floods caused by the broken bunds of the river and the wreckage on the road caused by the RAF's attack on the Irazhi reinforcements, the advance was to be led across the flooded area by the Mounted Legion. The relief column, still trying to get their breath back and bring failing vehicles back to efficiency, were to provide the reserves with a second column to follow in two halves, one by the same route as the main force, the second to head northeastwards across the desert to the Mandadad–Turkey railway, where it would turn south on to the road that ran alongside the track into the capital. Threatened on two sides, it was hoped that the officer directing the Irazhi defence would be in a flat spin and not know which attack to resist.

Already, resourceful civil engineers from Kubaiyah's Works and Bricks Department were constructing a bridge from commandeered dhows at Sin-ad-Dhubban to enable the pincer aimed at the railway track to cross the river. Craddock's lorried infantry were to lead the column and Craddock had been given the command – according to Jenno, because Lindley wanted him out of the way. The northern arm of the pincer movement was a lightweight affair and was intended chiefly as a diversion to draw resistance away from the main force advancing by the more direct route.

'Lindley's not forgiven him for that bloody silly charge of his at Hatbah,' Jenno said.

To assist the aircraft, the ground troops were to wear a white patch on their backs while their vehicles were to carry the same shaped patch painted on the bonnet, and the night was made hideous with the curses of men trying in a hurry to sew torn-up RAF sheets to their shirts.

As the sky began to pale three Heinkel bombers flew over, the black crosses on wings and fuselage clearly visible, and dropped their loads on the hangars. The Hurricanes took off after them but, while they were away, four Messerschmitt 109s appeared and sprayed the cantonment, followed by a mustard-yellow Messerschmitt 110 whose gun shattered the marmalade pot on the breakfast table in the officers' mess. It was a warning that they needed to finish the job before the Luftwaffe arrived in strength.

As daylight came, the vehicles containing the Loyals, Verity's levies and the Gurkhas began to assemble outside the gate. Engines drumming, they picked their way through palm groves past the blackened wreckage of the vehicles destroyed in the RAF attacks. The land was flat and mud-coloured under an open sky where kites were already soaring. By the roadside, an eagle, from God alone knew where, stood heraldic, defiant and quite indifferent to the passing vehicles, on the carcass of a pi-dog. Overhead they could see long strings of wild duck heading from the river area to the broad lagoons where they slept through the day.

Flat as a plate, the earth seemed to stretch away for ever, vast, desolate and pallid. There were occasional halts in the worst of the flooded areas but, led by Ghadbhbhan, the column picked its way from one patch of high ground to the next. Flocks of coots watched them as they went by.

Eventually, they reached dry land again and edged their way back to the road. Ahead of them now they could see the early morning sky over Fullajah was full of aeroplanes, the pale oyster colour crossed by rising columns of smoke. Alongside the road lay the charred wreckage of a Blenheim bomber shot down in one of the earlier raids.

The troops went in almost at once and captured the iron bridge across the river intact as Audaxes dive-bombed the trenches guarding it. The Gurkhas and the Assyrians swept forward, and as Porlock's 4.5s opened up, they found themselves in possession of the town.

Many of the Irazhi soldiers had exchanged their uniforms for Arab robes looted from surrounding houses and sniping was taking place. The Gurkhas were rounding up every Arab they saw and hoisting his robes to examine his knees. If they were sunburned, Jenno said, they were considered to belong to a soldier.

Word came down from Lindley to be prepared to move again in the morning and Boumphrey set off to round up his men. They were making the most of the capture of the town to raid a chicken farm and robed marauders were flitting about the runs among the flying feathers. Squawking fowls kept bursting into the air and every now and then one of the Belles made off with four or five birds hanging upside down from his hand, some of them still flapping hysterically. As Boumphrey bullied them away from their spoil, someone sent British soldiers to guard the farm, but he noticed that before they took up their positions they, too, helped themselves.

The river was edged by tall reeds standing in water that reflected the vast blue sky. As the wind grew stronger it brought a chorus of strange noises from the reeds – groans, whistles, wails, bleats, croaks and loud flatulent sounds. A flight of pelicans sailed majestically by on stiff wings, and they saw kingfishers in patches of electric blue, chestnut and crimson.

Boumphrey was just briefing his men for the final advance when whistles went and they heard a sudden burst of firing. Running to their vehicles, their weapons clanking, they moved towards the sound to find that, contrary to expectations, the Irazhis were counterattacking with determination and skill.

'German "technicians" showing 'em how to do it,' Boumphrey observed.

There were two light tanks in the attack but one became stuck in a bomb-crater and the other was knocked out by, of all things, a Boyes anti-tank rifle, a despised and outdated weapon which nobody with any sense dared fire. The screams for help brought aircraft from Kubaiyah to drop bombs behind the attack where the Irazhi reserves were trying to move up. As they struggled to hold the attack, a lorry burst out from among the houses and began to advance towards the bridge.

'That looks bloody ominous,' Jenno said.

'I bet it's full of explosives,' Boumphrey agreed. 'And the chaps in it hope to get into heaven by setting it off on the bridge and going up with it.'

Fortunately one of the Audaxes spotted the lorry. Whether the pilot realized what it signified or whether it was pure chance they didn't know, but the bomb stopped the lorry dead and left it rocking on its springs, its canvas cover in ribbons, its windscreen shattered, its crew dead inside. Then, while they were still looking up at the climbing Audax there was a tremendous explosion and the lorry disappeared in a sheet of flame. Mud houses alongside the road vanished in a shower of fragments, palm trees were flattened, and lorry wheels began to whack down in the fields on either side.

'My God,' Jenno breathed. 'I bet that carried the poor sods right into the arms of the Prophet.'

The explosion seemed to knock the stuffing out of the attackers and the firing died away. Soon afterwards the arrival of the British reserves settled the matter and they swept through the town while the Irazhis were still recovering. Pushing through more flood water, they reached the outskirts of Mandadad, only twelve miles from the city centre and Jenno found himself outside a police post.

It consisted of a quadrangle of yellow-plastered buildings set about with oleanders and the beginnings of a garden. On the walls were painted the markings of British and Irazhi aircraft and there were still prisoners in the cells who promptly exchanged places with the solitary remaining policeman, a stout sweating man wearing a Prussian spiked helmet from the first war. The place had been the headquarters of one of the recently ejected Irazhi battalions and there were all the signs of recent occupation, including a meal on a table and a pair of brand new shorts hanging on a line which one of Jenno's men took to replace his own ragged pair.

In one of the rooms was a switchboard and Jenno and Flight Sergeant Madoc leaned over it, Jenno holding the receiver while Madoc worked the switches and twirled the handle. Immediately a voice replied and Jenno almost dropped the receiver. Replacing it hurriedly, he yelled to one of his men to find Boumphrey.

'And tell him to bring Sergeant Major Ghadbhbhan with him,' he said.

With Ghadbhbhan holding the receiver, they tried the trick again and this time an agitated voice called in Irazhi, 'I've been trying to raise you for two hours. What's the matter?'

As Ghadbhbhan placed his hand over the mouthpiece and explained what he'd heard, Jenno grinned. 'Tell him the place's surrounded by the British, that the British have tanks and that they're already across the floods.'

Ghadbhbhan made his voice sound excited and frightened, and laid horrified stress on the word *bababa* – tanks. When it brought immediate consternation at the other end, it was decided not to risk any more for fear of being found out, but Ghadbhbhan went on listening, picking up snatches of conversation. It was clear the Irazhis had no idea the line was connected and they babbled to each other in greater and greater alarm. A patrol was ordered out to find the 'tanks' and soon afterwards, to everyone's delight, it reported back that there were fifty, fifteen already across the floods.

The line didn't go dead until late afternoon. One minute frantic orders and explanations were being yelled in Irazhi then the next there was a click and Ghadbhbhan found he was holding a dead instrument in his hand.

Jenno grinned at Boumphrey. 'Somebody a bit brighter than the rest's arrived,' he said.

As evening came, they could see two great domes ahead of

them glowing in the last of the light, and four tall minarets topped with gold. With the sinking sun touching them with crimson, they looked like flame-tipped torches. It was the Mosque of Holy Kadmaiani in the centre of Mandadad. Alongside it was the Palace of Flowers, the official residence of the ruler, at that moment occupied by Ghaffer al Jesairi, suffering, Boumphrey hoped, from a nasty case of indigestion caused by fright.

Civil engineers – rushed up from Kubaiyah's Works and Bricks Department – had collected dhows and planked them in to supplement the iron bridge, and a great gang of labourers was struggling to repair the breached river banks to allow the floods to dry out. One of the engineers brought news of what was happening at Kubaiyah. A complete squadron of Italian fighters had arrived in Mandadad and the RAF had laid on a welcoming party which had destroyed most of them on the ground before they could become operative, and an Audax crew, the observer the indefatigable Darling, had cut the telephone wires to the north by simply flying through them. For another set of wires which had looked too numerous for this treatment and seemed likely to bring up the aircraft with a jerk, they had landed and, while the pilot had climbed on to the main plane with a set of shears, Darling had set off with an axe and chopped down the poles, before swinging the propeller so that they could take off again just as an Irazhi armoured car hove in sight.

They were sitting at the side of the road listening to the engineer as they ate their rations when the Life Guardsman from Lindley's staff appeared, asking for Boumphrey. As Boumphrey rose, he produced a map. 'They tell me you know this area round here,' he said.

'I know all the areas round here,' Boumphrey admitted.

'Well, look –' the map was flattened out on the bonnet of Boumphrey's car '– there are floods to the north of where we are now, running alongside the Mandadad-Musol road and railway line. Is there any high ground along there which won't be flooded?'

'It might be possible close to the road.'

'You willing to take your chaps and try to get through to the northern column? They reached the railway line and turned south but when they reached Taji the stupid clots just sat down. The Brig wants them to pull their finger out and get moving. Can you do it?'

The Life Guardsman looked at Jenno. 'He says you're to go, too, with the armoured cars, in case anybody tries to stop you. Somebody's *got* to make it. If the clots had got away earlier and travelled all day without a halt they could have driven into Mandadad without meeting any opposition. The embassy got through to us and told us there was nothing on that side of the capital. Unfortunately, they've now found out and rushed troops up there. Your job's to stir Craddock into action. Got it?'

'Got it,' Jenno said with some satisfaction.

12

To their surprise, they found the water wasn't as deep as they'd expected because the flooding had been halted by local chiefs and headmen anxious to preserve their crops, and they were able to skirt it and push northwards parallel to the road, but just far enough away from it to avoid the attention of the Irazhi gunners deployed along its verges.

The situation was no longer as reassuring as it had been. The surprise had been lost and at any moment the Irazhi leaders would discover they were being attacked by about one-tenth of the numbers they could muster themselves. In addition, German aircraft were increasing daily and the radio brought news of constant bombing at Kubaiyah. It only required a couple of efficient bomber squadrons and a few fighters to stop the advance dead in its tracks.

They found Craddock in a headquarters he had set up in a private house alongside the road. He was in a bad temper and it soon became clear why. He had heard of Boumphrey's charge at Dhubban and was resentful of the fact that it had succeeded while his own at Hatbah had failed. He clearly thought they'd been attached to his column and made it clear that he was not going to allow anything of the same sort to happen twice.

'You're under my orders here,' he announced. 'So don't let anyone get any idea of acting independently.'

Jenno let him run on, cynically enjoying his comments before allowing Boumphrey to pass on Lindley's message.

Craddock frowned as he heard them out. 'Are they suggesting I'm moving too slowly?' he snapped. 'They should come up here and try for themselves. I can't move off the road because of the floods.' He looked at his map, then glanced up. 'How the devil did you get here, anyway? Surely to God you never went all the way back to Kubaiyah and then across the desert.'

'We came through the edge of the floods,' Jenno said bluntly. 'Boumphrey found a way.'

Craddock glared. 'I don't believe it,' he snapped.

Jenno shrugged. 'Better ask someone,' he suggested.

Craddock muttered something to himself then he straightened up. 'The Irazhis knew I was coming. They sent their navy up here, too. The river's only half a mile away to the east and their ships are armed with 3.7s. They can hit my people every time we stick our noses out. When do they want me to start?'

'At once. They want you to occupy the Irazhi reserves up here so they can get in by the south.'

Craddock's face was red with indignation. 'They just want to be first in,' he said. 'That's all. Very well. I'll set something up. What about you people?'

'Can't see much point in heading back,' Jenno said. 'By the time we arrive, they'll be pushing the last bit of the way in. They're at the end of the tram track. They could almost do the job on the public service. We might as well stay with you.'

Craddock looked bitter. 'We have to do something about the Irazhi navy's 3.7s first,' he said.

'Have you any guns?' Jenno asked.

'I have a troop of truck-towed 25-pounders.'

'If we can borrow one, I think we can get rid of those 3.7s.'

'With one gun?'

Jenno smiled. 'Two would be better.'

Jenno and Boumphrey spent the night discussing their plans with the captain in command of the guns. They had half-expected the move to start immediately, but Craddock was behaving like an old man afraid of making mistakes, afraid of

257

doing something which would detract further from the reputation he had built up. But the years between had taken their toll. He was an unimaginative man and all he could think of was to do again what he'd done in 1918 with Allenby.

'The bugger's never going to move unless he's nudged,' Jenno decided.

'If you can do what you claim you can do,' the gunner captain pointed out, 'we don't need him. Can you?'

Jenno smiled. 'Ten armoured cars can keep any amount of people busy,' he said.

The armoured cars led off, with Jenno in front, moving warily on to the open ground towards the river. The Rolls-Royce engines barely made a sound. As the first glimmer of light appeared, they halted and the two 25-pounders took up positions fifty yards apart. They were utterly devoid of cover but the Irazhis had not thrown out a picket and the guns and armoured cars were still obscured by the darkness. Not far away they could see the angular shapes of the Irazhi naval vessels. They were old-fashioned paddle-steamers and their great wheels were silhouetted against the faint lightening of the sky in the east. Small splinters of yellow showed where portholes were open, and one of them, obviously the flagship, was anchored against the bank, its hull protected by the bund.

'You open the bowling,' Jenno said to the gunner officer. 'You ought to be able to finish off the one against the bank with your first couple of shells. As soon as the crew appear on deck, we go into action. Just give us three or four minutes to get into position and try not to hit us.'

Their engines silent, the armoured cars moved to within machine gun range of the river and drew up in a long line. Flight Sergeant Madoc was humming softly to himself and Jenno was nervously fishing for a cigarette when the first of the guns came to life with an iron-throated bark.

'Here we go!'

The range was short. The shell struck the bow of the flagship

258

alongside the bank and they saw splinters fly into the air from the wooden stanchions that had been rigged to hold an awning. As flames began to lick along the woodwork, there were shouts and men began to appear. At once, Jenno set his car in motion. Madoc's followed him and the others swept forward one after the other until all ten cars were in motion. Hurtling along parallel to the river, they saw their tracer bouncing off the burning vessel's deckhouse and men running along the deck towards the silhouetted shape of a gun on the foredeck falling in a heap. As they disappeared, the other 25-pounder fired and the shell burst against the bridge.

'Lower,' Jenno muttered. 'Lower.'

All the cars were in motion now, moving along the line of paddle-steamers, their guns preventing the crews from reaching their weapons, just as they had against the machine gunners on the escarpment at Kubaiyah, keeping heads down, never remaining still for a second. The second shell from the first gun tore a hole in the side of the flagship and the third hit the engine room so that an enormous jet of smoke and soot shot from the funnel and came down in a shower. A pipe began to screech as steam escaped and more men appeared on deck; but Madoc's car was racing back now, and they dived out of sight again at once. As the car passed, they reappeared, but this time they were making not for the gun on the foredeck but for the gangplank and were fighting to get ashore – it dawned on Jenno that the vessel was beginning to list.

The guns were banging away now at the steamers in the river. One of them was already on fire near the bridge, and men could be seen taking to the boats. Then they began to range at will over the remainder, as the armoured cars, making enough dust for a squadron of tanks, cavorted effortlessly along the bank.

Waiting with his dog near the Mounted Legion, Boumphrey saw the first flashes and heard the crack of the guns and the rattle of machine gun fire. Almost immediately, firing started in front and he saw tracer bullets whipping overhead. Rifle fire stuttered and a gun banged, the shell screaming past to explode somewhere behind them.

'Come on, come on!' He turned to look at Craddock standing near his staff car, peering anxiously towards the river where the first rays of sun were beginning to push a golden glow into the sky. 'Now!'

But Craddock seemed hesitant. His second in command, waiting near Boumphrey, turned his head. 'For God's sake –!' he said.

Suddenly, unexpectedly, one of the lorries caught fire and Boumphrey was just about to climb into his car to urge Craddock into action when something whirled him round, throwing him to the ground. Sergeant Major Ghadbhbhan was by his side in an instant.

Boumphrey lay for a moment, dazed, the dog anxiously licking his face. He felt as if someone had delivered a tremendous kick up his backside but he decided that at least, since he was thinking, he couldn't be dead. He put his hand to his rear and it came away covered with blood.

'Good Lor',' he said. 'I think I've been shot up the bum!'

When he was hoisted up, he found he could stand and he held on to the side of the car, trembling a little with shock, while his blood-drenched trousers were cut away.

'I don't think it's serious, sir,' Ghadbhbhan said portentously. 'It seems to be only a flesh wound.'

'Where?'

Ghadbhbhan's handsome actor's face lifted and his white teeth flashed in a smile. 'Fortunately, where there is most flesh, sir. I don't think you will miss the little that has gone.'

Still holding on to the side of the car and craning his head round in an effort to see, Boumphrey became aware of engines roaring to life. Craddock had climbed into his car and was waving his arm. As the car moved forward, it was followed by the lorries carrying his cavalrymen. The Mounted Legion vehicles roared to life and Boumphrey swung in alarm on Ghadbhbhan.

'Ghadbhbhan,' he said painfully. 'This is going to go wrong! He's left it too late! Get the boys on foot and well dispersed.'

As Craddock's car swept past, Boumphrey stared. What should have been a steady advance on foot was being turned into a cavalry charge.

'Get me in the car,' he told his driver.

He made it to the front seat, his face twisted with pain, and grabbed the top of the windscreen.

'Take it slowly,' he said. 'Until I get the hang of it. I don't want to sit down suddenly.'

As they moved to the smoke ahead, they saw flames and realized the advance had already come to a standstill. Ghadbhbhan appeared, blood on his trousers.

'It's been stopped, sir,' he announced.

Craddock's lorries were already trying to retire and Boumphrey noticed that they were empty and the cavalrymen were lying on their faces behind any scrap of cover they could find. For a moment, Craddock, on foot, his car burning, tried to urge them on, upright in the middle of the firing, then Boumphrey saw his hand jerk and the riding crop he was carrying flung away in a spatter of blood. Slowly he sagged to his knees and, just as slowly, subsided until he lay on his face.

'Oh, you fool,' Boumphrey said softly. 'You poor bloody old fool!'

13

When Jenno arrived, Boumphrey was face-down in the rear seat of his car, his feet in the air, his backside swathed in bandages, the dog sitting by his head, industriously licking his face.

Jenno was in a rage that Craddock's stupidity should have stopped them in their tracks just when they had overcome the opposition from the Irazhi Navy.

'After all we did,' he snarled, 'to get nobbled because of a stupid old fart trying to pull off a double!'

But he also had news from the British embassy, picked up on his radio, that the German and Italian ministers and Ghaffer and all his pals – even the Grand Mufti – had bolted for Persia, and by the time Boumphrey was moved to an ambulance, the northern arm of the attack was roaring down the road between the now silent Irazhi guns. They passed the wrecked Lafwaiyah Club at a rush – hardly noticing the charred furniture and fittings stacked in the garden, the smouldering buildings and broken windows – and when they came to the tram track they simply commandeered the trams and continued to head southwards, bells clanging, Bedou Legionnaires and British soldiers clinging to the sides and yelling with delight.

Great clouds of dust hung over the column and Irazhi soldiers tramping to the rear eyed them sullenly. A little man with glasses appeared in front of Jenno but no one took any notice of him and he was moving from truck to truck pleading for someone to listen to him. It was only later that Jenno learned he was trying to surrender the city.

As they reached the city centre, they ran into the southern column and from then on they moved together. A gang of young hooligans in plus-four Ruftwah uniforms threw a brick into a truckful of Gurkhas, but the Gurkhas promptly threw it back and jumped out, kukris in their hands, to wipe up the opposition, which immediately disappeared into the back streets. In some parts of the city, a riot was developing. It had started round a liquorice factory, and a bazaar had been stripped and shop owners were barricading themselves in.

Because he knew the way, Jenno was the first to reach the embassy. As he arrived, he saw people in the tiled courtyard, a fountain playing behind them. It looked a little like a country house party, especially when the ambassador, in white drill suit and topee, stepped forward to shake his hand.

It hadn't been too bad, he said. They had been surrounded but the water and electricity had never been cut off and enterprising traders had sold sweets, tobacco, cosmetics and even out-of-date issues of the *London Evening News* at the gate.

In no time the place was full of soldiers seeking people they knew, and Jenno found himself facing Christine Craddock.

'So you made it,' she said.

'I made it,' he agreed.

'What about my idiot of a husband? After stirring up trouble here he disappeared into the bloody desert. What happened to him?'

'He was badly wounded early this morning.'

Her face remained expressionless and Jenno half-expected her to produce some sneer. But she didn't.

'I'll get my things,' she said, turning away. 'I suppose I'd better go to him. He'll need me.'

Now that it was over, the clearing up started and the injured were hurried to hospital at Kubaiyah. Boumphrey found himself in bed, the roof above him still pitted with holes from shrapnel, bomb splinters and machine gun bullets, but outside now there was no sound more violent than the growl of lorries and ambulances, and the trumpeting of the band of Verity's Assyrian levies playing a triumphant tune that was a mixture of braying Western music and ancient Arab notes.

By this time, men of the Indian Division, flown up from the south, were appearing everywhere, complete with tents, folding baths, polo sticks and fishing rods, as if they were prepared for a two-year campaign and didn't intend to miss any of their usual comforts. To their amazement they found that the Irazhis had three-inch mortars which they did not have, and Bren guns with the Skoda mark still on them, while the British were armed with Hotchkiss guns used in the Boer War forty years before.

They had found aeroplanes grounded on Irazhi fields for lack of spare parts, their swastikas painted over in Irazhi colours, their German or Italian crews vanished northward to Turkey on the Taurus Express. Jenno's cars had even rounded up German and Italian fitters, a few officers and a whole host of German 'technicians', still in sports coats and flannels and grimly clutching cameras in the vain belief that their identity was still secret.

But Boumphrey was under no delusions. Despite what the BBC was saying, they'd been very lucky. The timing of Ghaffer's rising had been wrong and the Germans had procrastinated when procrastination was foolish. But even so, the rout of an organized enemy by a makeshift air force of unpractised crews in training machines had been a pretty good effort. They had saved Kubaiyah, rescued the relief column, and captured Mandadad with less than two thousand men against twenty thousand.

Now it was just a case of getting the place in running order again. The Engineers had taken over the one surviving paddle-steamer of the Irazhi navy as an officers' mess and the only thing that marred the sweet feeling of success was the knowledge that in Crete the Germans seemed to be winning, though the British had invaded Syria to make sure that it would never again be used as a base for Nazi activities.

Boumphrey sighed. He couldn't stand up for long and when he grew tired he had to return to the hospital so he could lie on his face to recover. The man who had preceded him in command of the Audax flight and suffered the same indignity, gave him tips on how to handle it.

A few gongs were said to be on the way and Boumphrey had made sure that Darling would get an immediate award. He had disappeared now to the Middle East but not before calling to see Boumphrey, walking with his elbows out so that nobody could miss the brand-new chevrons on his sleeves.

'I'm being sent straight on to ops, sir,' he had said. 'They waived the rest of the training.'

'There can't be many people,' Boumphrey had observed, 'who arrive on an operational squadron for the first time with a DFM and a couple of dozen sorties under their belts.'

Jenno had also been with the news that Craddock was going to pull through. As he turned to leave, he paused. 'By the way,' he said, 'I thought you'd like to know. The young storks have left the nest at last.'

Boumphrey smiled. 'Oh, good show! All right?'

'Unfortunately, no. Take-offs were a bit premature. The first one made it over the wire but it lost flying speed, crash-landed and was grabbed by a jackal.'

'And the second?'

'Broke a wing. It was brought to the hospital for servicing but when it found itself about to be x-rayed it gave up the ghost.' Jenno smiled. 'Pity, really. They were a sort of symbol of this place.'

Finally Ghadbhbhan appeared with a wilting bunch of flowers and the information that the legion had come out of the scuffle outside Mandadad with no more than a few minor wounds. Boumphrey was still thinking of the sergeant major's shy happiness when Prudence Wood-Withnell appeared. She was brisk and cheerful and Boumphrey was damned if he didn't think she was more good-looking. She had come out of her shell a lot since the fun had started and had revealed qualities nobody had been aware of. The siege had shown many people what they and their friends were made of. Her shyness had disappeared and she was no longer afraid to look people in the eye. Knowing each other seemed to be good for both of them.

'How are you today, Ratter?' she asked.

'Feels as if I'd been to see the headmaster and had six of the best with a very thick cane,' Boumphrey admitted. 'I shan't be able to sit down properly for a long time and even then I shall have a list to starboard. Will you mind?'

She smiled. 'I'll lean the other way to make things even,' she said. 'You were jolly lucky, actually, Ratter. An inch further to the right and you'd have had *four* holes in your bottom instead of just two.'

Boumphrey looked up, surprised, and she laughed.

'Read the report,' she said. 'It's all there. You'll be on your feet before long and there's talk of flying the wounded to Egypt.'

Boumphrey nodded. He knew it was so, because Vizard had been to see him. 'What about you?' he asked. 'Are you staying here?'

Prudence shook her head. 'Father is. I'm not. I'm joining the WAAFS. Then we'll be in the RAF together, Ratter. I'm going with you to Egypt. I can join there.'

'That's jolly sporting.'

'Father told me you're going to get a gong.'

'Really? An army one for flying, or an RAF one for ground operations?'

'You put up a splendid show, Ratter.'

He reached out and touched her hand. Her fingers curled round his. 'It's been quite a business, hasn't it?' he said. 'One of the derring-dos that didn't win the Empire. I think we did rather well, under the circs, though. I expect when they look into it, they'll discover that things were more in our favour than we realized but, all the same, it was pretty good, considering the tools we had.'

He paused and grinned. 'Just a sideshow really,' he ended. 'But I think they'll give us full marks. If nothing else, ten for effort.'

Bestselling War Fiction and Non-Fiction

☐ Passage to Mutiny	Alexander Kent	£2.50
☐ The Flag Captain	Alexander Kent	£2.50
☐ Badge of Glory	Douglas Reeman	£2.50
☐ Winged Escort	Douglas Reeman	£2.50
☐ Army of Shadows	John Harris	£2.50
☐ Up for Grabs	John Harris	£2.50
☐ Decoy	Dudley Pope	£1.95
☐ Curse of the Death's Head	Rupert Butler	£2.25
☐ Gestapo	Rupert Butler	£2.75
☐ Auschwitz and the Allies	Martin Gilbert	£4.95
☐ Tumult in the Clouds	James A. Goodson	£2.95
☐ Sigh for a Merlin	Alex Henshaw	£2.50
☐ Morning Glory	Stephen Howarth	£4.95
☐ The Doodlebugs	Norman Longmate	£4.95
☐ Colditz – The Full Story	Major P. Reid	£2.95

NAME ....

ADDRESS ....

....

....

U.K. CUSTOMERS: Please allow 22p per book to a maximum of £3.00.

B.F.P.O. & EIRE: Please allow 22p per book to a maximum of £3.00.

OVERSEAS CUSTOMERS: Please allow 22p per book.

Whilst every effort is made to keep prices low it is sometimes necessary to increase cover prices at short notice. Arrow Books reserve the right to show new retail prices on covers which may differ from those previously advertised in the text or elsewhere.

Bestselling Non-Fiction

☐ The Gradual Vegetarian	Lisa Tracy	£2.95
☐ The Food Scandal	Caroline Walker & Geoffrey Cannon	£3.95
☐ Harmony Rules	Gary Butt & Frena Bloomfield	£2.25
☐ Everything is Negotiable	Gavin Kennedy	£2.95
☐ Hollywood Babylon	Kevin Anger	£7.95
☐ Red Watch	Gordon Honeycombe	£2.75
☐ Wildlife of the Domestic Cat	Roger Tabor	£4.50
☐ The World of Placido Domingo	Daniel Snowman	£4.95
☐ The Sinbad Voyage	Tim Severin	£2.75
☐ The Hills is Lonely	Lillian Beckwith	£1.95
☐ English Country Cottage	R. J. Brown	£3.50
☐ Raw Energy	Leslie & Susannah Kenton	£2.95

NAME ....

ADDRESS ....

....

....

U.K. CUSTOMERS: Please allow 22p per book to a maximum of £3.00.

B.F.P.O. & EIRE: Please allow 22p per book to a maximum of £3.00.

OVERSEAS CUSTOMERS: Please allow 22p per book.

Whilst every effort is made to keep prices low it is sometimes necessary to increase cover prices at short notice. Arrow Books reserve the right to show new retail prices on covers which may differ from those previously advertised in the text or elsewhere.

Bestselling Humour

☐ Picking on Men Again	Judy Allen & Dyan Sheldon	£1.95
☐ Carrott Roots	Jasper Carrott	£3.50
☐ A Little Zit on the Side	Jasper Carrott	£1.75
☐ The Corporate Infighter's Handbook	William Davis	£2.50
☐ The Art of Coarse Drinking	Michael Green	£1.95
☐ Armchair Anarchist's Handbook	Mike Harding	£2.95
☐ You Can See the Angel's Bum, Miss Worswick!	Mike Harding	£1.95
☐ Sex Tips for Girls	Cynthia Heimel	£2.50
☐ Lower than Vermin	Kevin Killane	£4.95
☐ More Tales from the Mess	Miles Noonan	£1.95
☐ Limericks	Michael Palin	£1.50
☐ Bodge It Yourself: The Beginner's Guide to BIY	Jeff Slapdash	£2.95
☐ Dieter's Guide to Weight Loss During Sex	Richard Smith	£1.95
☐ Tales From a Long Room	Peter Tinniswood	£1.95

NAME ....

ADDRESS ....

....

....

U.K. CUSTOMERS: Please allow 22p per book to a maximum of £3.00.

B.F.P.O. & EIRE: Please allow 22p per book to a maximum of £3.00.

OVERSEAS CUSTOMERS: Please allow 22p per book.

Whilst every effort is made to keep prices low it is sometimes necessary to increase cover prices at short notice. Arrow Books reserve the right to show new retail prices on covers which may differ from those previously advertised in the text or elsewhere.

A Selection of Arrow Bestsellers

☐ A Long Way From Heaven	Sheelagh Kelly	£2.95
☐ 1985	Anthony Burgess	£1.95
☐ To Glory We Steer	Alexander Kent	£2.50
☐ The Last Raider	Douglas Reeman	£2.50
☐ Strike from the Sea	Douglas Reeman	£2.50
☐ Albatross	Evelyn Anthony	£2.50
☐ Return of the Howling	Gary Brandner	£1.95
☐ 2001: A Space Odyssey	Arthur C. Clarke	£1.95
☐ The Sea Shall Not Have Them	John Harris	£2.50
☐ A Rumour of War	Philip Caputo	£2.50
☐ Spitfire	Jeffrey Quill	£3.50
☐ Shake Hands Forever	Ruth Rendell	£1.95
☐ Hollywood Babylon	Kenneth Anger	£7.95
☐ The Rich	William Davis	£1.95
☐ Men in Love	Nancy Friday	£2.75
☐ George Thomas, Mr Speaker: The Memoirs of Viscount Tonypandy	George Thomas	£2.95
☐ The Jason Voyage	Tim Severin	£3.50

NAME ....

ADDRESS ....

....

....

U.K. CUSTOMERS: Please allow 22p per book to a maximum of £3.00.

B.F.P.O. & EIRE: Please allow 22p per book to a maximum of £3.00.

OVERSEAS CUSTOMERS: Please allow 22p per book.

Whilst every effort is made to keep prices low it is sometimes necessary to increase cover prices at short notice. Arrow Books reserve the right to show new retail prices on covers which may differ from those previously advertised in the text or elsewhere.

Bestselling Thriller/Suspense

☐ Voices on the Wind	Evelyn Anthony	£2.50
☐ See You Later, Alligator	William F. Buckley	£2.50
☐ Hell is Always Today	Jack Higgins	£1.75
☐ Brought in Dead	Harry Patterson	£1.95
☐ The Graveyard Shift	Harry Patterson	£1.95
☐ Maxwell's Train	Christopher Hyde	£2.50
☐ Russian Spring	Dennis Jones	£2.50
☐ Nightbloom	Herbert Lieberman	£2.50
☐ Basikasingo	John Matthews	£2.95
☐ The Secret Lovers	Charles McCarry	£2.50
☐ Fletch	Gregory McDonald	£1.95
☐ Green Monday	Michael M. Thomas	£2.95
☐ Someone Else's Money	Michael M. Thomas	£2.50
☐ Albatross	Evelyn Anthony	£2.50
☐ The Avenue of the Dead	Evelyn Anthony	£2.50

NAME ....

ADDRESS ....

....

....

U.K. CUSTOMERS: Please allow 22p per book to a maximum of £3.00.

B.F.P.O. & EIRE: Please allow 22p per book to a maximum of £3.00.

OVERSEAS CUSTOMERS: Please allow 22p per book.

Whilst every effort is made to keep prices low it is sometimes necessary to increase cover prices at short notice. Arrow Books reserve the right to show new retail prices on covers which may differ from those previously advertised in the text or elsewhere.